Hiding from her father's people in plain sight, Mala has made her living repairing starships to showroom condition. When a handsome Guardsmen offers her a new life using her talents to their limits, how can she refuse it, or him? She becomes Fixer, he becomes Shade and together they are the core of the Sector Guard.

Running Wyld

Nominated for the post of Guardsmen by the planet she was raised by, Agreha is surprised to find a Guard from Morganti base waiting to take her with him as his partner. With her ability to shift her shape and his telepathy, Morph and Thinker become a team when tested by an assignment on a clone world that becomes more dangerous than Aggie had imagined.

Hael's Fury

Minimizing natural disasters was all that Liv Hael lived for. When she meets the dragon of her dreams, and he offers her a position in the Sector Guard, she can't believe her ears. Only one thing stands in the way of Liv and Vasu joining. Will she accept his house as her nest?

Seering Order

Reva was born a slave, her commanding voice her largest asset. When an Enjel buys her from the insects that own her she has a choice, unfocused freedom or life as a Guardsmen. Seer is her companion, and he wants to move up to lover. Reva needs to deal with her past so that her future can begin.

Star Breaker

With an asteroid heading to Morganti, Kale volunteers to retrieve the Star Breaker, a weapon that has the ability to shatter anything in its way. When it breaks open he meets the woman who has spent the last four hundred years waiting for this moment with the soul of a star in her body. The *Star Breaker*.

This book is a work of fiction. Names, characters, places, and incidents either are products of the author's imagination or are used fictitiously. Any resemblance to actual events or locales or persons, living or dead, is entirely coincidental.

Sector Guard Collection 1
Copyright © 2012 Viola Grace
ISBN: 978-1-77111-184-3
Cover art by Martine Jardin

All rights reserved. Except for use in any review, the reproduction or utilization of this work in whole or in part in any form by any electronic, mechanical or other means, now known or hereafter invented, is forbidden without the written permission of the publisher.

Published by Devine Destinies
An eXtasy Books Inc imprint
Look for us at www.devinedestinies.com

Library and Archives Canada Cataloguing in Publication

Grace, Viola, 1971-

Sector guard : collection 1 / Viola Grace.

Short stories.

ISBN 978-1-77111-184-3

I. Title.

PS8613.R333S42 2012   C813'.6   C2012-902929-7

SECTOR GUARD COLLECTION 1

BY

VIOLA GRACE

FREAK FACTOR

CHAPTER ONE

"You know, the kind of repair that you are requesting will cost you." Dock master Vin nodded wisely as he spoke into his com unit. "I have a specialist who can do the job, but not at the price you want."

"Whatever. Your station comes highly recommended. As long as your specialist can do the job, we will pay. If I bring in this thing in this shape, I'll get fired." The male voice was tense and it made Vin smile.

The commander of the vessel was obviously concerned and Vin was fully willing to take advantage of that concern financially. Kaddaka station was out of the way, but his secret weapon was making them known for their perfect repairs.

The com crackled again, "And, just so you know, we are coming in hot. We have no engines and are moving at speed. If you don't send out your specialist, we are going to hit the station."

"Mala! Get that lazy ass of yours out of bed and get down here. We have a repair and it is coming in hot!" Her com unit shrieked her awake as it had several times this year.

Struggling to wake, she rolled out of bed, "Geez, Vin. How long do we have?"

"They are inbound and they have no power. Your team is on its way."

She was hopping up and down on one foot to get into her coveralls. A few sharp tugs and it was covering the bodysuit that she slept in. "Get the cradle ready, Vin. I am gonna take it to them as soon as I get there."

"Then get your ass moving. We have less than an hour to do this." The click of the com was enough. He was serious and she was moving.

Her tiny quarters on the station were sparse. The money she had saved by doing impossible fixes for incredible prices was piling up nicely. She bolted through the halls, crew and vendors backing up against the walls to let her pass. The screaming scarlet of her repair suit was enough of a warning to them and so she passed dozens on her way to the repair bay.

Gergar was holding out her space suit in two of his four arms. She jumped into it and started slapping the closures. He sighed, took her hands away and slowly sealed her suit for her.

"You keep doing it that way, Mala, and you are going to be breathing nothing out there."

"I know. Sorry. It's just that Vin sounded so excited on the com. It seemed urgent." Her understatement was marked by a roar.

"Get your asses in gear and get out there."

"You heard the man. Let's get our asses out there." She clipped her helmet into place, checked her tanks and stepped into the mag boots. "Checking interior coms."

"Check." Gergar gave her four thumbs up.

"Check," Rihal hissed through her mic. Her suit had a tail extension and she pressurized it to make sure it was sealed.

With her small team ready, Mala nodded for them to take their scooters and she took driving position on her pride and joy, the cradle. The cradle was a connected network of rockets that expanded to surround and lock onto a powerless ship to steer it back to the station.

"Coordinates coming up," Vin's voice echoed in her helmet.

Mala flipped the toggles that would get her up and running. As soon as the data flashed in front of her, she was out. This was her favourite part of duty, the thrill of the race through space. Vin had cleared the path outbound so her team could really haul ass, so haul they did. Traffic was steady around the station, but no one was dumb enough to get in their way. A broadcast had gone out to keep private ships out of the area because an emergency ship repair crew was coming. Everyone knew what that meant.

It took fifteen minutes of dodging debris and terse communications, but finally they were at their prize and it was a beauty.

"Lady and gentleman, do you know what this is?"

"It looks so new." Rihal was in awe. Gergar was silent.

"Oh, it is, very. That is a Reflex ship." She was already jockeying for position. "Ahoy the ship!" It was tricky, suddenly hitting reverse to match the speed of the approaching craft.

"This is the Class One. Please identify."

"Repair crew from Kaddaka Station. Please be advised that we will be fastening rockets to the hull for manoeuvres back to the repair bay."

"Do you have confirmation of your identities?"

"No. But we do have a rocket assembly. How many pirates would be out on scooters with an engine cradle? My name is Mala, you can check with Vin." She sighed and looked at the sleek hull of the ship. "I will be using magnetic attachment so as not to mar the hull, please have your pilot notify me of any discomfort." She started to move fast. Her boots enabled her to walk the ship's surface and, in only a few minutes, she and her team had locked the magnet grips into place and were climbing back into their respective conveyances.

"Uh, we will. Thank you." The masculine voice sounded amused. "Let us know when you hook up."

"I am attached and we are heading for Kaddaka station. Estimated arrival time, three minutes."

The male voice was a little stressed. "I thought you were going to attach rockets."

"I did."

"Then why are we still moving at this speed?"

She chuckled. It wasn't the first time she had gotten a panicked call from a ship at this point. "I am not going to hit the brakes until we are within easy pushing distance of the station. What would be the point?"

He didn't seem happy, but replied, "You are correct. Or at least I hope you are. If not, we are going to make a large splat at the station."

"I have been doing this for years and have never lost a shuttle or ship."

He was suddenly suspicious. "How many years?"

She laughed, he had caught her. "At least two. Whoops. Prepare for braking." His chatter had distracted her and she winced as she triggered the front thrusters to slow the ship. This was the one moment she was worried about the connections. Traffic was still steering clear of their path, so Vin was doing his job.

She slowed the ship down to a controlled float and eased it toward the open repair bay. Gergar and Rihal floated in beside her, keeping the ship from bumping the edges of the doorway. It wouldn't do for them to put more damage on the ship. It would come out of their pay.

With finesse and not a little pride, Mala landed the cradle in the docking area. Clamps came out to hold the ship and she disengaged her pride and joy. The rockets folded together and another clamp came out to bring the cradle to storage. She climbed out before that could happen.

Mala stood and smiled at her crew through her helmet and gave them both a thumbs up. Mission accomplished. Now for the hard part. "Team, prepare for complete scan and repair of the ship. Be warned. Reflex ships are wired to a living operator. The operator can feel the ship like their own body. Be gentle." She crossed the floor and grabbed a data pad. It was time to make some notes.

"Blast damage on the forward nacelle," Rihal piped up.

"Blast damage on the nose, indicative of a battle," Gergar was decidedly cheerful.

"Blast damage on left engine port," she put in her own two cents.

"Blast damage on right engine port."

"Tail broken and metal fatigue throughout rear portion of the hull. Yup. This would keep them from flying straight, all right." It was a final confirmation of the damage. She sent the report to Vin and he told her he would forward it to the occupants of the ship. She looked forward to the go ahead. She wanted to get her hands on her first Reflex ship.

CHAPTER TWO

Inside the ship, Isabi was busy removing the results of a cold sweat from his body. "Did you know she was going to cut it that close, Helen?"

The pilot leaned against the frame and smirked at him. "From what we have heard, yes. I did think that she would conserve her resources until the last moment. I didn't know you were this twitchy, Isabi."

"Only when my life is at stake and an unknown quantity is controlling whether I live or die. I am funny that way." He stretched and flexed muscles that had grown taut. The repair woman had almost killed them and Helen Taline was remarkably calm about it.

"Didn't you read her histories? She is incapable of damaging a ship. She knows every inch of every ship she has ever seen, she knew that this was a Reflex as soon as she saw it. That is not an identification that most techs in the Alliance could have made."

"Fine. How did she know?"

"That is what we are here to find out." The ship shifted and it began its slow progression into the detail repair bay. They would soon be in a breathable atmosphere with access to the station amenities, including restocking their galley. The light to the outer airlock went green. "Now, we will see what she can do."

Taking off her EVA suit was a lot easier than putting it on. Boots first, then helmet and finally, she unsealed the baggy thing. She stumbled free and stretched just as the hatch opened to reveal the occupants of the ship.

"Holy mother of stars," Mala whispered it as quietly as she could, but there was no getting around the fact that the male Selna was one of the most attractive things she had ever seen. She shook her head. Of course he was. All

Selna put out pheromones causing compatible races to want to mate. Mala's mixed bloodline was no exception.

She stayed out of their way and merely nodded to the pilot as she passed. It was easy to determine that she was the controller for the ship. The ports in her wrists gave it away. The pilot looked with a smile between Mala and Isabi. Apparently, Mala should have been writhing on the floor in front of the Selna. That just wasn't her style.

Her repair crew helped her look busy as the occupants made the long walk to the end of the repair bay and they waited until the Selna and pilot were out the door. The instant that the coast was clear, Mala stripped off her gloves and ran her hands over the hull. The minor and major damage caused by the blasts ceased to exist at her touch, the metal joining, sealing and healing under her fingers.

This was why she made the credits that she did. The money was compensation for the perfect repairs she was capable of. It was her one skill, this repair talent, her freak factor when it came to blending in with other techs.

She moved slowly along the ship, inch by inch, clearing and eradicating all trace of the battle. Whatever had hurt this beautiful ship had been brutal. The damage had been deliberate and designed to turn the ship into a paralyzed meteor, and it had worked. The poor baby.

She was murmuring to the ship when she reached the engine damage. "Gergar, I need some metal here." She stroked the superficial damage on the exterior of the housing and waited for the hand to tap her shoulder. She took the metal sheet blindly and held it in place, feeling it melt into the surface of the ship. She could repair anything as long as she had enough materials to patch up the holes.

"I am going to need three more of those if this engine was any indication." She clambered over the ship, keeping her focus on feeling the entirety of the ship at all times. It took her two more hours, but at last she was finished. Dizzy and terribly pleased with herself, Mala sat heavily next to the ship and turned to face her crew. Dismay filled her.

"You know, if I hadn't seen it for myself, I never would have believed it."

The Selna from the ship leaned on one of the pylons and played with one of the chunks of metal she had been using to reconstitute the engines.

"The report was quite insistent that she was capable of it. I am glad to see that it was not exaggerated." The pilot was smiling.

Whatever race she was from was in Mala's own makeup. She could feel kinship with the strange pale creature with its wide eyes and cheerful grin. Her crew was huddled together near the door, mouths gagged and arms and tail confined. "Let them go and tell me what you want."

The beautiful Selna moved close to her and whispered, "We want you."

CHAPTER THREE

"For what? Your ship is fine, you have already paid, so you can just go." She kept her back to the ship and reached out to support herself. She was always weak as a kittling after a repair.

"Is there somewhere we can speak? Privately?" The Selna was still close.

Too close for her peace of mind and he smelled too damned good. "Sure. Give me a few minutes to refresh myself and we can go to one of the station diners." She needed a cleanse and she definitely needed food. "Untie my crew first."

The pilot simply nodded and, with a few economical movements, she released the workers. Rihal's tail was the last thing unfettered and the pilot jumped back as she triggered the release, narrowly missing the swipe of retribution.

"Rihal, Gergar. Leave it. It will be fine," she barked the order and they immediately stood down. She didn't often throw her weight around, but when she did, she meant business. Her discomfited crew slowly left the bay, leaving Mala with the two newcomers.

The Selna came toward her again, seduction in every line of his body. "I would rather we talked immediately."

"Well, I would rather be half a meter taller. It isn't going to happen." She took a deep breath and strode for the door. "My quarters are this way, I need a cleanse and a change of clothing. Then I can eat." She moved through the halls with a weary plodding gait. All she wanted was a way to eat as she slept, but that wasn't going to happen. Her two shadows stayed with her up one hall and down the other. When they finally reached her quarters, she stopped. "You can't come in."

He blinked at her. "Why ever not?"

He was completely clueless. "I have one room and a small cleansing unit. No room for dressing in there. I am not stomping around naked with you in there."

The pilot stepped between them. "Isabi. Just stay outside. I will go in and keep my back to her."

"Good compromise." Mala headed into her room and, as soon as the pilot crossed the threshold, she triggered the lock. "Just in case he gets nosey."

"He is really too cocky for his own good. He is far too used to women just flopping onto their backs and spreading their thighs."

Mala blinked. "Uh, that is quite the image. I will be right out." She headed into the cleanser and stripped. She had lied, there was room in the chamber for clothing, in fact it was where her wardrobe was. To conserve space, she had opted for the gel cleanser and now she took a deep breath and stood under it as it covered her from head to toe and then hardened into a shell. She waited for a three count and then the sonic blast hit her, blowing the gel into bits. A quick swipe with a towel and she was ready for fresh clothing. She used the com unit in the room to place an order at her favourite diner for lunch for three. It would be ready when they arrived.

One baggy jumpsuit and some clean boots later, she was ready for company. "Sorry for the wait." Oh, she was so glad she had dressed in the cleansing chamber. The Selna was inside her room. A quick glance told her two things. One, her door was still locked and two he was looking very disappointed that she was wearing a jumpsuit.

She opened and closed her mouth in surprise. Something was going on here and she didn't know what. Never mind that, she was still hungry. She said nothing, merely led the way out of her room and down the hallway. Her favourite diner had private rooms. As soon as they were behind the silence screens, she was getting to the bottom of this. It was one weird day.

The brighter light of the commercial halls made her blink and she stumbled for a moment until she acclimated. The instant that her footing became uncertain, she felt a hand under her elbow. She didn't need to look to know who it was. The Selna had an unusual fascination with her and she was going to disabuse him of that idea as soon as she could. Men were a department of her life that she wanted to leave dormant. She straightened her shoulders and simply moved out of his grip. They were at their destination.

"Mala! How nice to see you. We have your room ready." The Ontex nodded, his small silver frame and enormous black eyes incongruous to his voice.

"Hey, Milton. Thanks for being so attentive." She followed him to the private room she had reserved and sat on a floor cushion next to the low table. Her guests sat to either side of her. The food arrived while they were staring at each other. As the host, she portioned out the food and filled the beverage cups.

The Selna looked surprised by the courtesy.

"I wasn't raised in a field. We did have manners where I came from."

"My apologies for the surprise. You seem to be a woman of many talents." He took a sip from his cup and the pilot did the same.

Mala was now clear to eat. She ate as rapidly as she could while maintaining her manners. It was a tricky proposition. She managed to stifle the belch that was trying to escape and deliberately put her utensils down. She wiped her hands on a small towel and took some of the berries that were available for dessert. A sip of the tea and she was full.

The pilot was about to speak when Mala held up one hand for silence. She got to her feet and touched the privacy screen that would ensure that no one could listen in. A subtle manipulation of the wiring and she deactivated the recorder that Milton had in place. Sneaky little bugger. "Now we can speak. Milton has more greed than good sense, just like the other facility owners on this station. Money leads the way. Now. Who are you and why are you here?"

CHAPTER FOUR

"First. I am Helen Taline of the Alliance Protectorate of Terra, pilot of the Class One. This is Isabi Reda, Master Companion of the Selna. We are both members of the Sector Guard. But let me first tell you why we are here." She took a deep breath and then looked to Isabi. Clearly he wasn't going to help. She hated public speaking, but he was far too interested in their new friend to give her the background. Twit.

"The dramatic rise in pirate activity in the outer sectors has been a concern for the Alliance planets. The representatives of the various mother planets discussed their options and it was suggested that groups of agents be selected to act on behalf of the Alliance. Volunteers were selected by their governments based on their talents and divided equally amongst the sectors. Bases have been set up and there is only one missing piece to complete the project."

She knew it was a rush of information, but she tried really hard to make it make sense. Mala seemed nice enough, but it hadn't made sense to her when they had explained it, well not until she arrived at the Base. Then she had met Hyder and it had all made sense.

"The Base for this sector is located on Morganti. We currently have a crew of six, including myself. Our mission as Sector Guard is to answer distress calls and to assist in any planetary evacuations and such." There. It had almost all been said.

Isabi decided to contribute. "Do you have questions?"

"One. Why are you here?"

As soon as the words were out of her mouth, Mala knew. They wanted her to join this project, this Sector Guard.

"We want you. Your talents with repairs are phenomenal and could be of tremendous help when we are assisting stranded vehicles." He smiled.

There it was again. He wanted her. Parts of her shivered in response and she internally slapped them into calm. "Why would I join you? What benefit is there to me?" It sounded mercenary, but a woman on her own couldn't be too careful with her financial future.

"The annual salary for the guard is three times what you earn as someone in ship repair, even on this station." He smiled again. "We checked all your records, official and not." His eyes were a dark gold, and when he smiled, they crinkled in the corners. The full pouty lips that were moving... "So will you join us?"

"What? Oh. Can I think about it?" Mala's mind was whirling. She wanted to follow him to the end of the universe, but she didn't know if she could work with him.

"I am afraid not. We are on a schedule and the others are picking up the last of our team members." He didn't seem sorry at all—in fact, he seemed to relish her distraction.

"I'll do it." The words shot out of her mouth without any additional prompting. Helen and Isabi looked surprised and then pleased.

"Do you need to collect your things?" Helen was speaking again. Her voice was stronger now.

"Give me five minutes. I will meet you at the repair dock." She nodded politely to them both and rose to her feet. She waited until they had preceded her out of the diner and then paid for the meal. Watching Isabi walk away was almost too difficult, but knowing that she would see him in a few minutes was heartening. She broke into a trot as soon as they were out of her sight. She didn't want to waste any more time.

Her jumpsuits were ready for travel, and two small duffels later, she had wadded up her entire three years on Kaddaka station. It was funny, really. She had lived here, but never been at home. Home was still where her mother was, halfway across the galaxy. Chuckling to herself, she closed her door and started down the hall with a quick stop at Station Registration so they would know her room was empty. She wasn't expecting to greet Vin on her way back to the repair dock and she certainly didn't expect him to be holding a blaster to Helen's head.

"Go back to Registration and get your room back, Mala. You aren't going to leave me." His voice trembled, but his hand stayed firm on the blaster.

"I am not leaving you, Vin. I am just getting on with my life. You remember life. It is something you do when you are not working."

"But the money! You can't leave me. The station repair dock is famous and it's all you, you and that freaky talent of yours." He shifted from side to side.

Mala saw a shadow flicker behind him.

"I have tried to duplicate what you do and it doesn't work!"

"Of course it doesn't. I can't do underhanded deals like you can. We all have our talents. And besides, Rihal and Gergar can do the jobs, no one has to know I am gone. The cradle still works just fine. Now let the nice lady go." Mala had her hands open and she was stepping toward Vin when he went down.

The shadow became solid and Isabi stood there, fists clenched.

Helen worked her way free of Vin's unconscious body. "What took you so long? He wanted to fire and he was going to, you twit!" She gasped for a moment and then punched Isabi in the arm. "Jackass."

Mala was just blinking. She had seen something that should have been impossible. Isabi had become shadow and then solid again. It was weird. Freaky. "What did I just see?"

Isabi grabbed her bags and took her by the arm. "I will explain on the way to our base. For now, let's get off this damned station as soon as we can."

She didn't have a chance to argue for an immediate explanation as she was dragged through the halls and to the repair dock.

Helen sprinted in front of them and was warming the engines as they arrived.

Isabi ran Mala through the entryway and sealed the door behind them. He stowed her bags, then shoved her into a seat.

"Sit still until we are away."

She sat and watched Helen become one with the ship. The pilot's seat was curling around her while cables descended from the ceiling. She plugged her wrists, knees and the back of her skull into the ship and it came to life at the contact. It was beautiful to watch. Mala clung to her seat as the ship lifted with a whisper of sound and began to move through the docks to the outer repair bay.

"Alliance priority override, Class One." Helen's voice was strong. The doors hissed open and they flew through to face the great doors opening out into space. This time, no one had cleared the lane for the ship, but it didn't matter to Helen. The Class One was wheeling, dipping and spinning through the traffic, sliding with the ease of a fish in water. "Prepare for jump."

Mala's eyes widened. "Jump? A ship this size? Are you nuts?" No ship this small had ever received a jump engine. It was the ultimate feat of engineering just to get an engine into a midsized freighter.

Isabi grinned at her. "Hold on. This is going to be rough."

He wasn't kidding. As soon as Helen barked *jump,* space folded around them, putting them in two places at the same time. Time stretched around them as they saw where they had been and where they would be. With a wrench, they were in a new star system.

Mala shook. Her body was in shock.

Isabi assessed her then moved swiftly to the rear of the ship. He returned in a minute with a hot cup of sweetened tea. "Drink it. It works wonders on your species."

She sipped a few times and then sighed as it did indeed help. "I have no species. I am a mutt. I have no idea who or what most of my ancestors were."

"If you are interested, we can help you with that. Our medical systems have most of the species specs for the Alliance and surrounding races." He held one of her hands and stroked her palm with his thumb.

She sipped at the tea. She took a deep breath and relaxed. She made no move to withdraw her hand. "I know my mother and knew my father. Few on Cadith could say as much."

"Knew?" He was close now, very close.

Stars, he smelled good. "He died five years ago, skimmer crash. It was when I had to go abroad to make enough credits for my mother to live comfortably." It had worked and she had sent enough money home to provide for her mother the rest of her life. A few lifetimes, actually. Her job had paid very well.

"A laudable activity."

He was almost kissing close now and it took all of her shaken self-control to hold back.

"Back away from the trainee, Isabi. No touchy feely until you are safe at home, and even then, she may not want your particular brand of attention." It wasn't Helen's voice. It was a male voice emanating from the com unit.

He did back away from her and released her hand. "Shut it, Hyder."

"Is that any way to speak to your commander?"

"It is the lesser of the comments that I could have given so yes."

Mala piped up, "Who is that?"

Helen half-turned. "That is Hyder Mihal. He is our team leader. Azon by birth, he has a talent for organization." There was a bit of pride and something else in her voice.

"And he is her partner in the Guard. So she is biased about his talents." Isabi's tone was dry and based on the look that Helen gave him she would punch him if she could reach him.

"Shut up, Isabi." Helen and Hyder's voices were in sync.

Mala giggled. Isabi's head snapped up as he stared at her and she felt herself blush from the roots of her hair to the middle of her ribcage. Fortunately for her, he couldn't see past her neckline.

"You have a nice laugh, Mala. You should laugh more often."

"And you should sit down for the landing. We are home," Helen barked the order and Isabi scrambled for the other seat. Her warning had come just in time as the small ship rocked and bumped in the outer atmosphere.

Mala fumbled with her empty cup and the straps, finally clamping the cup between her thighs as she buckled herself in. "We are going to the surface, not an orbital station?"

"Nope. The planet proper. Our facility is on the Western Continent."

Isabi had his eyes closed against the dizzying sight of the cloud cover whipping past their ship. Mala loved it—it reminded her of home. She hadn't been on a planet's surface in five years. She was looking forward to breathing unprocessed air.

She looked over at him again when she could tear her gaze away from the view out the main screen. His hands were curled around the armrests and he was extremely tense. "I am guessing that you don't like re-entry, Isabi."

"Not particularly. I have been in one too many crashes to be comfortable with it." The ship rocked and he clenched again.

As suddenly as it had started, it stopped. Helen guided them through the sky and toward a large group of structures on the far edge of a town. "Ladies and gentlemen, we are home." She did a slow loop around the facility before heading in for a landing.

They landed with nary a bump and unbuckled themselves. Helen had the ship retract the connections and she stretched. "That was a nice little jaunt. Hopefully the others will have similar luck on their recruiting runs."

"The others?" Mala remembered something about there being six members of the Guard on Morganti.

"Yeah. We need a full complement before we start operations. Once you go through your entrance procedures we will have seven."

"What procedures?" She should have asked a lot more questions before agreeing to come with them.

"Level testing, medical testing and of course, you need to go shopping."

"Shopping is a requirement?"

Helen winked at her. "It is in my book."

CHAPTER FIVE

Helen wandered off, leaving Isabi to lead her where she needed to go. He had recovered his calm and picked up the two duffels she had packed. "You really don't like flying do you?" She was trotting to keep up with him. She breathed deeply of the unprocessed air and smiled. Nothing like being on a living world.

"No. It is not a comfortable experience for me."

"I love it. There is nothing in the universe like flying through the stars." She smiled in remembrance. Had it only been that morning that she was on the cradle rushing to their ship? Right—their ship. "How did Class One come to be damaged? Was Helen damaged when it happened?"

"I will let our medical officer explain that. He knows more of it than I do."

The topic was clearly closed, and she could tell it made Isabi uncomfortable by the way he turned away from her. Silence fell between them as they walked the halls. Living on the station had helped her orient herself in grey expanses, but the brightly coloured doors and stripes in the halls made it ridiculously easy. MEDICAL was printed in large letters on a door in Alliance Common. It made it simple to find if you were in the right hallway.

"Hyder, we have our newest recruit, reporting for duty. Mala Deeha, this is Hyder Mihal, our commander chief and medical officer." Isabi stood aside and bowed formally to both of them as he completed the introductions.

"Welcome, Mala. Glad to have you here." The Azon was tall, muscular and covered with a fine bronze velvet. His feline features glowed in the interior lighting. "I am sure that you are familiar with the standard exam so just hop up here on this table and we can start the scanner."

She moved forward slowly. "I am not familiar with it. Will it hurt?"

Isabi blinked at her. "You haven't had an exam before?"

"No. I repeat, will it hurt?"

Hyder came and took her hand in his. "It doesn't hurt. It is a standard scanner, the same as you would use on a ship to check the wiring, which is basically what is being done here."

He helped her sit on the scanning table. She lay back at his gentle prodding and the hood began to slide up and down the table, beeping and chirping as it collected data. He kept his voice calm and she remained quiet as he explained the variety of tests that the scanner was running.

"It seems you have a minor mineral deficit as is to be expected if you have spent a few years without being planet side. No major defects of the respiratory or immune system, and oh…"

Isabi was still in the room. He straightened from his leaning posture against the wall and looked concerned. "What? What is wrong?"

"Isabi. Wait outside." It was an order and he backed it up with a glare to the Selna. As soon as the door closed, Hyder looked over at her worried frown. "Don't worry. The scanner just confirmed that you are a virgin. I didn't know if you wanted Isabi to know so I sent him outside."

"So a hymen will keep me from joining?" She couldn't see the problem.

He laughed. He had a good laugh. "No, not in the least, but Isabi is a male with considerable experience. If you two ever interact on that level he may expect you to be on population control."

"Why would you think that? That he and I would be. Would do. That."

"You are his partner. You will be sent on missions together without Helen, which will take considerably longer than if you are in the jump ship. You will be alone in a small ship for weeks at a time and a sexual relationship would not be unexpected." His eyes were kind and non-judgmental.

"Do you and Helen have a sexual relationship?" She sounded a little truculent, even to her own ears.

"Yes. We had been paired on a few assignments for the Alliance and it evolved very naturally."

"Do you love her?"

He looked surprised by her frank question, "I don't know. I know we are meant to be together, but I have not looked at it beyond that."

"How do you know?"

"My talent is the ability to see patterns. I see patterns in data, in living beings and in the stars. It was how I knew Helen when I saw her and how I matched you and Isabi as well as the others."

She looked at him suspiciously. "How often are you wrong?"

He moved the scanner hood off the table and helped her sit up. "Less than half of one percent of the time. And I have never been wrong about interpersonal relationships."

Mala mulled it over for a moment. "Does Isabi know? That we have been matched, I mean."

"He knows. It was why he was sent to bring you to us." He checked and doubled checked the results and waited. "How can you be of Terran blood?"

"What?"

"Your mitochondrial DNA is Terran by extraction. There is also some Nyal, Enjel and Moreski in there."

"Ah, according to my mother, my great-great-great-great-great-grandmother was stolen from Terra centuries ago and made a slave in the Nyal Empire." She bit her nail and looked at him seriously. "Is this what triggered my talent? The Terran DNA?"

"Well, it certainly helps to have all that diversity in your bloodline." He laughed and tapped at his data pad. Then frowned and tapped it again. "Stupid thing."

"May I? This is one thing I can do without prompting." She held out her hand had he placed the pad in it. She checked the workings and fiddled with it a bit. "Stop hitting it, for one thing. The electronics can't handle it." In her mind, she pictured it fixed and rewired. She could feel the mechanics squirming inside the box as it fixed itself. "That should do it." She handed it back.

He prodded it gently and then smiled. "It's faster. What did you do?"

"Simply rewired it a little. I took out some of the unnecessary components to use for the new bits." She shrugged. It was always a little weird to fix something and then have to try and explain what she did.

"You can do this with any mechanical devices? Make repairs, reconstruct?" Suddenly he was all business. He had switched from doctor to commander in seconds. "Will you demonstrate?"

"Something else? Something broken? Sure. It's what I do." There was comfort in it. In simply building, fixing, repairing with a mindless focus. "Lead the way, commander."

He nodded, helped her from the table and held her until she got her balance. He also held the door open and caught Isabi as he fell into the open doorway. "Listening at doors lacks a certain amount of decorum, Companion."

"But it lets me hear what is being said, most of the time anyway."

"You could have just shadowed through the door."

"*That* would have lacked decorum. I would not have interrupted the physician visit. The commander kicking into action, however, is fair game."

He scooped up the duffel bags and gestured for Hyder to lead the way.

They trekked through the halls and judging from the echoes up ahead, they were approaching a hangar or workshop of some kind. It was a workshop.

"This is your new office, Mala. When not on assignment, you can come here to work on repair projects or create your own. For now, I want to see your work on something that I can watch."

"Sure. What do you have?"

"A food dispenser. Some light engines. And Helen's toaster. Please, please fix Helen's toaster. It popped up and I struck it in reflex." A little sheepish, Hyder handed her a mangled piece of metal.

She had to hold it for a moment to determine its purpose. An image of bread came into her mind and she analyzed the process of the heated elements and the temperature trigger for the popping that Hyder mentioned. She took a deep breath and began to fix it. Her skin tingled and she felt Isabi behind her. He was watching her, almost touching, but not. His scent enveloped her and she finished the repair in record time. "There all done. Test it out."

Hyder whipped out some bread slices and shoved them into the toaster. They all waited pensively as it heated the bread and they heaved a sigh as it ejected with the distinctive pop that Helen must like. They examined it.

Hyder nodded. "Yup. That is what it is supposed to look like."

Mala jumped to her feet. She gave Hyder a brilliant grin and then turned to Isabi. *The turn was a miscalculation.* Everything went black.

CHAPTER SIX

Her voice was a harsh croak, "How embarrassing." There was a cold compress on her head and she was back in Medical. She tried to sit up, but was held back by Isabi's arm across her chest.

"Stay still, Mala. You fainted."

His voice was a warm rumble in her ear. She enjoyed it for the few moments required for the scanner to complete its rounds. "Huh. Two scans in one day. Lucky me." She laughed. "Usually I sleep for a while after I fix something, but today that just didn't seem to be in the cards. I think I was just tired."

Isabi was staring at her, but she didn't know what she was seeing. Concern, fear, exasperation and a strange tenderness that she shouldn't have been seeing crossed his features. "Hyder, did you tell him?"

"What? That you were exhausted and need some rest?"

"No, that I am a virgin." The words were out of her mouth before she remembered that she tended to feel like she had been given a few stiff drinks when she was tired.

Isabi blinked several times. He smiled, his teeth blazing white against the black velvet of his skin. "Virgin, huh? That explains a few things." He seemed almost relieved.

"Save it for later, Isabi. I need to get her chemistry balanced." Hyder shoved him out of the way and pressed a spray canister against her neck.

She flinched at the cold spray that invaded her and swatted him away when he came back for a second round. "I just need sleep and some food. I haven't had any rest and have done quite a bit more than is usual for me. The damage to Class One was extensive and it took a lot out of me. I just need to rest." She paused for a moment. "Maybe a sandwich, first."

He looked at her with his physician's face on. "Is this kind of collapse regular?"

"The larger the repair, the more it takes out of me. If I have the ability to rest after the initial exertion, I am fine. If not, I will collapse within twelve to twenty hours. Is that enough for your records?"

"It is a start, but I will require you to wear monitor pods for the next few days to continue your observation. I want to know what your talents do to your body and how your body reacts in turn."

"Fine. But I still want a sandwich." She was still lying flat and simply flinched as the tabs were put on either side of her neck. When Hyder moved to open her jumpsuit, Isabi stopped him.

"Hands off. I will do it."

Mala looked over at Isabi to find that he was almost bristling with hostility.

Hyder looked at him for a long moment and then nodded. "Fine. I will point the positions out and you need to apply the monitors."

"Do I get a say in this?"

"No." Both males were distracted by the monitors as Isabi prepared the next one for application.

When he reached for the join of her jumpsuit, she glared at him as he slowly opened it. He opened it to her navel and gently spread the centre just wide enough to get to the side of her left breast and attach a monitor pod, then attach one just below her collarbone. His fingers were warm and sure as they moved the fabric just enough to get the job done.

She felt unaccountably warm as he placed the monitors on her abdomen. There was something in his touch that she hadn't run into before, something that had her body reacting to him as if it knew him and wanted him.

The instant he pulled his hands back, she sealed her suit.

The monitors were sending signals to Hyder's data pad and he looked between the two of them speculatively. "Well, we can't do anything else. We will just have to watch and wait. You are dismissed. Isabi will show you to your quarters."

Hyder turned his back to them, but Mala could have sworn she saw a smile as they left. She stumbled a bit and Isabi swept her into his arms. "I can walk. I just can't walk fast."

"Be quiet, this is faster and I enjoy the feeling of you in my arms."

She decided to be direct. "Why is that? A guy who looks like you could have any woman he wants, why me?"

"I have been a Companion for over ten years and have met many women, but not one of them made me feel like you do." He kissed her forehead and smiled at her dumbfounded expression. "Is that so hard to believe?"

"Yes!"

His laugh was wonderful. He threw his head back to expose the cords of his neck and howled. He was still walking the halls with her while he chortled and they passed several support staff who looked startled to see the Selna laughing. It seemed to be an unusual occurrence. "Here we are."

It took a moment for it to sink in. *We,* he had said. Not *here you are.* As the door opened, she whistled in admiration. It was a common room with couches and a vid screen. Several doors led off the main room and Isabi carried her to one of them.

"This is your room. The sanitation chamber is to the left behind the bed. A personal vid and com unit is inside the wall. Your palm will trigger it."

She was feeling disoriented. "What about my sandwich?" It was all she could concentrate on, it was either that or start nibbling on her companion.

"I will take you to the dining hall now. I just wanted to drop off your luggage."

His blinding smile flashed at her in the shadows. He released the duffels from his shoulders and moved to one of the walls. A stroke of his fingers and the wardrobe released from the wall. Before she realized what he was doing, he had started to hang her collection of jumpsuits and undergarments up in the wardrobe. It took him less than two minutes.

"You don't worry about your clothing much, do you?"

"Not really. On the station there was nowhere to go and at home, well, my matchmate died twelve years ago and on Cadith you don't get a second chance." She shrugged. "Home and family was never in the cards for me after Jin died."

"Did you love him? The man you would have mated to?" Suddenly he was next to her, his golden gaze burning into her mossy green eyes.

"No. I didn't love him. I liked him well enough. We were friends first, a match second. If he hadn't died in a shuttle crash, we would probably have had a few kids by now." She laughed lightly, trying to break his concentration. His form fuzzed slightly as she mentioned kids, then solidified.

"Did you grieve for him?"

She reached out to touch the smooth velvet of Isabi's cheek. "I did. I mourned him and the life I could have had. It wasn't meant to be and then I went to Kaddaka, where you and Helen found me. Perhaps fate was involved." Mala leaned up until she could feel his breath mingling with hers. She cupped his jaw with her hand, loving the feel of him.

He leaned forward, trying to close the kiss.

"Where is my sandwich?"

CHAPTER SEVEN

"So this is our main dining hall. All of the support staff as well as the Guards eat here. Let's see what we can find for you."

He popped her into one of the seats at an unoccupied table and wandered off to make selections from the dispensers. There was an actual person behind one of the counters and he stopped for a moment to speak to her. Of course it was a her. Mala sighed and kicked herself for her foolishness.

Companions were known for their sexual prowess and he had probably slept his way through most of the female staff. In their conversation, they stopped and looked at her for a long moment and the woman smiled brightly at her, waving. Bemused, Mala waved back.

The woman gave Isabi a plate of something. He nodded formally to her, then returned to the table. "Here we go. Something here should qualify to fill that belly of yours. Stal gave me some of Helen's private stash of something called peanut butter and jelly."

Oh. So that is what the conversation was. She reached for the white fluffy sandwich with brown and purple paste, then bit in to it. Heaven. It was just what she needed. She scarfed it down and continued on to the rest of the tray. Her manners deserted her and she grabbed everything that looked like food or a component of food. When the tray was finally empty, she reached for the tea that Isabi held out to her with wonder in his eyes.

"I have never seen a woman eat like that."

"It's the downside of my talent. I can fix anything, but I lose my manners. I apologize." She nodded to him, but blinked sleepily. Her body was sated, now it needed sleep. She leaned her head on her hand and smiled. "Thank you, by the way. That was just what I needed."

"I live to serve. Now, I am going to get you back to your room before you fall asleep on me."

"That's nice." Everything was getting warm and hazy around her. When

Isabi got closer, she climbed into his arms without any complaints. He would keep her safe. Safe and warm.

She woke from the most restful sleep she had had in a while. She turned to see where the light in her room was coming from and couldn't. There was a masculine body blocking her way. Whoa. Isabi was watching her sleep. "Is it morning?"

"It is. You slept for twelve hours." He stretched.

She blinked. He was naked, beautifully and deliciously naked. She wasn't. She was still wearing the monitor pods, nothing else. "Did you undress me?"

"Of course. We are partners. We have no secrets." He pulled her down on top of him.

She stiffened for a moment until his warmth relaxed her. His erection was hot and very noticeable against her belly so she froze again. "Good morning, partner." It was her first kiss and it was enough to shake her world. At first the gentle brushing of lips had her sighing in pleasure, but as she began to feel the rise in her blood, she wanted more. She wove her fingers into his hair and held him still as her mouth duelled with his. When she parted her legs to get friction where she desperately wanted it, she moaned. It was the sound of her own voice that snapped her out of the sensual daze she was in. She jerked free of him and rolled off and onto the floor.

For a while they simply stared at each other, panting and then Isabi uttered a curse and swung off the other side of the bed. "I am sorry to have rushed you."

"I rushed myself. It felt so good that I forgot I had the monitors on. I am sorry for leading you on." She rose to get her clothing from the wardrobe, blushing and certain he could see every inch of it, including the spots that marked her spine and shoulders. That was the residue of her father's genes, a Moreski. Anyone who knew about their mating habits would have taken the spots as the easiest way to arouse her. Stroking, blowing or licking them would have her climbing the walls. But he had not.

"Do not apologize. I knew it was foolish to stay here last night, but I wanted to be near in case you needed me." He was putting on his trousers and tunic.

Damn. All that beautiful muscle covered by cloth. It wasn't fair. "Uh, I have to use the sanitation chamber. I will be back in a moment."

"If you say so." He smiled and let himself out the door.

With that cryptic comment tumbling in her mind, she went into the sanitary chamber and stopped short. The facilities were beautiful, an enormous tub, a waterfall shower and a lavatory that looked carved of granite. A door that didn't open at her touch perplexed her, but she was far too eager to take the shower for a test drive.

It was bliss. She spared a thought for her monitors and then decided that she didn't care. If they washed off, they washed off. The pounding of the water soothed her muscles, but more than that, when she turned her back to it, the water caressed her spinal marks in a way that had her shaking. She staggered forward and sat on the stone bench across from the fall. No wonder her mother had always insisted that she use the gel.

Shaking with her heart pounding like a drum, she staggered to the towels and dried herself. She jerked on a breast band and underwear then closed up one of her baggy jumpsuits. She fell to her knees under the power of her hormonal reaction and was getting up when the locked door burst open. She widened her eyes, but still couldn't see.

When Hyder called him, the urgency in his voice was unmistakable, "There is something wrong with Mala. Go to her now."

Cursing in every language that he knew, he ran from the common room, through his room and into their shared bathing chamber. She was on the floor with eyes gone blind with lust. The thick smell of her pheromones in the bathing room almost took him to his knees. He tried to calm her, "Mala! Are you all right? Hyder called me and told me you were in some kind of distress."

"Goddamned shower! Goddamned spots!" She was shaking uncontrollably and tears began to snake down her face in fat tracts.

"Your Moreski spots?" It finally came to him. She had showered in less than five minutes on the station—she must have been using gel showers. If she had never had a shower, then she would have been over stimulated when the water pounded against the spots. It would have set off every hormone she had.

"Damned spots." It was a sob. "Can't even wear my hair loose because of the damned spots."

Her hair looked down to him. "What do you mean?"

"I have a confinement net on my hair. The surface cut is what you see, but my locks are underneath."

She didn't move to undo the net, but he found himself wondering exactly what she looked like with her hair spilled around her, preferably on his pillow. Damn. He had never thought to find a mate and when he joined the Sector Guard, he had thought that it was an impossibility. After the orientation he learned, as did the others, that they were expected to pair off to create a foundation for the Guard. Romantically involved teams had their problems, but they were much more stable in small group assignments. No lover would leave their other behind.

"So your father was Moreski?" He had thought the blood was further back and that the spots were a throwback. He was mistaken. He felt himself smile. No wonder she wore loose fitting clothing on the deck. Normally it would be suicide for a repair specialist, but for her it was self-defence. She couldn't have anything pressing on her back. Her breathing slowed. She was calming, he could smell it. Slowly, sanity was returning to her eyes.

"Yes, he was of minor nobility, and marrying my mom made it impossible for him to keep his title. She was descended from slaves, you see, not worthy of him."

"But he took her as his wife anyway."

"Yes. Their love was one thing I never doubted. It was comforting when my talents developed." She blinked hard, then stood on her own.

Her suit gaped open in front and he was unabashedly staring at her breasts in their pretty blue band. "I hate to say this, but you may want to check your suit closure." She flushed that delightful pink again and fumbled her jumpsuit closed. Pity. All that creamy skin and now it was hidden. Damn. "Shall we return to medical? Or did you want some breakfast?"

"Breakfast sounds…"

She didn't finish her sentence, or perhaps she did and he didn't hear it. A claxon rang in both of their rooms. He grabbed her arm and pulled her along, "Come on. We have an assignment." He headed for the meeting room and sure enough, Hyder and Helen were waiting for them.

"I know we told you that we would not be engaging in any assignments yet, but we have an emergency. There is a ship foundering in orbit around Lexiss 3. It will completely lose orbit in the next two days if we don't render assistance." Hyder was all Commander now.

Mala piped up, "What is the problem with the ship?"

"There is a leak in the engines. The crew have been unable to stop the contamination and are now holed up in the shielded area on the main level."

She was aggressive and took a seat next to Hyder, looking at his report. "Are there any other ships who could render assistance?"

Isabi had to admit that he didn't want his *partner* that close to the Azon.

"Nothing in the area. The ship is a freighter and can't be towed. It is far too fragile and will shake apart if it hits the atmosphere."

"Do we get a pilot?"

"No. It will be just you and Isabi on this one. The planet is too close for a jump and Helen can't help inside the ship. So you two get to run solo in Shuttle Arion. Can you fly?"

His delicate little partner snorted.

"I had to catch ships in mid-flight before they crashed into the station. I can fly."

His pride in her skills was unwarranted, but it still warmed him. She slapped him on the shoulder and he looked at her curiously.

"Come on, Reda, let's go."

CHAPTER EIGHT

She brightened and wanted to get the show on the road, but it wasn't that easy.

Hyder moved to block her. "We have not yet settled the matter of your little incident this morning."

"I need a gel shower installed. I have a problem with the water pressure on my spots." She reached into her suit and pulled out all of the monitors one by one. The two she pulled off her neck were easy, but the one in her bra had been a bit of a struggle.

"The Moreski spots? Oh. I see."

He seemed to blush a little under her frank gaze. She guessed that he, too, thought the spots were for decoration. He knew better now.

"Isabi, keep an eye on her. Mark any change in her health and expect to have another scan when you return, Mala."

"Fine. Where is Shuttle Arion?"

Isabi grabbed her arm. "I will take you. We should get going." He led the way to the shuttle hanger.

She whistled in surprise. "Another Reflex ship?"

"Sort of. We are working on making it useable with a person who isn't wired like a pilot."

They entered the machine and she immediately headed for the pilot's seat. She ran her hands lightly over the controls, learning them one at a time until she was confident that she would be able to hit the correct button at the right time.

"You really enjoy flying, don't you?"

"I do. My father taught me as a teenager and I would engage in any number of manoeuvres that turned his hair black while we were going over our properties. It is one of my favourite memories. Shall we go?"

"Has Hyder given the ship the coordinates?"

"He has."

"Then by all means, terrify me." He gave her a grin and a wink, then strapped himself in. He had a package tucked in his hands, which he held on to firmly.

She backed out of the hangar and made for the launch ramp. "Do I need to contact ground control or anything?"

"No. No other ships are cleared for unsupervised takeoff and landing. Launch at will."

His eyes were closed so she did what she needed to do. She launched the shuttle as gently as possible. They floated upward through the atmosphere as lightly as a leaf on the wind.

He opened his eyes in surprise. "When did you launch?"

"Five minutes ago. You were too busy remembering all the women you have had in your life to pay attention." She was grinning at him so he would know that she was joking. Some people missed out on her sense of humour. The upper atmosphere was slightly rougher, but no more so than ripples on a pond. The instant they cleared the planet, she programmed the ship to take it to their destination at full speed.

She released her harness and stood to stretch and explore the shuttle. "I am going exploring." There was a tiny lavatory, a couch for two or more, a small counter for food and a dispenser for beverages and snacks. She had one immediately. The small repairs she had made to the ship while flying were enough to make her hungry, but not exhausted. A dry fruit bar and a hot cup of tea satisfied her craving and she went back to the pilot's seat with a sigh of relief. "Sorry. I got hungry."

"You will need this."

He held the package out to her and watched her carefully as she opened it. Inside was a bodysuit. It was blue and silver with a small SG intertwined above the heart.

"And you will need to decide if you want the people we meet to know you as Mala Deeha or as something else."

"Why wouldn't I want to use my birth name?"

"Will your family be safe if it is known that you are in the Guard? That you can fix any technology?"

His voice was serious and she had to think it out. "I want my mom to live in peace so I think I will go with an alias. But what?" She chewed her nail and he took her finger from her mouth.

"Stop that." He smiled at her. "I have a name for you, Fixer."

"Fixer?" She liked it. "But if my name is different, my face is still the same, that will be a problem, I think."

"Look at the complete suit. Try it on. Your identity will be safe."

He knew something about what she was about to put on. But she was going to have to try it on to find out. She walked to the back of the cabin and then stood for a moment, deciding whether to do it or not. "What the hell, you have already seen me naked," she muttered under her breath and then peeled off her jumpsuit. She had his full attention now so she turned her back to him, unconsciously showing him her spots. She heard his sharp intake of breath and shimmied into the new suit as fast as she could.

A cowl folded around her neck and she pulled the hood up over her head, then down over her face. So this was how she would protect her mom. By not being herself. By becoming Fixer and embracing her freak factor. Her dad had always laughed when he mentioned it. She had come home complaining of being called a freak by the other kids. He said her freak factor made her special, that it was part of her and that it was why he loved her. The arms of her suit left her palms open, but hooked around her middle finger to cover the back of her hands.

"There are boots to match it, in the couch storage area."

Curious, she flipped the seat of the couch up and sure enough there were some female boots. The masculine versions were right next to them, along with another suit. "Who are you when you are not Isabi?"

"I have no name. I have no one to protect."

"I think you need a name. Shade. You are Shade." She crossed her arms over her chest and smiled at him.

"Why Shade?" He was stripping off and putting on his own suit, black with just the tiniest black embroidered logo on his chest.

She wanted nothing more than to run her fingers over it. "Shades are ghosts, but shade is also the place I fell asleep as a child, knowing that the sun couldn't burn me there, that I was safe. In the shade." He had frozen halfway through her explanation and looked into her eyes as a wave of emotion ran through him. She saw lust, fear, envy and a deep caring. Going up on tiptoes, she put a gentle kiss on his lips. He grabbed her waist and pulled her against him, deepening the kiss until they were both panting and the fit of his suit around his groin was no longer as precise. She backed away regretfully. "I don't think this is the time or the place. Dammit."

He scrubbed his face with one hand and stepped back himself. "You are right. But one day it will be the right place, and right time, and we will have a door that stays locked."

"Right. Right. I wonder how much time that will take?"

"Hopefully not long or parts of me will be turning blue."

"Right. A distraction. So does my suit have any extra features?"

"It is radiation resistant and the fabric is stiff, it shouldn't bother your spots. Let me know if it does."

"If it does, what will you do?"

"Find a time, a place and a locked room."

The devilish look on his face made her laugh out loud. "It isn't fun, you know."

"What isn't?"

"To know that someone touching you in the right spot will make you theirs until they tire of you. It was always something that my parents taught me. Watch my back." She stretched and looked back over her shoulder, catching her reflection in the view screen. It was not her. It couldn't be.

The creature looking back at her was strange, sexy and had eyes that were wide in surprise in the confines of the mask. She started to run a hand down her suit and then stopped. It was far more form fitting than it had any right to be and her breast band stood out noticeably. She turned to Isabi. "Is it supposed to look like this?"

"Well, it wasn't designed to be worn with undergarments." He eyed her up and down, then nodded.

"Well, I am not stripping again." Mala mulled it over for a moment, then parted the centre closure. She simply undid the front binding and released the band, then drew it out of the suit. For her underwear, she reached into the pocket of her old jumpsuit and withdrew her knife. Cutting the bands on either side released them and she took them off. The closure of the suit was smooth and when she looked at her reflection again it was better. No unseemly lines to mar the sweep of the suit. "Better?"

Isabi was sitting down and swallowed heavily. "Much. Do you cut your clothing off often?" He wasn't hiding his erection, but it was fighting with the fabric of his black suit, one more shadow on the darkness.

"I have gotten stuck in engines a few times. It has been a necessity. Part of the problem with wearing the baggy suits." She turned from left to right and enjoyed the feel of the suit. "I can't feel this one on my back at all. What is it made of?"

"I have no idea. I only know that it is impervious to slicing, fire resistant and insulating. The researchers have also created a few other specifics for other talents. Mine, for example, moves as I move."

"You mean when you go shady and walk through things? I noticed that you made it into my quarters on the station without opening the door and you snuck up on Vin in the hallway when he had those eyes in the back of his head. It wasn't too hard to figure out." She shrugged and winked at him.

"And here I try to be a man of mystery." He smiled. "It made me very good as a spy on Companion assignments."

Mala headed back to the pilot's seat. "A spy? Is that what you were?"

"Amongst other talents. Yes." He took the navigator station and turned to her. "So, Fixer. What is our ETA?"

"Two hours. What shall we do?"

"I think that we should engage in a time honoured method of wasting time."

She raised one eyebrow in surprise. "Really?"

He raised his hand holding a small object. "I thought a little card game would be in order. Winner buys dinner when we make it home."

"The winner buys? That is a little counter to regular rules."

"I like to walk on the wild side." He popped a table up between them and shuffled the cards. "Would you like to cut?"

She reached out to take the slick cards from him. "You have no idea what I would like at this point."

CHAPTER NINE

The proximity alarm went off after the ninth round of cards. "I win, so dinner will be on me."

Isabi shook his head and smiled. "You have no idea what image that puts in my mind."

Mala swung around and looked at the freighter through the view screen. "Don't be so sure of that," She muttered it under her breath, but his reflection in the screen gave her a startled grin, followed by a wink.

"Freighter Dunlap, this is the Sector Guard shuttle Arion. Please confirm status." He sounded so calm and controlled as he spoke a small thrill went through her.

The signal crackled, but was audible, "This is Captain Anar of the Freighter Dunlap. The crew have taken shelter in the secure hold, but the leak in the engines has contaminated most of the ship. We are falling into the planet. Can you help?"

"I have a repair specialist onboard who should be helpful. We will contact you once we have more information on the repair."

"I look forward to it. Dunlap out." The connection was broken.

"Fixer, can you put us down near the engines?"

Her lips twitched, "Shade, it would be better if I moved that chunk of debris over there against the damaged engine."

"Why is that?"

"If there is a breach I need to seal, it would be better if I have inert material to use for the patch, rather than our shuttle."

He turned to her, surprised. "You do that?"

She winked. "When I have to. It is rather draining. Bring a sandwich." She was still chuckling when she had another thought, "Do we have environmental suits?"

"Third cabinet on the left."

She nodded and concentrated on using the nose of the Arion to move chunks of debris up against the engine, careful not to block the flow of radiation. She had to embed them in the ship so she shoved hard. A resounding dent in the nose of their shuttle was the result. "I will fix it later, I promise."

Now, all she had to do was to set the shuttle up against the nearest airlock, but out of range of her talent. One quarter of a kilometre should do. She had the side of the Arion kissing the hull of the Dunlap and engaged the mag locks. The two ships gravitated to each other with a clunk. "Honey, I am home." She smiled and turned to her partner, half dressed in his environmental suit, "Are we ready to go?"

"I am, Fixer. Suit up."

"Fine. Don't forget my food."

He patted a pocket on his thigh. "Have it right here."

She clambered into her suit and then waited impatiently as he checked her seals. She put on her helmet and snapped it into place. "Let's go." She was hopping from foot to foot with impatience, but stopped him long enough to check his seals. "Safety first."

Their enviro suits were colour coded the same way their bodysuits were. She was in blue and silver and he in solid black. She imagined that they made quite the striking couple, bubbleheads and all.

The Dunlap was in rough shape. She could have spent a year in it and still had more to do. For now, her focus had to be on fixing the engine and getting the ship able to run. First task, keep the environmental system up and running. Isabi led her through the ship and gave her the run of the repair. From the bridge, she accessed the enviro controls and turned up the oxygen, then made sure that the food dispensers were working. No stupid deaths on her watch.

After she was sure that the existing crew was fine, she moved to the problem area. Behind her, she heard Isabi in contact with the Captain of the ship. He was updating the man as she moved through the ship. The tears in the hull were obvious to her senses and she felt the *wrongness* of the state of repair that it was in. "This ship is in crappy shape. It hasn't been inspected in years." She was murmuring to herself, but he heard her.

"If you fix it, how long will it last?"

"*When* I fix it, it may have one year left. It needs a full overhaul. The metal fatigue alone is appalling." She was muttering. "Okay, time to earn my pay." She turned to Isabi. "You might want to wait out here. There is a lot of radiation in there and you don't need to expose yourself."

"I will expose myself if I wish." His grin was easy to read. "When I shift, I am impervious to the effects. These suits also defend you longer than a standard suit."

She paused in front of the engine room door. "Well, here we go." The blast of heat that rushed from the room almost took her breath away. "That has to go."

She rushed to the cracked and bleeding power supply and pressed her hand against it. Nothing. Aw hells, she couldn't do this with gloves. Sneaking a glance at her escort, she peeled off one of her gloves and held her hand against the glowing metal. She hissed in pain, but kept the contact as she sealed the leak. Rubbing at her palm, she took a deep breath and concentrated on what needed to be done next. Propulsion was needed to move them from orbit so she had to bend her mind to the most efficient means of repairing it.

"What did you do to your hand?" Isabi was scowling at her, his gold eyes shooting sparks.

"I had to make contact to fix the containment. Now I have to crawl around in the ducts to make enough repairs to the engine to make it suitable for propulsion. See you in two hours." She gave him a cheerful pat on the arm and opened the access panel. With both gloves back on, she scooted into the bowels of the ship.

She was glad that she had placed the debris in contact with the ship. Her repairs ate half of them in the first hour. Wiring had to be replaced, new ducts generated, coolant replenished and cracks sealed. She had no idea how long she had been in the engine itself until her stomach growled. Time to go.

The engine was in working condition. It would get the crew to the next repair station, but she had not done the full overhaul that the ship needed. It was no longer her job. She was here to get them out of danger, not to rescue them from their own stupidity. She crawled along her new ducts and had to admit that the engine was in better shape now than it had probably been in for twenty years. She did good work.

Coming out of the crawlspace was a relief and Isabi's hand had never been more welcome. She smiled up at him through her bubble and then unsnapped the seals and took off her helmet. "All clear. You can tell the captain that as soon as we are away, he can fire it up and get out of here." Her environment suit was trashed. It was covered with soot, coolant and some things that she didn't want to identify too closely. She grimaced and peeled off the suit. It was limp so she turned it inside out to confine the stains. "Sorry. I hate grubby suits."

He shook his head and took his own suit off. "So that they won't think you are the only one impervious to grime. The Captain is on his way."

The stomping of feet on metal grating let her know that it was more than just the Captain coming to greet them. The crew stopped short just inside the door of the engine room.

Mala whispered to Isabi, "I am not naked, am I?"

"Nope. But that suit fits you very well." He wrapped one hand around her waist and moved toward their audience. "Captain Anar. I am Shade, this is the Fixer. Your ship will make it out of orbit and she has sealed the leak. The engine will not be at full power, but should get you to a repair station."

"*You* fixed the ship? I thought that Shade was the repair person."

"Uh. Nope. And you should kick yourself for letting your engines get in that kind of shape. They haven't been checked in years. No wonder the power housing cracked." She stood with her head up, shoulders back, chest out. No one could tell her that her work wasn't precise.

"I thank you and the Sector Guard for your help, then. We should be on our way. Will you remain in the area until we are sure that the repairs will hold?"

Isabi's fingers tightened on her waist and she kept her voice controlled, "Of course we will. It wouldn't do to have you falling back planet side after I did all that work. Shade? Let's head out."

"We will be in contact the instant that we reach our ship and separate." He nodded to their audience and simply walked straight through the group. Not around them. With his arm around her, he walked *through* them. She wobbled a bit when they solidified, but was able to keep her balance as they made it to the airlock. She had it cycle once and then open, the lightest touch of her hand controlling the seals. With her worksuit and helmet under one arm and the other wedged against Isabi, the instant that he let her go, she hit the floor knees first.

"Fixer, are you all right?" He picked her up.

"Just hungry. Get me in the pilot's seat and get me a snack bar. I have a feeling these jerks aren't going to wait until we are off to fire up." He dropped her into the seat and she strapped in. A few toggles had the mag locks releasing, but she had to wait until they drifted off before firing her own engines. Their drift took them right into the path of the newly repaired engine exhaust ports. She counted down as Isabi slapped a snack bar into her hand. She munched and watched the distance from the ship grow second by second.

"Strap in. This is going to hurt."

He buckled in then snorted, "Isn't that my line?"

"No, your line is it will only hurt for a moment." She grabbed the controls and hit the throttle less than a second before a blaze of superheated gasses hit the mooring spot that they had occupied. "Assholes!"

"Captain Anar, what the hell are you playing at? You almost barbequed us!" Isabi was furious. Apparently he hadn't actually thought that the crew of the Dunlap could be that stupid.

"Almost? Then I was too slow. No one shall know of our presence here."

"Aw hells." Swallowing the last of the bar, Mala gripped the controls and gunned her engines. The Dunlap was way too heavy to follow, but she now knew why their ship was in such bad repair. They were Travellers. It explained the brightly coloured clothing that she had seen and the off the charts oxygen consumption. There were women and children on that ship. Whole families. "Anar, I have no quarrels with the Travellers and would not report you to the authorities. We *are* the authorities and we don't care who you are. We simply came to help. We wish to leave without incident as well."

"You are serious, you do not wish to have us hauled to the nearest secure facility?" The disbelief was obvious in his tone.

"At this point I simply want you to get the repairs that the ship desperately needs. I will send you the specs and those repairs will take you to a conclave. You are putting your people at risk in such a minimally active transport." She kept her voice calm, but she was watching the movements of the ship closely. If they set up for pursuit, the freighter would never make it. Mala was not going to have those people's deaths on her conscience. She would go back to the ship if it was necessary, but she was hoping that Anar would see sense.

Long moments of silence ran between the Arion and the Dunlap. Finally, "I apologize for my impulse. It is seldom that we meet someone willing to offer assistance without an ulterior motive."

"Your apology is accepted and I wish you the luck of the stars." Breathing a sigh of relief, Mala turned to Isabi and gave him a wink. "Now, follow the directions I have sent and get those emergency repairs as soon as you can. Sector Guard operative Fixer, out." She closed the com and sat back looking at her partner, "How was that?"

"Amazing. How did you know that it was a Traveller ship?" He was leaning back in his chair and observing her closely.

"They were consuming much more oxygen than their official tally should have been using. That and the seventeen ear piercings on all of the men over twenty." She set the autopilot and left her seat. She was halfway to the small galley when she fell to her knees.

He was at her side in an instant, lifting her. "Mala? What is it?"

"How long was I in the engine?"

"Five hours or so. I checked on you a few times, but you didn't respond."

"Isabi, I really need some food. Now." The world was growing brighter, large spots swimming in her vision. He deposited her on the couch and went to the galley.

"You know, I should request extra pay for being a waiter."

"Ha ha. Make with the food." She flopped her hand weakly. "You can take it out of my hide later." She made the offer before she realized what she was saying, but his sudden spin and grin brought her impulsive words back to her in a moment. "Hells."

He barked a laugh and returned to her with a tray of snacks. "I will hold you to that when we land. For now, I am more concerned with the fact that you just turned grey. Start with the fruit juice."

He ceased to exist as she took the tray. She needed to eat and this was food. When the tray grew empty, hands took it away and replaced it with some hot soup and bread. She finally was full after a third tray had been given and emptied. "I need some rest now." She put the tray aside and lay on the couch. Isabi was looking at her in concern. He tidied up the food trays then returned to her side, picking her up to move behind her on the couch, becoming a living bed for her to rest on. His breathing soothed her and she felt herself slipping away.

Isabi was sure that the food that she had consumed was going to swell her belly to enormous proportions, but her stomach was flat and there was no trace of all the food that he had seen her eat with dainty bites.

Hyder was going to have to investigate her metabolism. He suspected that her body used her own materials for certain repairs and the food was an internal replacement of the minerals and vitamins that she had lost.

It would explain why she ate thousands of calories at a sitting, but didn't gain any weight. Her body hummed gently on top of his and he wondered what was going on inside at the molecular level. Mala was a symphony of biochemistry all working together. The trust that she showed by curling gently against him had him shaking with the urge to peel her suit from her.

The suit was so form fitting he had had to stop himself from punching

Captain Anar in the jaw. The scent of masculine interest had been thick in the room the instant that they saw Fixer and his own reflexes had swung into the possessive range.

All those years as a Companion and he finally found the woman he wanted at his side forever, but she had no clue that his interest was this powerful. She would learn. There was no way that Fixer would get out of the Shade.

CHAPTER TEN

"So I hear that your first assignment went successfully." Hyder was waiting for them after she brought the Arion in for a landing.

"Apparently. They were on their way when we left. The engine should last them the better part of a year." It was hard to keep a serious conversation going when Isabi had her clutched to his chest like an infant.

"Isabi updated me on your condition. You consumed half a week's rations in one sitting. That is impressive. What is even more impressive is that you don't weigh three hundred pounds right now." They were on their way to their quarters. "Why aren't you taking her to Medical?"

Isabi snarled, "Because unless we monitor her during a large repair and then immediately after you won't have the full spectrum of information. So watching her digest her lunch is not really going to do you any good."

Bemused, Mala simply cuddled against the source of warmth that was Isabi's chest. They walked through the common room and into his quarters. "Your room? I thought I was going to sleep."

"You are. But from now on, you sleep with me."

He was being very alpha but she decided she didn't mind. It was just easier to let him carry her to his room and undress her. Wait. Undress her? Her skin pinked with embarrassment as he peeled her suit off her. He stopped to examine her hand and shook his head with a quirky grin.

"So you heal fast. I was wondering."

She had forgotten about her burn. Come to think of it, she had often fixed radiation leaks with her bare hands and been fine afterward. It had never occurred to her that it was part of her talent that fixed her body. She had simply put it down to not being severely injured. Apparently that wasn't the case. She healed herself. Interesting.

He moved back and stripped his own suit off. His interest in her was obvious and standing in a curve that almost reached to his belly, but he wasn't in a hurry. He simply pulled back the bedding, tucked her in his bed and then curled around her, guarding her. He was warm and she snuggled against him as if his heartbeat was soothing. A jaw-cracking yawn later and she was out.

Something was tugging at the back of her head. "Wha..." She batted at it, but it continued.

"How long is it anyway?" He was unravelling her hair. It slowly came out of the confiner and then he spread it out and across the pillow. "Wow. Pretty." His fingers were combing it smooth and he finished his task.

"My father would hate it. I had to cut it to fit in the confiner. It used to hang to my ankles in Moreski fashion, but I couldn't go onto a station like that." She was blushing again, she could feel it. His admiring look was far too frank for her.

"It is beautiful. Every colour of the rainbow is here—why do you cover it with such a drab dye?"

"Moreski nobles don't socialize with other species. It marked me as different and I had enough trouble with that already." He was nuzzling at her neck and inhaling her scent. She returned the favour and soon they were rolling together in a tangle of limbs. Mala's heart was pounding as he moved between her thighs and then she sighed in relief as he entered her.

He rocked into her, gaining ground inch by inch until he hit the barrier. He took her mouth in a kiss and reached behind her to stroke her spots. She moaned and arched to him, breaching herself on his turgid length.

He kept one hand on her spine and stroked her every time he withdrew. Her body arched up to keep him inside and they set a rhythm of attack and withdraw. A firmer pressure on her spots made her moan again as her body clenched around his and he moaned in return at the grip that her channel provided, milking him. A few short thrusts and he joined her in release.

He slumped over her for a moment to get his breath, then withdrew to lay beside her. His hands gently moved over her back, this time avoiding her spots, to sooth and relax her. He gave her a gentle kiss on her forehead. "Next time it will be better."

She was confused. "It wasn't good?"

A startled look washed his sated expression away. "It was amazing. But it was your first time and I didn't want to draw it out too much. You would have been too sore."

She thought about that for a moment, "All right, if you say so. But you are forgetting one thing."

"What is that?"

"I heal really fast." She gave him a quick kiss on the nose and watched his eyes as the ramifications of her statement washed through him. She gave a shriek of laughter as he rolled her beneath him again. "Do it better this time."

His mouth was on her collarbone and he was moving lower when he said, "Oh, I intend to."

She was giggling as he continued his exploration and it was almost an hour later when they fell apart again. "That was better. But next time, I want it to be *amazing*. Isabi, you had better get some rest."

"Moreski women, insatiable." He was muttering, but didn't seem displeased. In fact there was a certain pride in his tone.

"No, I am sated. I am simply optimistic." She couldn't help it, some laughter escaped. He delivered a swat to her behind and dragged her with him to the shower. A gel shower had been installed, but that wasn't where he towed her. He went straight to the waterfall and stood with his back to the pounding water, letting the mist and the water run off his body and onto hers.

"This is how you take a shower, Fixer."

"So I have to stand in the Shade." She smiled at him over her shoulder and enjoyed his ministrations as he soaped his hands and washed her back with smooth gentle strokes. He washed her hair with the same thorough attention and smiled as she ran her own hands through her locks. The dye faded away and the shortened hair grew out before his eyes to flow into the rainbow of hair that fell around her. "I am fixing it." She smiled at his surprise and turned to let him wash her front. That led to another round of frolicking and Mala learned why sex in the shower was such a popular fantasy for women. It was fun and then you rinsed yourself off for the rest of the day.

CHAPTER ELEVEN

"So you used the Arion as a battering ram?" Hyder was not too impressed with the dents in the shuttle. He hadn't turned to see them, he was caught up with the inspection.

"I had to move debris in place so that I would have raw materials to make the repair." She was wearing one of her jumpsuits. The baggy fabric was still serviceable, but she felt it was lacking a certain amount of style. She had really liked the new uniform, but it was being cleaned. She let her hair flow free today. It felt good. Even inside the open hangar, it caught the breezes and swung as she moved.

"You will have to explain to me how that works."

"Get me some sheet metal and I will show you." She passed him and moved to place her hands on the nose of the Arion. He stopped her with a hand to her arm and was spun around as Isabi grabbed him. Mala looked at her lover in surprise.

He looked down in embarrassment. "Sorry. Instinct."

Hyder actually looked at them, took in her loose hair and the possessive hand that Isabi wrapped around her waist. "It is understandable under the circumstances. Congratulations."

Isabi nodded and Mala felt a bemused expression cross her face. Men. Full of strange rituals that only another of their kind would understand.

"Your hair looks very nice, Mala. Your father was a royal?"

"Some kind of noble, yeah. He gave it all up for my mom and me." Tears welled in her eyes and she drew a deep breath, "Now, on to the mess I made of the Arion."

"I would like you to be wearing monitors while you work. Isabi, would you help her apply them? Hands, neck, heart, lungs, abdomen, temples and anywhere else you think she may have measurable power output."

Together they wired her up, his dark glances as she opened her jumpsuit was enough to cause a spike on her heart monitor the instant it was placed.

"Playtime is later, kids. This is business."

They giggled through the rest of the applications and then she was all fully dressed and ready.

"Sheet metal?"

"Does it have to be metal?" Hyder was curious—it showed in every line of his face.

"Did I miss it?" Helen came running up to them and Hyder grabbed her waist as she skidded to a halt in front of Mala.

Mala snorted. "No, you didn't miss it. I was just about to start. And in answer to your question, Hyder, it doesn't have to be metal, but the closer the repair substance is to the item I am repairing, the less tiring it is. Technically, I have repaired broken wiring using a sandwich."

Isabi let out a low whistle. "So that is why you have an obsession with sandwiches."

"Well, I was caught in a storm at the time so it was all I had."

Helen frowned at her. "I can't believe you would have let your wiring get into disrepair."

"I didn't. It was cut." She put enough firmness in her tone to let them know that the subject was closed. "Now. On to poor Arion. Where is that sheet metal?"

It was anticlimactic. They watched her repair the ship. She watched the ship become solid and beautiful again. Quietly she made a few improvements on the hull structure, but since they couldn't see what she was doing to the metal, it simply became a blip on the monitors.

She stepped back after examining her work and bumped into Helen. She grabbed the pilot's arm for balance and her talent surged to the fore. There was something wrong with Helen's wiring and her talent wanted to fix it. She released her hand from the jack with an effort. "I am sorry. Are you having problems with your jacks?"

Hyder looked at his partner, concerned. "Helen, are you? Why haven't you said something?"

"It is just some discomfort. Nothing that will stop me from doing my job. The implants have never felt right. You know that." Helen flexed her arm where Mala had grabbed her. "This one is suddenly pain free. What did you do?"

"I think, I am not sure, but I think that I changed the composition of the implant to something you weren't allergic to. If it works, I can do the same to the others."

"I am *allergic* to my pilot implants?"

"Of course. It is a common problem, but I have never gotten to touch a pilot before so I didn't know why." Her stomach rumbled in protest. "Now, we get to the fun part. Anyone want to follow me to the dining hall? The feeding frenzy is about to start."

Isabi chuckled and the others looked a little bewildered, but they followed her to the dining hall. Isabi ran shuttle for her as she ate, and ate, and ate. Hyder was looking at his data pad in confusion and Helen was just watching wide-eyed, sipping her tea.

When she finally ceased to eat and dabbed at her lips with a napkin, a group of support staff stood at one end of the cafeteria and applauded. Grinning, she stood and bowed. "Thank you, thank you."

Hyder was glued to his readout and eventually he blinked and looked up at her. "You didn't digest any of it. It simply broke down when it touched your stomach. It's amazing. Your body ate it, absorbed it, and there is nothing left."

Mala was fascinated. Because she didn't get sick, she had never been to a physician before Hyder. No one had even thought to examine her talent before today. "Whoa. I need a nap."

Hyder was on his feet, but Isabi picked her up before he could touch her. "Your body has gone into a dormant state. It seems to be processing the new material. You need to rest."

"Duh, what did I just say? I need a nap." She curled up and dozed off, trusting Isabi to take her somewhere safe.

"All right, sleeping beauty. It is time to wake up."

It wasn't Isabi's voice, it was Helen's. Mala glared at the woman through slitted eyes.

"We need to get you something to wear."

That perked her up. "Shopping?"

"Yeah, shopping. And then we can discuss the improvement you made to my implant." Helen threw the covers back to expose Mala's jumpsuit. "You have got to improve your style. That hair of yours demands a little more...oomph." Helen grabbed her hands and dragged her out of bed.

Mala stomped into boots and followed the pilot out to a skimmer. "Where are we going?"

"Into town. There are a few shops in there that I think you will love."

"Isn't there a supply station at the base?"

"Not for the kind of clothing I think you need." Helen sighed as she steered around traffic. "Mala, we are women who have dirty jobs to do. We put our lives and bodies on the line with every working day. We need to be women on our time off, with all the fripperies that we can manage."

"I used to dress in a more feminine manner before I had to start earning my way in the world. In our house, we dressed for dinner, attended local events and were a social family. That all stopped when my father died. With everything in his name, my mom was left with nothing when his family came to claim the body. We weren't even allowed to bury him."

Helen looked shocked. "You are can't be serious."

"I am, very. I had to find a way to make enough money to support my mother. She had never needed to support herself. So I took a job at the Kaddaka station and tried out for the Repair Specialist position as soon as it became available."

"And now you are here."

"And now I am here." Mala took a deep breath. "My mother is safe and stable and now my life can begin." She was no longer fighting tears. Her mercurial moods were courtesy of her father. Pieces of him were still left in the world. "So where did you want me to shop first?"

"Zalbeeliyah's. They have some fantastic gowns as well as daily wear." She set the skimmer down in a small lot and thumbed the lock. "I think we also need some footwear along the way."

"Perhaps shoes first?" She eyed her service boots and smiled grimly. "Definitely shoes first."

"Tal's, then. They can do wonderful things with leather and laces." She steered Mala down the street, waving at a few people that they passed. "The people here are so friendly. Over seventeen races are represented in the shopkeepers alone."

"Interesting." She dug her heels in and looked through some of the shop windows. "When we come back, I want *that.*" She was pointing at a gown for display in one of the windows.

"Well, it's a good thing that it is on our list. That is Zalbeeliyah's." Helen continued on her way and soon they were in the doorway of a shoe shop. "Tal! I have a job for you. She needs something for every occasion."

"I will do my best, but based on those hefty ship boots, I don't know if she will be amenable to my suggestions." He was rather snotty for an Ontex, but he was right about her boots.

"I will be amenable if you get your silver butt in gear and get my size, we will get along so much better." Mala flipped her hair and his large black eyes were immediately drawn to it as she knew he would be. She looked like Moreski royalty even if she wasn't.

"Yes, my Lady. What would you like to see first?"

Helen was standing back and just watching Tal fall all over himself to get the shoes as Mala selected them. She almost laughed at the pilot's face as the boxes piled up. It took more than an hour, but finally she had to ask. "Do you have something more stylish in a work boot?"

Tal's eyes lit from within. "I have just the thing." He brought out a long box and laid it at her feet. "Impervious to weight and pressure, heat resistant to six hundred degrees."

"Oh, they are lovely." She took one of the boots out and slipped it on. It hugged every inch of her leg, literally. "Masuo?" The leather caressed her and closed into a seamless fit. It was beautiful—it was alive.

"You are very discerning, Lady. It is indeed Masuo, generated by forced growth. Lab grown."

"You are lying. The striations here cannot be given in a lab. They are wild, the marks occurred in nature as a result of weather interference in the growth pattern, but as we are on Morganti, it is legal for you to sell them so why the subterfuge?"

Tal laughed. He chuckled and howled. "I have been waiting for someone like you to walk into my shop. Take the Masuo, with my compliments. We grow them out back."

It took her a second and then Mala chuckled as well. "And because you grow them, and it isn't legal to ship them, you sell them as cloned. Very smart. And, considering the business that I have given you today, I will take them with thanks." She chuckled and gave him the formal bow that she had been trained in since she was a child.

He bowed back and they took care of the little matter of paying her bill.

"Wow. That was a load off. Can you have the rest of the shoes shipped to the base? Except for those lovely casual slippers. I will break those in with the rest of my shopping." She gave him a brilliant grin, showing teeth.

"Yes, Lady. The Masuo and *these* as well?" He was gesturing to her work boots.

"Yup. All. Send them all to the base to the Sector Guard quarters, please." He looked up, startled and she sailed out wearing the new slippers, Helen giggling in her wake.

"How did you know all that?" Helen trotted to keep up with her. "About the boots, I mean."

"Masuo are highly prized on many worlds, but only grow wild on a few. You can't trade in the wild creatures, but can sell the clones."

"I mean, how did you know what they were? What are they?"

"A fungus and vegetable combination that grows wild. You can train them to take on a shape and then once you have them in that shape, you can coax them free of their mooring. The only down side is that you have to find them a host to live on within a few months or they die."

"A host?"

"Yup. They feed off of the auras of sentient beings. It is a painless process and they provide protection to their wearer." The new slippers were a good fit. They left no hotspots or other types of irritation on her feet.

"Oh. Neat." Helen took the lead and opened the door for her at the dress shop. "Now for my favourite part of our trip. The true experience of shopping."

Gowns of every colour and shape were all over the shop. It obviously catered to a large variety of species. When the l'nal came out of the back room to serve them, Mala suddenly understood the variety of the clothing.

"Zabby! This is my friend, Mala. Mala, this is Zalbeeliyah. Our resident l'nal and fashion maven."

"Oh my dear, is that what you wear with that hair and that skin? It cannot be!" The seven-foot spider scuttled toward her and measured her with a scanner. "I have just the thing."

"I would like to try on the gown in the window, if I may?" It was best to be polite with the carnivorous creatures. They were as quick to anger as they were talented.

"Excellent choice." She scuttled over to the window and had the mannequin stripped in seconds. "Come with me to the fitting area and take off that horrid jumpsuit." Her true voice emanated in a series of clicks and squeaks. The translator around her thorax did the speaking in Alliance Common.

It was an orgy of fabric, snacks and beverages. They spent hours laughing, twirling and even Zabby tried on some gowns. The result caused more hilarity. The gown from the window was a perfect fit after a few minor alterations and she was going to wear it home. The light rainbow effect of the fabric contrasted with the dark rainbow of her hair. It was so perfect that Zabby just stood looking at her for a long moment.

"You are giving me ideas. Come back in a few weeks, I may have something new for you to look at."

The financial matter was settled and she put in an order for some more suitable jumpsuits. Again, ordering the clothing to be delivered to the Sector Guard, she swept out of the shop wearing the rainbow gown and a matching shawl. Helen trailed behind her, shaking her head at the amount of money that Mala had spent. "I haven't shopped since before my father died, Helen. It was time."

Helen immediately brightened at that. "So this kind of binge isn't normal for you?"

"Hell no! I just needed to get everything from the skin out. The rest of my clothes are on Cadith." She saw a floating shadow near her and stepped into it. It moved away. "All right, Isabi. You can come out now."

His laugh appeared before he did. He was wearing a deep blue shirt tucked into black trousers that clung to him in a sinful manner.

Now that she knew the body behind the clothing, she was all in favour of voting for him to run around naked. His boots went from silent to gentle clicks on the paving stones.

"I had never imagined that you would look so elegant and so pissed off at the same time."

"I am a woman of many talents. See what Helen helped me pick out?" She twirled happily and he laughed again.

"Would you ladies do me the honour of accompanying me to dinner?"

Helen piped up, "Of course."

Mala met her lover's gaze with a solemn, "Of course."

He extended his elbows to them and together they walked a few blocks to a very classic dining establishment.

She sat next to Helen and across from Isabi. He watched her carefully as she made her selections. "What are you staring at?" It was curious. He was looking at her as if some mystery was about to be uncovered.

"I just realized that aside from that light repast for the sake of manners on the station, I have never seen you eat when you were not ravenous. This will be an education."

The eating sticks and prongs were all on the table, each used for a different food. He was testing her. Fine. If he wanted to play, she could play.

The sheer variety of food that was ordered, including appetizers, had them using prongs, sticks and fingers. They discussed the variety of foods on their home worlds and Helen regaled them with tales of something called a cheeseburger and fries. Isabi seemed pleased by her table manners and only threw food at her once when she asked him about the most disgusting thing he had ever eaten. That was not dinner table discussion, she was informed.

The only thing that kept her from launching herself at him was that he hadn't hit her new gown. The food glanced harmlessly off the hand she held up to deflect it.

To distract them both, Helen smiled at her. "So, when do you feel you will be up to working on me? The port that you repaired is feeling fantastic. I have no idea what you did, but the connection is faster than normal."

"We can do it when we get back to the base. I don't want to do it here." She grinned wickedly. "I wouldn't want to bankrupt Isabi—after all, he is getting the cheque."

Helen joined her in the laugh and Isabi simply thumbed the payment slip, shaking his head. They made their way back to the skimmer and found a one-man sled parked right behind it. He handed them up the steps into the skimmer and took up his position on the sled. He rode escort the entire way back to the base, then took their hands as they exited the skimmer on the landing pad.

Helen merely nodded to him with a smile.

Mala had to make a comment, "You are so getting lucky tonight."

He leaned down so that his lips were in the crook of her neck. "I already am."

RUNNING WYLD

CHAPTER ONE

If a Dhemon walks into your bar, you know you are in trouble, but when he asks for you by name, it's time to run. Agreha Wyld made her way right past the offending Dhemon. He didn't see her, but that was only because Aggie had put on her *makeup*.

Shifting her features was painful, but if it was only for a few seconds, she was willing to do it. Outside the bar, she let her face go back to normal and stretched her features to relax them. She was halfway down the block, winding her way through crowds and waving at friends in the market, when she noticed that the Dhemon was exiting the bar. His cloak was too heavy for the warm afternoon sun, but he kept it closed as he turned to follow her.

"Aw hells." There was nothing for it. She shifted her legs into a more efficient running configuration and laid on the speed. Moving with the speed of a four-legged animal, she sprinted for safety. She didn't know what the Dhemon wanted, but with the stringent morals of his species, she was sure that she had offended someone somehow. Avoiding him was the best solution.

She wasn't even breathing heavily when she looked back to see no trace of her pursuer. That made it easier for her to slam into the living brick wall in front of her.

He sighed heavily and crossed his arms over his chest, all patience and hard muscle. "Aggie, what have I told you about running through the market?"

She looked up from her vantage point on the ground. "To not do it? To do it when the market is empty? Sorry, Avatar. I was trying to avoid someone." The Avatar was the personification of the planet Cor. Cor used the body to carry his consciousness around when there were negotiations in the works regarding his planetary resources. The rest of the time, Avatar Lio was free to live a life and even flirt. Now was not one of those times.

It was Cor who spoke. "The Dhemon who was looking for you?"

"How did you know?" She stood up, brushing her skirt off and returning her legs to normal configuration.

"I sent him to you. He has a proposition that I believe will appeal to you."

"Well, I think I lost him, so better luck next time." She straightened her halter top and smoothed everything down.

"You didn't lose me. I simply tracked you until you stopped moving." The deep baritone was immediately behind her and she winced before turning around. His skin was so dark burgundy it was almost purple and his horns looked like they were made of silver. She paused for a long moment before meeting his eyes then almost keeled over at the blue-green orbs framed by thick black lashes. His eyes were so pretty it was enough to make her whimper. As she stared, fascinated, his full lips twitched in amusement.

"Wow."

"I beg your pardon?"

"Sorry. I have never seen a Dhemon close up. You are quite attractive." She did believe in honesty, but was sorry that she hadn't rearranged her face into a more pleasing affectation. Her regular features were just so…regular. Black hair and gold eyes were standard on Cor. She just blended in.

"As are you. But as Avatar Lio and Cor were telling you, I have a proposition for you. Would you care to hear it?" He held out his hand to her and waited. She had the feeling that he would keep that hand extended until the stars burned out if he had to. "My name is Haaro Denler."

Slowly, she reached out and put her smaller extremity in his grip. He closed his fingers gently over hers and gave her a smile that warmed her to her toes. Whoa. She had been hit on by better looking guys, but none had made her stomach jump like that. She gathered herself together and stood next to him. The top of her head barely reached his shoulder. She fought the urge to make herself taller.

If Cor was vouching for him, she was willing to listen to what he had come for. The fact that Haaro was fun to look at was a bonus for her.

As they headed through the market to the Great Hall, she waved at a variety of vendors whom she had known almost all her life. Their faces were familiar—they were family to her and her sister, Voreha, the only one that they had known.

Because of Cor's presence, they did not call her over, merely shook their heads at her and laughed. She had a penchant for trouble and every one of her twenty-seven years had been spent getting into trouble and having Cor pull her out of it. It was not an illustrious lifetime.

Inside Cor's private quarters, Agreha sent a message to the kitchen for water, juice and wine. Snacks were also requested, via the bell-pull system. They waited in silence until the food arrived.

Haaro started the conversation. "Agreha, I have been sent here to invite you to join the Sector Guard, a new division of the Alliance specializing in small events that can be handled by teams with special skills. You have been identified as one with those required skills and I am asking you to return, as my mate." His teeth almost gritted at that last one and she could only look on in shock.

Dhemons were notoriously straight-laced. For him to be asking her, a bar owner and woman of unknown morals, to mate with him, he had to be under some kind of pressure. "Why me?" Since Cor was in on this, she fixed him with her glare.

Lio took her hand and Cor looked out at her through his eyes, the black and silver swirl making the speaker unmistakable. "Agreha, your talents are wasted on this world, only helping a small portion of living beings in distress. I sent the Alliance your specs when they sent out an all-call for persons with odd talents. You and I both know you qualify."

Shock was short lived. He had given her that lecture time after time. "Do you have a copy of the information you sent out?" She wanted to know what she was up against. How much they knew. Haaro was looking bemused, probably because she'd deliberately ignored his mention of mating. She would tackle that next.

"Certainly. Would you like to see it?" Cor flicked on the view screen in the centre of his table. His planet was tech restricted, but as the living embodiment of the planet, he had some perks that were not for the general public and essential for inter-planetary commerce.

"Have you seen this?" Agreha looked to Haaro and he looked impassively back.

"No. I have not."

"So you just came across the galaxy to mate with a female you didn't know?"

"I trust my commander. He has the gift of foresight. It was he who viewed your video and pronounced us a match. Personally, I don't see it, but I will abide by his wishes." Wow, that was cold. Even for a Dhemon.

"So you have no interest in me whatsoever? Excellent. How about a marriage of convenience?" Cor was looking as if he would interject, but she waved him off. "Seriously. It will be easier on us until we can discuss it with your commander."

"I will agree to this." He inclined his horned head and they shook on it. The instant that their skin connected, she felt an electric charge go from her to him and back again. She felt her body try to shift and held herself back. It took far more effort than anything she had dealt with before. Her body was literally trying to find an optimum configuration to mate with him. She had to keep a tight rein on her body and reluctantly let his hand go.

Haaro was looking just as surprised as she was. Aggie felt a light prickle on her mind and slammed up her shields. He was a telepath, and right now, he had no right to her thoughts.

"Here is the information that I sent to the Alliance Representative. It covers every shift that you have made." Cor started the recording and Haaro tore his gaze from her to watch the information packet that the planet had assembled. "It is mostly sentinel footage, so pardon the angles."

Cor's voice came through the recording, "This is the candidate for the Sector Guard from the planet Cor. Her name is Agreha Wyld, and she is a metamorph of unknown power and potential. Her talents were first discovered when her family shuttle crashed into the Great Northern Ocean. Her parents drowned, but her sister was safe in one of the escape pods. Agreha herself shifted into a form that would allow her to survive in this hostile situation." Images of the crash and the rescue efforts flowed across the screen, including Voreha's emergence from the pod as a toddler, and the little infant, Agreha, being pulled from the water with gills and a tail. Two still figures were also removed from the water and Aggie did what she did every time that she saw this footage, she closed her eyes and wished for souls at peace for her parents.

Pictures flashed by of her with a snake's tail, wings, the running legs that extended her height by five inches. There were others, but none as powerful as that picture of Cor-Lio holding her with her little flipper of a tail and her sister clutching his leg.

The sentinels were flying security cameras, the only technology that was widely allowed on Cor. If there were people in the area, there was a sentinel nearby. Cor watched and protected those who lived on his surface.

Her father and mother were coming home from a trade expedition and a stray meteor had run through the main cabin, destroying air pressure. Voreha had known enough to move from her room to the pod when the alarms sounded, but her baby sister had been stuck in her crib until they had opened the main hull of the ship to attempt a rescue.

"You can really assume all of those shapes? Grow limbs?" Haaro was sounding part impressed and part horrified. She looked at him closely. Nope, he was intrigued. "What else can you do?"

She crossed her arms under her breasts and fought a smile when his gaze followed the motion and stayed put. "I assume a shape reactive to the situation. No matter what it is, my body shifts to accommodate my survival."

Cor smiled and took a long sip of wine. "Like the way that you grew wings." He grabbed some crackers and put some cheese and fruit on top. "She was out on a school trip and a stampede broke out amongst some local herbivores. They chased her and one of the other students off a cliff. She flew them both to safety." An image of Agreha with wide, white, Enjel wings filled the screen. Her shirt was torn to tatters and only the collar kept it in place. Not a great look for a teenage girl in front of an audience, especially when she was carrying the boy that she had a crush on. Simal had been her dream of a perfect boy, but once she shifted in front of him, he had avoided her by any means necessary.

One look at Haaro was telling her that he would not be scared if she grew claws in front of him, in fact, he might just find it fascinating.

CHAPTER TWO

"So you see, it will be in your best interest to join the Sector Guard, Aggie. I may have raised you from infancy, but I do not know how to help you make the most of your talents. You are wasted just remaining here, running the local tavern." Lio was holding her hand. Cor was there, but Lio's hand was several degrees warmer. His handsome features were arranged into paternal lines. She didn't want to disappoint him.

She decided that there was nothing left to lose. "Will you take care of Voreha? You know she is in love with you, right?" His surprise was answer enough.

"Me? She loves me? But she could have any man on Cor."

She sighed and slapped his forehead. "And she has wanted you, waited for you. So do something about it. I know you feel the same." She scowled at him. "You are over fifty. You aren't getting any younger. And if she says yes, please invite me to the nuptials."

Haaro stood. "That reminds me. Cor, are you authorized to officiate our marriage?"

"Of course. Now?" His eyebrows winged up into his hairline.

"She has agreed, there is nothing to delay us and we are needed on Morganti. I do not wish to travel as a couple unless we are wed." His harsh formality let her mind get back to the matter at hand—joining a group with special talents to help people in need. It was indeed a worthy cause, and if she didn't like it, she could just quit.

At a gesture from Cor, a sentinel came winging through the open window. The ball hovered at a six foot level and prepared to record the events.

"No sense avoiding the inevitable. Where do you want us?" Agreha stood and followed Cor's instructions to the formal dining room where they took up a triangular position with the sentinel hovering nearby.

Cor cleared his throat and turned to Haaro. "Take her hand in yours."

That tingling shot through her again and his fingers tightened around hers.

"Do you, Haaro Denler of Dhema, take Agreha Wyld of Cor, to be your lawful mate? Bound by the rules and strictures of the Alliance in all things?" Cor had taken on a serious tone, not like his usual banter at all.

The Dhemon looked down at her, considering. "I will be bound."

Cor let out a whoosh of air, "Do you, Agreha Wyld of Cor, agree to take Haaro Denler of Dhema, to be your lawful mate, bound by the rules and strictures of the Alliance in all things?" They waited.

Agreha looked up at the male she was binding herself to. There was something about him, something trustworthy and something hidden from the worlds at large. She looked over to Cor and saw his concern for her, even though his actions had thrown her into this situation. He would beat a path to Voreha's door the instant that she left and her sister would be in good hands, possibly several times a night.

She fought her grin. "I, Agreha, do bind myself to Haaro by the rules and strictures of the Alliance."

"You may seal the bond." Cor stepped back and turned away, leaving them to kiss, or not.

She prepared to step back and away from her new husband, but he had other ideas. Using the grip he had on her hand, he pulled her to him with gentle pressure. His lips were halfway to hers before she realized his intent and then she could only blink in surprise as he made contact.

A short shiver ran through her where they touched, that same blending of power and pheromones that she was becoming accustomed to. His lips were firm, warm and so sensual that she swayed toward him after only a few seconds of the chaste kiss. She stood still for a moment until Cor cleared his throat. Her eyes had closed at the kiss and Haaro was looking down at her with a satisfied smile on his lips. Whatever he had been testing was just proved.

"We must be leaving. The shuttle will return us to Morganti in short order." He turned, his cloak swirling around him dramatically. He still had his grip on her hand and didn't seem inclined to let her go.

"Now? You want to leave now?" She was shocked. For some reason, she thought she would have time to say farewell to Voreha and the rest of her pseudo family.

"We are catching a ride on a jump ship and must be at the rendezvous on time."

"What about my clothes? My stuff?"

"Cor will send them along when convenient. All that you need will be provided by the Guard." Haaro was almost dragging her along. He really was in a hurry.

"Wouldn't it have been horrible for you to have courted me first? You would have missed your flight schedule." Grim and grumpy, she allowed him to haul her along. She would honour her word, he was her husband. But if he looked at her the wrong way, she was going to kick his ass. She had just the hoofed form to do it.

With Cor's promise to take care of everything and Lio's promise to take care of Voreha, Agreha was able to leave with a clear conscience. Vor would not miss her much, she had always been a little afraid of her freaky sister, but Aggie knew that she loved her and that made up for a lot.

Haaro slid behind the controls of one of the most beautiful shuttles that Aggie had ever seen. The Cor shuttles were old, but in excellent shape. This one was new and practically hummed with its own energy. Someone had put a lot of love into this design and it showed.

"Shuttle craft Arcus waiting for clearance."

"Cor acknowledges. Clearance granted. Make us proud, Agreha, as you always have." Lio's voice came through the com and tears welled in Aggie's eyes. He always knew the right thing to say, usually after Cor backed him into a verbal corner with demands and orders.

"Best wishes to Cor and keep my bar running. I might want a retirement plan one day." It was through a tight throat, but she meant it. Cor was home. It would always be home.

Her companion was silent as he ran through the last of the pre-flight checks. As soon as all lights were clear, they lifted off. The ship didn't even shudder as it moved through the atmosphere, pulling and pushing itself into the blackness of space without any seeming effort. She couldn't help but admire the design and said so.

"Thank you. I was very happy with the way it turned out." His eyes were twinkling with amusement and pride. "It took two years of prototypes before the Arcus was ready to fly."

"*You* designed this? Wow. You have unimagined depths."

He laughed at her. "As do you. We will learn more as we continue to travel together. The close quarters of the shuttle are conducive to involved conversations."

She snickered. "Okay, you have me there. I have been sent on a few missions for Cor and each time me and my co-pilot ended up sharing more than we were comfortable with when we landed. Well, usually they stopped talking after they saw me shift for one reason or another. It seems most of them didn't believe the rumours about me."

"There is no other history of psychic or talented phenomenon on Cor?"

"Nope. They weren't designed to."

That had him freezing in his seat then oh-so-slowly turning to look at her. "What do you mean, *designed to*?"

Oh. He didn't know. She had assumed when he had been sent to collect her that he had been given a full briefing. "You weren't given that information before you were sent out to fetch me?"

"Apparently, if I was, I didn't read it very closely." They were just lifting through the stratosphere. He held his questions until they were out of the orbital range and had set a course for the jump rendezvous. He turned back to her and then asked again, "About the design?"

"Over thirty years ago, a Sethrin clone colony revolted from their duties as labour and miners, led by a few slaves from free worlds. The clones fought and many died for their freedom, but though they were successful, the Alliance agreed with the Sethrin that they were not entitled to keep the planet they were born on. They had to find another world to live on."

"Cor offered them a place."

"Not initially, no. My mother, Evain, was one of the slaves that the Sethrin had sent to entertain the overseers. She negotiated with Cor and an accord was struck. The clones would be welcome, provided that they agreed on restricted tech and no destruction of natural resources. It had to be a full replenishment cycle or nothing." Aggie smiled in fond memory of what she had been told. "She told the clones to embrace the conditions and to get their butts planet-side. They did it."

"Your mother sounds like a strong woman." His voice was soft with understanding.

"I guess she was. The people of Cor have certainly told me that she was often enough, and she wasn't even one of the founding clones." Aggie was sniffling lightly and, from under his cloak, Haaro produced a handkerchief. "Thank you."

"Do you know her lineage? Why she was a slave?"

Aggie smiled and nodded. "I asked Cor if he would let me access her Alliance records when I was old enough. He waited until I was seventeen before he would let me, but he had all of her breeding records going back to her great-great-grandmother's origins on Terra. Mom would have been so proud of the strides that they are making in the Alliance."

"What is your lineage?"

"Terran, Engel, Hickom, Wyoran, and Nyal, with Sethrin as the final addition." She smiled. "You have shackled yourself to a mutt."

"I will find a way to deal with it." She could have been mistaken, but she thought she saw a hint of a smile with the sarcastic comment.

"Apparently, my father, Seragha3, fell in love with her scrappy attitude, no matter her past as a whore. They became the ambassadors for Cor while Lio settled in as Avatar. That was part of the agreement as well, that one of the clones take on Cor. Lio6 was the volunteer and his body has been frozen in time since. He was my father's best friend, and when the shuttle crashed, he took care of us." She thought about it for a moment. "Actually, all three thousand colonists took care of us."

"Aside from when you were jumping off cliffs."

"Well, yeah, but Simal went first." She grinned and laughed. "You should have seen those beasts coming at us. The cliff was our only option."

"What incited the animals to stampede?"

"Can you keep a secret?" She giggled a little at the memory. "Simal had carved a whistle and was blowing it to cause the animals to squeal. They got mad and came to investigate the incursion into their territory. The stupidities of childhood."

"I would say so. How do you want to run the shifts? Only one of us needs to be at the con at any given time. We can trade off galley duties as well as sleeping shifts."

"That's fair. Did you want something to eat? You may as well stay at the con, I don't know where we are going."

"That would be lovely. Anything is fine, and some tea if there is any left." He nodded his thanks and turned back to programming their course.

She placed a few packets of food in the heater and started the tea. Now it was time to go exploring. The sanitary chamber was just large enough for Haaro to squeeze in, but not to stretch out at all. It was a gel shower, the thick substance solidifying on the body and shattering with a short sonic pulse into shards that were vacuumed up by the chamber. Common enough on shuttles, but she had never used one before. Agreha wondered how long they were going to be travelling.

The benches in the dining area folded out to turn into beds. Underneath each bench was a storage area. Deep burgundy and black fabric pooled around her hands and she lifted a suit free. It was obviously Haaro's, but it was veed in the back, as if for spines or wings. Mulling the possibilities over, she put it aside and pulled out another pile of fabric. This was in several sections and came with a schematic. It was black and gold, a halter, miniskirt and leggings.

She brought the fabric to Haaro, "Is this for me?" He blinked in surprise.

"Yes. That was manufactured based on video of your body in action. It does show a lot of skin, but we are getting a manufacturing specialist who may be able to do a better job."

"But why is it for me? Why do I need a costume?"

"It is more of a uniform. We all wear one. Some of us change our names for the safety of our loved ones. On my way here, I received notice that Fixer and Shade were our first couple after the Commander and Pilot. Until I see you in action, I don't know if we can speculate at your name."

"What is your name? Have you selected one yourself yet? And why does your suit have a slit in the back? What do you have going on under that cloak?" She gave him a saucy grin. "Come on. Strip."

CHAPTER THREE

With the autopilot locked on at the flick of a finger, Haaro stood and walked past her to the common area. Maintaining eye contact, he peeled the cloak off his shoulders and carefully folded it over one arm. Stretching his neck with his horns flashing in the dim light of the cabin, he extended his wings.

Wings they certainly were. A beautiful burgundy and black opened and flexed in the small space.

"Wow. Pretty. And they really fold that tightly around you?" She approached him and then stopped as the heater beeped. She retrieved the hot ration packs and poured the tea. A pressed button had a table extend and she gestured for him to take a seat. "Doesn't it get tiring, wrapping them around you like that all the time?"

"I have to say, I thought you would be more surprised. I am a genetic throwback to the days when the warrior class of Dhemons had wings." He blew on the pack and she kept an eye on the readouts as she leaned on the food prep counter.

"I have seen my own skin turn black and hard in space until they could reel me in. Nothing physical scares me." His at-rest wingspan covered about twelve feet. "Those wings are more for gliding than they are for flying, aren't they?"

"Yes. They were traditionally used for low altitude drops. It was a battle tactic." He smiled at her insight. "The gene was expunged, mostly. Occasionally, it crops up. You really know your biogenetics for someone raised low tech."

"Well, Cor did give me access to all of the databases and I was a ravenous learner. Plus, with my body sprouting alien limbs, it was a good idea to get familiar with the different configurations so that I wouldn't freak out when it happened." She glanced at him. "My winged form is feathered and not nearly as wide. More muscular though, I think."

"Show me." He crossed his arms and sat back.

"Doesn't one of us have to be at the con?"

"No. Not as long as all signs are good. The alarms will warn us if we get close to anything." He smiled encouragingly. "Go ahead."

She smiled and had a silly thought. "I haven't done this since I was old enough to know better."

"Done what?"

"Played *I'll-show-you-mine-if-you-show-me-yours.*" Agreha took a deep breath and a final look at the control panel. It was clear and she had some time. She stretched and pulled the form of wings out of her mind and through her ribcage. The wings burst into life suddenly—white feathers glowing in the light of the shuttle. It was painful, but worth it for the look in Haaro's eyes.

He was shocked.

"What? You didn't think I could do it?" She knelt, turned her back to him and let him run his fingers through her feathers. *Oh.* That felt fabulous. She was almost purring with the smooth touch of his hands through the flight feathers, moving them delicately, precisely. It was less of an exam and more of a worshipful awe. When he trailed his fingers down her spine, she shuddered. Okay, that was way too close to foreplay for her peace of mind.

"Okay. That's enough of that. Your tea is probably toxic by now and my dinner is cold." She leaned forward and stood on limbs that had turned to jelly. Her wings retracted grudgingly, leaving her skin smooth and pale once again.

He swallowed heavily. "That was impressive. Do you shift into that form often?"

"Only when falling off cliffs. Or out of shuttles, or out of trees, though that last one didn't actually do me any good." Agreha reheated her food slightly and dug in while sitting in the co-pilot's seat.

The companion seat was soon occupied and a cup of hot tea was placed on her half of the console. "Agreha, we are three hours from the jump ship. We may as well get comfortable. If you want a nap, you are welcome to take one."

"Nope. No thanks. I would rather get a lesson on the ins and outs of this shuttle, if that is agreeable to you."

"It certainly is. Let's proceed." Haaro's burgundy skin skimmed lightly over the controls as he explained each and every one. She asked questions and he answered each without hesitation. He knew every inch of the shuttle and, by the time they arrived at the ship, she was getting almost as familiar with it when a voice interrupted their lesson.

"Shuttle craft, this is the Alliance ship, Bakoral. Please identify."

"This is the Arcus of Morganti, Sector Guard shuttle two. Requesting permission to tag along?"

"Come aboard, Commander Haaro. We look forward to escorting you to your destination." As he spoke, the belly of the great ship opened and the Arcus slipped inside. They locked into a bay and waited. Within an hour, the red flaring lights started to indicate the jump.

Haaro breathed deeply, his eyes closed and fists clenched. This was obviously not his favourite method of travel. Agreha loved it. That moment when they were in two places at the same time was exhilarating. She hadn't been through a jump before, but shouting *wahoo* was out of the question. Especially considering Haaro's sudden lack of colour. He went from burgundy to a greyish-pink in seconds. Considering his bravado earlier, this sudden change of attitude was almost unnerving. Aggie thought about it for a moment and then reached out to take his hand.

The grip that greeted her would have broken her hand if she had not been made of sturdy stuff. It still caused a wince, but she didn't pull away. He needed this and she could give him what comfort her touch afforded.

It took less than five seconds from jump to calm, but Haaro did not let her hand go. Instead, he raised it to his lips. "Thank you. The psychic talents don't deal well with displacement."

"So I have heard. I suppose I am lucky that my talents are strictly physical." The grin she gave him tried to dispel the heated look in his eyes.

"No, I am. Thank you for your assistance." He released her hand, but not before a warm wave had started to wash through her. It was a sensation that she barely recognized, but she knew it when she felt it. Pleasure. A blush crept across her face in a trail of heat and now it was his turn to smile.

The snap and crackle of the communicator separated their gazes. "Commander Haaro, we are out of jump and over Morganti. Whenever you are ready."

With graceful and economic movements, he took over the shuttle controls and set them for release into Morganti space. "Shuttle Arcus, ready to drop." Seconds later, the shuttle was free of the jump ship and moving slowly toward a jewel in the blackness of space.

Morganti, home of the first Sector Guard outpost, and Aggie's new home.

CHAPTER FOUR

"Your first stop will be a trip to Medical. Our Commander, Hyder, is also our medical officer." Haaro was picking up a small duffle from a storage compartment and gallantly escorting her from the shuttle.

"I heard the jump ship address you as Commander. Who outranks whom?"

"He outranks me. I abandoned my rank when I chose to join the Guard. Hyder Mihal is an excellent medical technician with an uncanny ability to see potential. When he received your file, he immediately matched you with me. From what I have seen of you so far, we will be an impressive partnership."

She looked up at his horns, his skin, and his smile. "I am going to agree with you there. There is something about you that draws me. Beyond your impressive wingspan." She grinned and winked.

He laughed and then told her about the Drae that was also in the guard. His wings were far more functional, but he had been assigned to another female.

"Oh. Poor me."

"And lucky me." He gestured to the main building of the complex they had landed near. "This is our home. Your room and mine adjoin with a common room for the Guard when we are off duty. Though, that being said, there are quite a few places in town to have dinner or go dancing."

"Oh, you dance?" What he had said about accommodations sunk in. "Adjoining rooms?" Her voice came out as a squeak.

"We remain in a marriage of convenience. Do not worry. Should you choose to change your mind on that front, I am willing to renegotiate." They were inside the complex and he stopped in front of a door that read Medical. "I will introduce you to the Commander and then will go to obtain some clothing for you. Helen or Mala will be called to give you a tour of the facilities."

"Oh, alright." So he was just dumping her and running. "I suppose I will see you later."

"You will." He tilted her head up with the back of his knuckles and the kiss that he left her with had her heart pounding a distress call against her ribs. He grinned smugly at her bemusement and opened the door. "Commander Hyder Mihal, this is the newest recruit to the Sector Guard of Morganti, Agreha Wyld of Cor."

The Azon smiled at her gently, his eyes kind and a satisfied wisdom in them. "I am glad to meet you in person, Agreha."

"Aggie, please."

"Aggie then. The data that Cor sent was fascinating, but seeing you in action will be a definite thrill." A knock on the door interrupted him. A woman with bright eyes and a wealth of rainbow hair walked into Medical. "This is your chaperone. Haaro won't leave you alone without another woman in the room. Like Helen wouldn't castrate me if I strayed." He shook his head. "Mala, this is our newest recruit, Aggie Wyld of Cor. Aggie, this is Mala Deeha, or Fixer as her spouse has named her."

"Pleased to meet you, Mala." She extended her hand and enjoyed the firm no-nonsense grip that the other woman replied with.

"Pleased to meet you as well, Aggie. I am going to have you in my clutches soon. I think you need some special design assistance in your uniform. The trampy little outfit that they sent out with Haaro was ridiculous. We can do better."

Seeing that she was in good hands and her chaperone in place, Haaro gave her a short bow, a kiss on the back of her hand and left Medical silently.

"Well, that wasn't odd at all." Aggie turned to Hyder and smiled. "Shall we get started?"

He blinked rapidly and recalled why she was there. "Of course. Just hop up here on the table and we will start the scans."

The next few minutes were taken up with scans, idle chatter and having Mala place the recording pods on her torso while Hyder watched the placement on his palm scanner. "Don't worry. I have had to wear more of these things than I could count. Isabi was just as bad as Haaro when it came to having Hyder touch me. He was in here doing it himself. At least Haaro called me in." The last pod went on and Mala pulled the halter top back into place. "Do you always dress like this?"

"It makes it easier to shift. I need a certain freedom of movement and I can't get it from standard fabrics. They tend to rip when I shift and leave me almost naked when I shift back. I don't like that." Hyder was still writing notes, but Aggie swung her legs off the bed.

"Aggie, can you shift something? Just so I can get a baseline." Hyder had his eyes down on his readouts and they widened as she took a deep breath and grew some wings and some extras. "Whoa. That is fabulous. The shifting in internal organs is amazing."

Aggie winked at Mala who was looking at her in stunned admiration. Wings of snowy white protruded from her back and vicious spikes came out of her forearms.

"Hyder, look at her, you moron!"

"What?" His feline eyes widened in surprise as he took in her shift. "Oh my. I registered some pain. Does it hurt?"

"Only during the shift. If I shift my face, it is more difficult and hurts until I relax it." She pulled her features into something resembling that of an Azon and he whistled softly. She relaxed back into her normal features as quickly as she could, pulling the wings in with a sigh and letting the spikes sink back into her body.

He looked to the information and his eyes began to glow as something fell into place for him. "You are bio-kinetic. Telekinesis restricted to making your body shift its shape. Fascinating. Please keep the pods on as long as you can."

"Uh. Sure." That was a new one. She just thought it was something her body did. To find out that her mind was doing it was illuminating.

"Come on, Aggie. Let's see if we can't get you a suit that doesn't make you look like a low-rent Companion." Mala took charge of the new recruit and headed out of Medical. Aggie had no choice but to follow—Mala had her by the wrist.

There were support personnel all over the complex, running errands of varying degrees of importance. A few waved at Mala and she waved back. "Most people here are friendly if you give them a chance. They only people I ever have any trouble with are the staff in the commissary. They run when they see me coming." She laughed heartily and Aggie wondered at the joke she was missing.

Mala looked perfectly ordinary. Aside from her rainbow of hair, she looked like a standard bi-pedal humanoid. Nose, eyes. Everything seemed normal. "Why?"

"A side effect of my talent is that I get very hungry. Extremely hungry. Pounds and pounds of food hungry. When I am working on a project, they all have to pull overtime to keep me fed. My talent runs off my body mass, so I need to replace it." They had arrived at a hangar and with the variety of accoutrements in the area, it was obviously Mala's workshop. In light of her comment, the snack machine was now also explained. "Now. Let's get you a proper uniform. Are you up to doing some shifting?"

"Sure. How are we going to start?"

"There is a screen there and a jumpsuit over it. We are going to start with that. I will make the adjustments as you shift." Mala gestured to the back of the hangar and sure enough, there was a modesty screen with a one-piece body suit in it.

Aggie did as she was told and shucked her skirt and top, climbing into the bodysuit that fit her faithfully. Mala's voice called out over the screen, "It isn't meant to be worn with underwear."

Aggie closed the front and replied, "Good. I don't have any." She loved the colours—the same white and gold as the ones in their shuttle. "I also don't have shoes."

"Whoops. Sorry. Helen is bringing them. They might even shift with you. Masuo grow on Morganti and we have struck a deal with the local cobbler to provide them to us. For a bit of business, of course." Mala was eyeing the suit intently. "Shall we begin at the top and work down?"

"Sounds good. You may want to create an opening in the suit so I don't rip the back open."

"On it. By the way, my hands will be touching you throughout your shifts. I hope that it is okay?"

"Sure. No one has ever wanted to get close enough, but I have no issues with contact." She shrugged and turned her back to the perversely eager Moreski. Fixer began to live up to her name. It took three shifts, but the suit now parted of its own accord and resealed itself when her wings were no longer in evidence. "That feels wonderful."

"Thanks. Now, what next?"

"Well, you saw the forearm spikes. I also pair that with claws when fighting animals. Occasionally a tail for balance."

"Let's start with the spikes. We can use the same thickening and memory fabric technique that I used on your back." Mala was holding her forearm with one hand and eating an apple with the other. "Go ahead."

"Alright." Aggie drew an invisible line down her arm. "The spikes will appear here. You may want to avoid that area."

"Thanks for the heads up."

Hours passed and Aggie was exhausted. She had shifted individual limbs more times in one day than she had in her life. Doing it on command was tricky, but good practice.

They had gained an audience. Hyder was watching his readouts, a woman sat next to him with a set of boots, that must be Helen, and Haaro was watching her with a fascination that bordered on obsessive. Mala's mate was standing by with a basket full of snacks that he occasionally popped into her mouth while she worked.

"Alright. Have we missed any forms?"

"The non bi-pedal ones. I can grow gills and a tail." Aggie was slumped back in a chair that Haaro had brought out to her. "And I can grow four legs and carry a passenger."

That brought Hyder upright. "Really? There was no evidence of that on the data reels."

"I didn't demonstrate everything. I used to carry kids around when they had gotten too tired to walk all the way home. The skirt made it easier."

"Can you shift to the tailed form? I would like to have a chance to shape the suit for that." Mala was almost vibrating with eagerness. It could also have been fatigue.

"No. Not unless you have a tank of water and you can swim. The instant I shift, I need to breathe water."

"What about the four legged form?"

"That I can do, but only once. I am really wiped out." Aggie was honest. She was enjoying shifting in the open, but it was tiring.

"Please. Just this last one." Mala had her hands together and was begging. She was almost done with her fabulous creation and there was this one thing standing in the way of completion of her project.

"Fine. Hands on my hips and here we go." Taking a deep breath, she started the shift. Her lower body had feline aspects, four paws and a tail. That tail was lashing as she waited for Mala to work her magic.

Her tailor shifted the split seam from the two legs into a train that lay across her back. It looked like it should work. And would be quite dashing in her fin form. "Now for the true test. You done, Mala?"

"I am. And starving." Isabi popped another cheese and meat cracker combo into her mouth and whatever else she would have said was lost in munching.

More deep breathing and she shifted back into her bi-pedal form. It worked! The seams of the bodysuit slid back into place and sealed as she stood on two legs again. "That is fabulous! Thank you, Mala."

"Hello, Aggie, my name is Helen. Or Pilot. Whatever you like. This pair of

Masuo is for you." The woman held out the boots and Aggie put them on with shaking hands. She extended into her running feet and back again quickly. The boots shifted with her. Fantastic.

"Thank you, Helen. I am glad to meet you, but I really need to sleep. This has been wonderful, but I am exhausted." She turned to her husband. "Haaro, can you show me to our quarters?"

"Whatever my lady wishes." He took her hand and tucked it into the crook of his arm as they walked down the hall with his wings sweeping back like a cloak and her sparkling bodysuit proclaiming her status as a Sector Guard. The Masuo were taking on the pattern of the suit as well, the little joiners.

He was giving her a complete tour, but she was too exhausted to hear any of it. She simply listened to those magical words, "These are your rooms," and wandered away from him and to the large and inviting bed.

Day one as a Guard was exhausting and she hadn't even done anything yet. She barely had enough strength to strip and climb between the sheets before she remembered nothing at all.

CHAPTER FIVE

"Aggie. Wake up. We are needed in the conference room." A hand shook her shoulder and she batted at it without opening her eyes.

"Shut up, Lio. It isn't a school day." She grumped and rolled over, wallowing in the warmth and softness of the sheets and blankets.

The masculine laughter did not belong to her guardian. She peeped up to see Haaro looming over her with a smile on his sensual lips. "Morning, wife. We are needed in the conference room. Kale has our first assignment."

"Kale?" She sat up slowly, keeping the sheets covering her from neck to toes.

"Morganti's Avatar. It, too, is a sentient world. The soul of the world is named Gant." He turned and lifted the wadded remains of her uniform, fluffed it out briskly and handed it to her.

"Oh. Got it. Morganti. Gant's world." She started to squirm into the uniform and it went off without a hitch. Well, it went on with a few hitches, but she managed to get everything tucked into its proper place and all closures sealed properly. As soon as she was sure that she was decent, she threw off the covers.

Haaro looked a little disappointed, but he controlled it well while she pulled on her boots. Her eyes felt gritty. "How much sleep did I get?"

"About three hours. Gant received an emergency signal from one of his sister worlds in this system and we are needed."

She stumbled and took his arm as he led her to the conference room. "Why us? Why not Mala or Isabi, or Helen?"

"Gaffin is a level one restricted tech planet. No tech is allowed on the surface outside. That means you and me."

She couldn't contain her yawn and it was while her mouth was wide open that they entered the conference room and she met Kale-Gant. "Hullo. You must be the Gant Avatar, Kale."

"Yes, my lady. And you are quite lovely for someone disturbed from their rest." His features were undecipherable. There was no clearly identifiable race, but he had violet blue eyes that sparkled with every word. He took her hand and kissed the knuckles, then released it as Haaro scowled at him. "Cor has spoken very highly of you."

"Well, I speak highly of him, so fair is fair." She was seated in one of the chairs positioned around the large table and turned to watch the display. Haaro kept a hold of one of her hands and she welcomed the warmth. He stroked his thumb along her palm and something else woke in her as well. Mala and Isabi were also seated, but they were keeping quiet.

"Gaffin is my sister world in this system and six hours ago I received a distress call. A couple who had travelled to the mountains on their honeymoon has not been seen or heard from in six days. They were to have returned to their village, but they have not. Gaffin is worried, it is unlike them."

"And you would like us to investigate?"

"Please. Gaffin has only recently decided to take in colonists and has gotten very attached to them. Losing these people might throw Gaffin into depression, and a depressed Gaffin is a volcanic Gaffin." Gant grimaced. "Do you think you can find them?"

"We can only try. I have a few tracking abilities that I can use paired with some orbital scans. Hopefully, we can bring them home." Aggie tried to put confidence into her tone. "Do the colonists have any religious leanings? I don't want to use a form that may get me into trouble."

"No. Nothing like that. They are another Sethrin colony. It seems that the clone projects did not end with the Cor colonists."

Haaro squeezed her hand lightly. "That is comforting, at least. The last thing I need is someone trying to burn out the evil."

"So you have been to Enjel worlds before?" She was laughing at him. It was common knowledge that the Enjel had whitewashed their own history of enslaving other races and blamed the order-loving Dhemons who tried to set the enslaved races free.

"Once or twice. Remind me to show you the scars." His grimace was wry. "Is the Arcus ready for the trip?"

Mala blinked at him. "Yup. Ready and waiting. Tons of fuel and ready to go. When you get back, I want to ask you about a few improvements I have in mind."

"Fine. Then we are off." Haaro helped Aggie up. "Can you create some extra uniforms for her? I have a feeling that she is going to be hard on them."

"A spare has already been put in the Arcus. Off you go now. I need my beauty rest." Mala waved them off with a hand and turned back into Isabi's arms, snoring lightly.

The golden eyed, velvet black Selna was apologetic. "Hyder stopped her feeding cycle to get you the extra suit. She's exhausted." He stood and scooped his mate into his arms, carrying her to their quarters. She snored the whole way.

"Wow. If he puts up with that snoring, he must be a saint." She was still yawning, but she followed Haaro to the Arcus, towed in his wake by his hand linked to hers. "How long to Gaffin?"

"Two hours. And you are welcome to sleep on the way." He led her back into the shuttle and tucked her in on the couch-bed. "I will let you know when we are in orbit."

With a smile of trust on her lips, she let him take them both into the blackness of space.

"Aggie. It is time. We are here." A gentle caress of fingers across her forehead brought her back to her body. She had been floating around a waterfall and playing tag with the mist generated by the pounding water. A dark shadow had begun to draw closer and closer, and she could feel the welcome in her mind as it approached. And then, Haaro was waking her.

He handed her some water and tooth cleanser. A short grin and a scrub later and she was ready to help form a plan of attack. "Okay. Where are we going to start the search?"

"The co-ordinates that Gaffin sent put us over the Western continent. We have a fifty kilometre radius to check."

Aggie thought for a minute. "I picked my name. Morph. I am going to be Morph. And I think you should be Thinker, 'cause your telepathy is about to get a workout."

He looked pleased, but curious. "How so?"

"Sethrin minds stick out, or so I am told. They should be easy to find. How close to the area are we allowed to land?"

"We have to land in the designated shuttle area. It is twenty kilometres from the search area. We will be having some travel on foot or via beast."

"Are we allowed communicators?"

"No."

"Can you read and speak to me via telepathy? If so, what is your range?"

"On this style of uninhabited world, perhaps twenty-five klicks. We could extend it, but I don't know if you are willing."

He was serious. There was something that would increase his ability to reach her, but he didn't want to ask.

"What is it? I am willing to increase our chances of finding these two alive by whatever means necessary."

With blinding speed, Haaro grabbed her and shoved her up against the wall of the shuttle. His lips took hers in a kiss that left her breathless and she wrapped her legs around his hips for stability. She tasted blood, hers, his, she didn't know. Her heart was pounding and her hormones were running riot in her nerve endings. Everywhere they touched, her skin was aflame. Suddenly, she felt the presence in her mind that had the same taste as the tongue that teased hers. Haaro was part of her, touching her in the most intimate way she could imagine, mind to mind.

When he pulled back just enough to separate their mouths, they were both gasping for air, chests heaving. The fabric of her suit was thick enough to hide her aroused nipples, but she knew he could feel the pulse of her interest in her mind.

"I can now find you anywhere on Gaffin. Our blood and minds have mixed." He bent his head and nuzzled the side of her neck. The heat of his breath made her shake. "You taste like a dream I had once."

"I hope it was a good dream."

"It was the best dream possible." He reluctantly let her slide down his body, her legs unlocking and releasing his wings as she relaxed into a loose stance. "The dream of my mate."

She didn't have anything to say to him, merely looked up into his eyes and tried to read the hundred emotions that were there. "We have to find the couple, and I think you have just given me the tools to do it."

"Please. Share." He began to take packs out of the storage areas and counted out ration packs and water.

"You will drop me."

His shocked look spoke volumes. "I will not."

"We will do a fly over and you will pinpoint the couple as well as you can. I will take rations and medical supplies in a pack, strap them to my front and drop out of the shuttle, flying to the area. You will fly the shuttle to the landing zone, gather a group to assist in carrying the couple, and head out to find me. Hopefully, we will collide somewhere midway between the two spots."

He looked over at her and considered.

"Make up your mind, Thinker. I am much better suited to ground travel than you are, and since you can find me and not the other way around, it makes the most sense." She rested her hand on his shoulder and he relaxed a little at her touch. "You can't think your way out of this one. It has to be. We can't spare the time walking and trying to find them. It may take days. Lives are at stake here."

He dipped his horns in acquiescence. "I agree. Let's make sure that you have everything you need."

The next few minutes were spent loading a pack, strapping it to the front of her torso and testing it for balance. When he was confident she would be able to handle it comfortably, he started his search.

They were on their third pass of the suspected area when Haaro suddenly sat up straight. "We are close. Very close." They were also two thousand metres above the ground.

"Give me the controls while you find a landmark." She took the con and held them in a slow circle as he pinpointed the area.

"Foothills. A three hundred foot tree. A brook." His eyes snapped open. "Tev has a broken leg. Sela won't go on without him. She has been keeping him alive for the last week with hunting and gathering. She has no idea which way to head."

"You have to love base level colonies. At least they can feed themselves." She felt pride at the survival of the female and her ability to keep her mate alive. "Which way is the village?"

"Southward, from the rock. As direct a line as you can make it. Use your compass and hold a southerly course. I will find you." He took the controls back and nodded for her to assume the jump position.

"You had better. If he has an infection, the clock is ticking." She took her courage into her own hands and gave him a kiss to sear her taste on his mind. He was just reaching up to hold her when she skipped out of his reach. "Later. You now have incentive to find me."

If his eyes could have started a fire, she would have been ablaze. He moved the Arcus over the drop zone and hovered, keeping as still as he could. The cargo doors opened and she held to the sides while sighting her target. A secondary protective lid flashed into being over her eyes. Taking a deep breath, Morph flew on her maiden flight.

Well, she dropped like a rock. To get a straight line, she kept her bi-pedal form as she fell, until the last moment, when her wings sprouted to catch her. It hurt, but not as much as the sudden stop would have. She circled until she found a glimpse of a woman near a stream and then she flew in for a landing nearby.

The woman hadn't seen her, so she pulled in her wings and kept them tightly against her back. "Sela? Sela of Gaffin?" The call was strong. Aggie was proud of her ability to keep her cool, the woman looked so worn and frightened. "I have been sent by the Sector Guard, summoned by the Avatar of Gaffin. My name is Morph."

The woman simply stood there, her jaw slack and her eyes disbelieving.

"Your mate, Tev? Is he nearby? Does he need help?"

That snapped her out of it. Sobbing, she ran to Aggie and gripped her hand, pulling her into the woods. "He broke his leg. Slipped on some rocks. We thought we were going to die out here. We weren't supposed to go this far."

"I know. But the newly mated need their privacy and villages are not known for that commodity."

Sela laughed a little, snuffling back tears. "That they are not." Her mate was lying in a cosy tent. The swelling in his leg was frightening, but this was not the first such mission that Aggie had been on.

"He seems to be running a fever, but the break looks clean. Did you try and reset it?"

"No. I didn't know how." Sela was fidgeting. Her fingers were twisting in her matted hair and Aggie sighed. She had given her full attention to her mate and ignored herself in the process.

"I do know how. I have done it half a dozen times, but it will hurt him and I have to rebreak the bone to straighten it."

"Why? It's already broken."

"But it has started to heal crooked. It needs to be straight." She looked over at the packs. "Go and take a bath, brush your hair and braid it up. As soon as you get back, you are going to help me get him ready to travel." Giving Sela something to do was all she could think of. She didn't want the woman there to see what was coming next.

Aggie waited patiently as Sela gathered her bathing items, and as soon as she was out of sight, shifted her fingers into a formation that few knew of. Paralytic venom came out through tube like protrusions under the fingernails. She pressed them against the swelling tissue surrounding the break. Opening her pack, she got out some folding splints and gauze. She laid all of the supplies within easy reach and tapped the break with one finger. He was numb. Aggie took a deep breath, shifted her musculature so that she could do the job and re-broke the bone, setting it rapidly into the proper alignment.

Tev moaned as she wrapped the leg into a rigid fix. It was straight, it would heal, as long as he survived. In contrast to his mate, Tev was clean. She had probably been hauling water to him the whole time, never thinking to take a quick dip.

Aggie sat near his head and waited until his eyes flicked open. "Hiya. I am here to transport you back to your village."

"Who? What are you? Where is Sela?" His eyes were worried. Aggie immediately moved to calm him.

"She is on her way back. I sent her to bathe while I fixed your leg into a more natural position."

"What? Can I see?" He struggled to sit up and she helped to support his weight as he looked at the matching limbs, aside from the swelling. "Thank you."

"Don't thank me until we get you home. It will be a long trek for Sela through the woods. I can only carry one person at a time, I think. I may be able to find a new configuration that will do the job." She propped Tev into his sitting position and left the tent, heating some meal packs and smiling at Sela as she re-entered the camp, clean and hopeful.

Tev's voice called out to his wife and she cried her relief as she ran to the tent. Aggie let them have their moment, feeling the slight tingle of Haaro's mind on her own. He was on his way. "Alright you two. Come on out here. We need to have a talk before we start moving. And we all need something to eat."

Tev's feet appeared first, but soon Sela had him upright and was acting in place of his damaged limb. Shifting her torso into a more effective bundle of muscle, Aggie shoved at a large tree and it formed a high bench for Tev to sit on. He looked exhausted from that tiny bit of exertion across the camp.

She handed food to the couple and waited until they had started on their food before eating her own. She was shocked when she realized that her last meal had been on the way to Morganti. She had to watch that. Her talent was not as dependent on food as Mala's, but skipping meals would weaken her.

When all the food was gone and everyone was sipping at water, Morph began to outline her plan. "As soon as you are ready, I will shift into a form to carry you both and we will begin our journey Southward."

"How will you do that? You are Sethrin, we can see it." Tev's glazed eyes were confused.

"I am not pure Sethrin, and I can do it. You will just have to wait and see." Sethrin were notorious for not having any sort of talent. They had no appeal to psychic races as there was no genetic benefit in breeding with them. "But I will not harm you, no matter what you see. I am sworn to protect you."

Curiosity lit both of their faces, and in that instant, Aggie saw how young they were. Tev had brought them out of the standard range to prove his manhood and had ended up almost killing them both. "Are you two ready?"

Sela scrambled around the camp, getting her pack together. All the food they had brought along had been eaten long ago. Tev grew a little white around the mouth, his skin taking on a greyish tint.

"Tev, you are obviously in pain. Can I give you something for it? An analgesic?" Aggie approached him slowly.

"Will it get better when we are moving?" His voice was tight with pain.

"It will probably get worse. This is not even ground we will be crossing. I will have to move in between trees and over rocks. The ride will be rough."

"Then whatever you can do would be welcome." Sela's voice was strong and she took Tev's hand in hers. "Pain isn't bravery. And it is stupid to distract our rescuer with it if there is another option."

Relieved, Aggie took out the painkillers. It was in a powdered form, so she mixed it with some water and handed it to Tev. Sela helped him drink it all. "He will need more every six hours. I want to keep traveling as long as we can. The faster he gets back to a bed, the better."

"I will keep the powders with me and give them to him as needed."

Aggie nodded, strapped her kit back onto her chest and started to shift. An idea had come to her, a picture of a creature called a centaur from one of the stories of Terra that Cor had shown to her. She grew the legs, the back and then walked carefully around to get the feel of the body. Walking with six legs was tricky, but she had fortunately gotten used to it years ago.

Sela's reaction was a little surprising though.

CHAPTER SIX

"That is fantastic! Wonderful. No wonder your name is Morph!" Sela walked around her and looked at her legs, the tail and hesitantly reached out to touch her barrel. The back of her uniform was across her back and formed a blanket.

"Go ahead. Touch. You will be sitting on me soon enough. And you are going to have to help Tev get up here." She turned and patted the flat expanse of her back. She would have to remember this form if it was as successful as it looked to be. She could always go back to her feline form, but then she could only carry the one passenger, which would have to be Tev.

It took a bit of effort, but finally the two women managed to get Tev onto Morph's back. The first few steps fully loaded were a little odd, but she eventually picked up a rhythm. Tev was right behind her and Sela behind him, supporting him as he slumped in his drugged stupor. It was just easier to keep him doped while she broke into a flat out run through the meadows on their way south. It was a brutal pace, but she wanted to get closer to the tingle in her mind that was getting stronger. Day and night ceased to have meaning, her hunting eyes making navigation in the dark simple.

Sela finally begged her to stop. She let them slide free of her and then shifted to help make camp. That didn't work. With her regular legs under her again, she found it impossible to stay upright. "Sorry, Sela. I am going down." She slumped against some timber and nodded off as Tev and Sela tended to their needs. She roused briefly to eat a ration pack and then drank some water. The tree trunk was surprisingly comfortable.

Fingers gently caressed her forehead and trailed down her nose. "Morph, sweetie. You made it."

"Shut up, Lio. It isn't time for school." She batted at the hands and the laugh that ran through the male in front of her was familiar. She was about to say his name and then remembered, "Thinker? How did you get down here?"

"We have steeds, and we have some very relieved parents with us right now." He was scooping her up and carrying her to one of the beasts that had been brought into the small camp. Somewhere in the camp, women were sobbing and some men as well. Effortlessly, he swung into the saddle with her still in his arms. She snuggled in close and fell asleep, the tingle of Haaro's presence warming her mind.

When she woke, she was alone, and butt naked. She was in a standard Sethrin cottage with gauzy curtains letting in some morning light. She felt rested, hungry, and scummy. The bathing chamber was off to one side of the bedroom and she made full use of it, relieving all pressures and scrubbing herself from head to toe, twice.

She was forced to a strange realization then. She had nothing to wear. Wrapping a swath of the towel linen around her, she tried to find the tingle in her mind that was Haaro and bring him to her. She was left pacing, fussing. Combing out her hair took a little of her pressure off, but she was still fidgeting when there was a knock on the door.

"Come in." A little girl of around twelve had her uniform and boots. "Hello, little one. What is your name?"

"Seva, Madame Morph. I am Sela's sister and very grateful that you found her." The tiny creature slammed into her with enough force to knock the wind out of her. She returned the little girl's hug as she sobbed out her relief. "We were so scared."

"Seva, did you know that your sister kept Tev alive and hunted for them both when he was injured? She deserves as much credit or more for her rescue. If she hadn't been a tough cookie, she never would have been there for me to find. She is a great woman who needs to know it."

Seva wiped her nose with the back of her hand. "But she said it was all you."

"That is what true heroes do. They take the focus off themselves." The little girl nodded wisely. "They act when it is needed and forget it when it is over." She smiled brightly at the little girl who looked a lot like the children she had left on Cor. "Did you wash my uniform?"

She nodded. "I also brushed your boots, they purred when I touched them."

"Yeah. They are alive." She grabbed her uniform and ducked into the bathroom. "Wait a moment." She quickly got dressed and made sure that everything was covered. Aggie padded out of the bathroom on bare feet and slid them into the Masuo.

The colors shifted to match her uniform and Seva squealed and clapped her hands. "You look so pretty. But how did you carry Tev and Sela?"

"Well it is too small in here for me to show you that form, but how about this one?" Knowing that it was pretty and impressive, she sprouted her wings. "I change my shape. It is why I am called Morph."

The little girl's eyes glowed. "Can you fly?"

"Yes. I can. So can Thinker."

"But he's a Dhemon and you're a Sethrin. He's supposed to be able to fly, isn't he?" Seva was reaching out to touch the wings so Aggie extended them and ruffled one down her cheek. She giggled and backed away.

"No. Dhemons aren't born with wings anymore. Thinker is special. And my mom was not Sethrin—she had her own talents, and she passed them on to me." Aggie retracted her wings and winced as her stomach growled alarmingly.

"Oh. I am so sorry. I forgot to tell you that lunch is in the main square. Thinker is waiting for you." A blush covered her cheeks.

"I am glad we had a chance to talk." She touched Seva's hair and remembered being that age herself—confused and frustrated by a body that would not obey her. Seva would never have to face that, but because of what Aggie was, she now had her sister back.

Some things had to reveal themselves in time.

Together, they walked through the village and headed for the square. Tables had been laid out and were filled with villagers. Haaro was seated near the Avatar, who stood out like a sore thumb. His coloring was reversed for a Sethrin. His hair was gold and his eyes were black.

Aggie headed for her husband and was stopped by a woman throwing her arms around her with profuse thanks. Another woman was in line behind her to embrace Aggie in a similar manner. She then shook hands with both fathers and a number of siblings. She was bewildered and extremely hungry by the time she reached the Avatar and Haaro.

"Ah, the infamous, Morph. I am glad to meet you. I am Wil, Avatar to Gaffin. Thank you for coming and abiding by the tech restrictions. It will make me more eager to seek assistance in the future, I can assure you." He was going to take her hand in his, but Haaro beat him to it, embracing her with a public display of affection that left her knees weak.

"Thanks for that, Thinker. I think you sucked out one of my teeth," she whispered it into his ear just to hear his husky laugh. "Can I eat now?"

"She's a little hungry. May we eat?" Haaro asked the Avatar who stood with a slightly unhappy look on his face.

"Of course. By all means. Begin the feast!" His eyes flared red as he spoke and Gaffin started the festivities.

The children brought out platters of food and carried pitchers of water and wine. Aggie stuck to the water. She wasn't up for getting drunk in public. "How are Tev and Sela?"

"Tev is recovering and Sela is at his side, as is proper." Something in his tone set her off. She could feel a sort of predatory hunger emanating from the Avatar.

"Ah. I thought she would enjoy the company of her community. She did, after all, keep him alive and fed for the whole of their journey. She did the hunting, kept him bathed and as comfortable as she could make him." She dug into some bread with enthusiasm, tearing a slice of meat to ribbons with some finger enhancements that she engaged in by reflex. The food was good, but the silence that fell after her pronouncement was obvious.

It was only when she and Haaro had eaten their fill that she got impatient. "I thank you for your hospitality, but we need to return to Morganti." The scowl that covered Wil's face took her aback.

"You must stay for the dancing that will occur this evening." A nearby villager looked startled at this announcement.

Haaro tried to smooth things over. "I am afraid that we must return to duty. Sector Guards are always on duty."

"You stayed to eat."

"Eating is a necessity. Dancing is not. If we are needed again, we cannot be reached here as we can at our home base." She was setting down the rules and Haaro sent her a questioning thought. "Good day."

She sent one back. *Fly.*

He moved fast. The instant that she sent the command, he stood on the bench he had been seated on, crouched down as low as he could and launched himself into the air. His great wings beat a steady pulse in the sky and Aggie narrowly missed being caught by Wil as he lunged for her.

She launched herself similarly, if somewhat more slowly into the air. As she gained altitude and caught the currents, she drew even with Haaro. He directed her to their shuttle and as soon as they landed, they ran in, sealed the hatch and lifted off.

They dealt with some shudders in the atmosphere of Gaffin, but for the most part their escape was uninterrupted. As they got into the dark expanse of space between Gaffin and Morganti, Haaro finally turned to her, "What the hell was that about?"

CHAPTER SEVEN

Aggie squirmed a bit in the co-pilot's seat. "Wil was in the mood to mate. He's a reversal of the standard Sethrin genes, and therefore is not a viable mate for any of the villagers. With my skewed heritage, it made me a candidate." She pursed her lips. "Because you and I have not mated, I was fair game."

"You are serious."

"Dead serious. Unfortunately, force is not unheard of in Sethrin society. Either in forcing a marriage, or a mating to force a marriage." She shrugged. "The clones of Cor adopted Alliance Regulations for mating guidelines. They acted as equals, male and female. Some of the clone colonies think that if they can hold to Sethrin values, they may one day be allowed back in to their societies."

"So if we had mated before we had landed?"

"I would have been mate marked by Sethrin standards. One of the only senses that they do have is to sense pheromone bonds." She fiddled with some of the targeting sensors, distracting herself from his fixated attention.

The cursing that emanated from him was creative and colourful.

She turned and looked at him in surprise. "I didn't know that Dhemons used that kind of language."

He gave her a wry glance out of the corner of his eye. "Only when we think we won't get caught. So if we hadn't run, he would have tried to rape you?"

"He tried to grab me when we left. I don't know what other plans he had." She shuddered. It had been far too close for comfort.

"Then we will have to remedy that, if you are willing."

"Willing?"

"To be my wife in truth and not just name."

"Ah. That. I thought about that while I was running through the woods with that young couple on my back. There is no one I would rather have creeping around in my mind than you. So you are welcome to creep around my body as well." The grin formed before she could stop it and her phrasing didn't slow him down—a gleam formed in his eyes that burned her from head to toe.

"As soon as we have some privacy, I will take you up on that. When you least expect it." He piloted them back to Morganti, the charged atmosphere of the challenge she had thrown down inside the shuttle making the air almost hard to breathe.

The Arcus was steered into its position in the landing bay and they disembarked. In silence, they made their way past Hyder, Helen and a number of other staff members. They went straight to their quarters. Her quarters. Still not speaking, they removed their respective body suits and then stood, naked and aroused, looking at each other. It was then that Aggie couldn't hold the seriousness any longer. She began to giggle and simply walked over to her husband and pressed herself against him from neck to knees. "Can we stop the silent treatment?"

"Well, conversation is not the first thing that enters my mind with you pressed against me like this." He stroked his hand down the pale curves of her back to cup her buttocks, pulling her against his unmistakable interest. With both of them naked, it was quite apparent. She squirmed lightly against him, learning the feel of his flesh against hers. It was more than nice.

He backed them up and laid her on the bed. "Know that we do this because we wish it, and not because of the Gaffin incident."

Aggie reached up and pulled him down to her, punctuating each word with a kiss. "I know that each woman has a first time, and I am glad that my first time is with a male of my choosing in a manner of my choice. Are you going to make me wait?" He was stroking her neck as she spoke and he groaned as she finished.

"I don't think I have the strength. Your charms have overpowered me and I am helpless before them." Breathing deeply, he rested his forehead between her breasts.

"Those aren't charms. Those are breasts. You Dhemons are easily confused, aren't you?" Her laugh was the last one she would have for some time. He kept her too busy to laugh. His kisses covered her torso, delved between her thighs and back up again. Each arm, each finger was caressed and as she gasped and wanted something she had not yet experienced, she felt the bond between them grow stronger.

When he entered her, it was a complete joining of bodies and minds, his flowering love for her touching every part of her soul. As he rocked them to completion, she fed him her love, her needs and wants with every thrust. Her body was trying to tell her something and when her release was upon her, she screamed in reaction, overcome.

As she writhed under him, Haaro embraced his own moment and roared his triumph, exposing his teeth and biting the joining between her neck and shoulder. With pleasure still rippling through her, she only absently noted the flicker of pain. Her mind was full of him, his thoughts and his satisfaction.

A voice broke into their subsiding haze. "Haaro Denler, your claim to Agreha Wyld is recorded and logged for the Dhema Mating Archive. Consider this your witness moment." Hyder's voice was wry. "Have a nice night."

Aggie lay under her husband for a moment before asking, "What was that about?"

Haaro shifted free of her body and cuddled her against him, covering her with a wing. "A Dhemon tradition. We require witnesses to the first claiming. With the women of our world at a premium, the witnesses serve as honour guards until the couple leaves the bedchamber. It is also a fast way to formalize a wedding. The witnesses file the notice with the Mating Archive so that all of our offspring will be classified as legitimate."

"Whoa. Offspring? I wasn't planning on any little Morphs running around that soon." She tried to back away from him, but he wasn't having any of it.

"They will arrive, if they arrive, in their own time. Our duties as Guards will be altered to fit our duties as parents if that happens." He cuddled her close again. "For now. Let's just enjoy our moment of pseudo privacy, wife."

Wife. She hadn't thought of her relation to him, only his to her. "What about the biting?"

"Mating marks, several species with similar physiologies engage in them. They look lovely on you by the way." He stroked the bite marks with his finger and she felt the reaction of his body against hers again. His head dipped as he kissed the marks he had left and soon they were enjoying their compatibility in the most basic of ways.

Aggie enjoyed the fact that she could use his horns to keep him where she wanted him, and she did, until the stars lit behind her eyes once again and she felt the bite of his teeth seconds after. As the pain and pleasure blended into one, she knew why there were so many children on Cor. It would be a hard habit to break, now that she had become addicted, and she had no intention of breaking it.

It was far too much fun.

CHAPTER EIGHT

Aggie woke with a start. She was trapped in the bed and for a moment could not remember why. The light hissing of breath on her shoulder soon reminded her as Haaro asked her, "What's wrong?"

"I am not used to sharing a bed."

"We will use the one in my quarters from now on. It's larger." He shifted lazily, running his hand across her belly while nuzzling at her neck. "Good morning, wife."

She stretched against him. "Good morning, husband. I am thinking that a visit to the bath would be in order. I feel decidedly sticky."

"Ah, a side effect of our nocturnal activities. I will assist you." He released her from his loose embrace and stretched, gloriously naked.

"Wow. You are really quite pretty."

"So you said on our first meeting. Was it less than a week ago?" He scooped her up and carried her to the bathing chamber. He filled the pool of water and set it to churn as he slowly lowered her in. The care that he took with her was amusing.

He hadn't been so delicate with her body last night. She bore finger imprints on several parts of her legs and buttocks, and her thighs pulled with every movement. It had been quite the wedding night. She smiled.

"Why the smile?" He pulled her into his lap and started to soap her from head to toe.

"I was just wondering why the thought of a marriage of convenience had ever entered my mind." She nestled against him. "It is obvious that I was deluded."

"I certainly thought so at the time. Just seeing you there on the ground, I was getting hard." He chuckled at his own reaction. "Your skirt had flown up and was exposing half your thighs, and your cleavage was exposed from my vantage point."

"Pervert." She splashed water at him, watching the drops dance across his horns. She watched a second too long. A water fight that doused the majority of the bathing chamber left them gasping and in each other's arms once again. "Perhaps we are done bathing. I don't think I can get more pruney. My fingers are shrinking." She held up her puckered fingers and grinned.

"Well, bits of me are not shrinking, but I agree. It is time to dry." He carried her out of the water with a whoosh of displaced moisture and carefully wrapped her in bath sheets until he had finished flapping his wings to dry them.

She stood and picked up a dry sheet, gestured for him to turn, and gently patted the last drops from his wings. She stroked the smooth skin of his back and then trailed her lips down his spine, kissing from shoulders to his tailbone. His taut buttocks flexed as she neared them and Aggie gave them a nice pat. "Turn around." She dried his arms, horns, chest, abs, calves, feet, thighs and finally the erection that was demanding her attention.

She gave him a final caress and stepped back. "Let's save something for later. I am a little sore."

His face went from narrow-eyed lust to concern. "Are you alright?"

"Just normal reaction from unaccustomed friction, or so I was told." She patted his arm. "The women on Cor had the responsibility to explain the facts of life to me. Lio kept choking when he tried to explain it. Everything seems normal to me." Linking her arm through his, she led him back to the bedchamber. "Let's get some clothes on and you can show me the cafeteria and the beauty of Morganti."

"That sounds like a fine idea. Mala donated some clothing for you and altered it to fit." His lips were twitching. "You are a little taller than she is." He gestured to the wardrobe and she made a beeline for it.

"I know. It was nice of her to offer them." The clothing was a welter of bright colors, some of which Aggie couldn't even describe. She slipped into a dark gold tunic with a black sash and a black skirt, then put on her Masuo. "There. Am I presentable?"

Haaro had sat back to watch her wandering around the room naked, holding the clothing up in the mirror and then returning it to the wardrobe until she found the clothing she now wore. He made no effort to hide his interest, but in light of her physical restriction, he would also not make any overtures until she told him she was ready. Pity.

"You are the loveliest lady on Morganti. It will be my honour to accompany you on your tour of the village." He moved to the connecting door and opened it and then it was her turn to trail after him and watch him dress.

She was as fascinated as he had been by the process. His muscles bunched, shifted and glided under his skin. Her mouth watered and she had to take a deep breath for control. "It is hard for me as well, no pun intended," he commented as he finished sealing the closure on his tunic. His erection was hidden in the overlap of his tunic to his trousers, but she knew it was there. Knew it and was frustrated by it.

"Why are women's bodies assembled in such a stupid manner? It is not like I needed a hymen. I wasn't putting writing implements up there or anything," she grumped as they walked through the halls. Only a few staff members were there this early, but the cafeteria was ready for business. Haaro was laughing too hard to answer her.

They made their selections and were seated. The food tasted especially good to Aggie, who had munched her way through cold rations for the last few days. It seemed like forever.

She was just on her second round of fruit when a light on Haaro's belt lit up. "What is it?"

"Hyder needs us in the conference room." He grabbed a tray and piled their breakfast on it, and to Aggie's surprise, carried it out of the cafeteria and down the hall. When they got to the conference room, he unloaded the tray at one end of the table and nodded for Hyder to start. A bleary eyed Helen sat next to her spouse, but was on alert for her portion of the meeting.

"Go ahead and eat, Morph. It may be your last fresh meal for a while." That Hyder was addressing her by her call sign was a signal that she didn't miss.

She nodded her thanks. "Thank you, Commander. I was just enjoying the fresh fruit when you called."

"There is a situation that calls for Thinker's telepathic expertise and your ability to shift." Hyder nodded to a screen that was displaying a tank with a Delean inside it. "The Delean's have requested your presence, because Morph can act as a telepathic conduit while Thinker engages in the treaty negotiations with a colony of Pela who want to settle on the dry land of Dele. Are you willing? It may take some time."

She looked to Haaro. *I am willing if you are. It has been a while since I have spent any large amount of time underwater though.*

He nodded in understanding. *If you are unsure, tell me now. If not, it is an excellent way to be together without ripping each other's clothing off.*

Aggie grinned. *Excellent point. I say we do it. But why is Helen here?*

She is the Pilot of the Class One, a shuttle sized jump ship. She helped

Isabi to bring Mala here, but the others and I had to take regular shuttles and catch jump ships to get us to our mates.

Huh. How many others?

Two. A dragon and a seer. They each agreed to let Hyder choose their mates, so let's see how happy everyone is with the process when they arrive back at home. Hopefully we will have returned by then.

So we will do it? Go to Dele?

We will. Haaro nodded and turned to Hyder. "We will go and assist in the negotiations."

The representative from Dele looked relieved and set up a stream of bubbles in response. Aggie looked to her husband and grinned. "I guess everyone is happy then. When do we leave?"

Helen nodded to them both as she stifled a yawn. "As soon as you can get to the Class One. Or as soon as you finish your breakfast. You will be needing your strength." She leaned up against her mate and looked like she would catnap. He stroked her hair and whispered in her ear for a moment and then the Commander and Pilot had left the room.

Aggie looked to her own spouse. "They look happy."

"As happy as they can be with him stuck here running the outpost. It frustrates him, but there is no option for the Alliance at present. We are fortunate in him, with his talents we stand to be the first complete complement of Sector Guard in the galaxy. The other outposts are taking auditions and following rumours to find their mates."

"Why mated pairs?"

"With the intensity of our talents, it keeps us from distraction. No seductress can compare to a true mate in every sense of the word. No man is as attractive as one who can truly understand you on all levels." He laughed. "Isabi has told me that Mala calls it *compatible freak factors.*"

"She may be right about that. Our talents do seem to mesh well, although I would not have thought it when we first met." She finished spooning the fruit into her mouth and stood. "I guess we should get our suits and report to the Class One."

"I wouldn't be in too much of a hurry, if I were you. Helen and Hyder know they are going to be separated for a while. They might just be spending some time together."

"Are you peeping at them?"

"It is hard to ignore. Touch my mind, you will see." He held still as she took his hand and looked into his eyes. She could make out the flare of thoughts in the complex, and a supernova of love and need near the joint quarters.

"Wow. Do we look like that?"

"Yes. Together we blaze as bright as the suns of Agregor." He ran his fingers through her hair and pulled her against him.

"I was named for those suns. My sister for the moons." She enjoyed the moment of tranquility, her body next to his, relaxed and satisfied to be in his arms before their mission.

"This is the Sector Guard shuttle craft, Class One, calling Dele Base. Requesting permission to land." Pilot was plugged into her ship, the wires and connections looking as natural as her hair.

"This is Dele Base. You are clear to land, Class One. Welcome to Dele and thank you for coming." The hiss and gurgle of the translator conveyed the warmth and enthusiasm of the species they were here to help.

Pilot flicked a few toggles. "Sector Guard Base, Morganti. This is Pilot. We have arrived at Dele. Morph and Thinker are ready to deploy."

"Commence the mission, Pilot. There are two newcomers when you get home. Be safe and get back here as soon as you can." Hyder's voice was strong as it came through the com. If there was a delay in communications, it was not detectable.

Pilot began to enter the atmosphere. "Okay, you two. I hope you packed your swimsuits—you are about to get wet."

The ship moved smoothly through the gas layers. Morph looked to her husband and grinned. "Who needs a suit?"

The first glimpses of the Sector Guards for the people of Dele were strong, tall, bi-pedals all laughing like loons. The one designated as Morph, by her dossier, separated from the other two and shifted forms into a mer form that they found most pleasing. As soon as she began translation for them, their delight grew. At long last they could make their wishes for the surface of their world known.

They would forward their gratitude for these beings to the Alliance. They were an asset that would be treasured.

HAEL'S FURY

CHAPTER ONE

"We require attendance by Customs Agent Mornil." The voice coming through the speakers was obviously agitated. This was why Livin Hael was here.

"I am sorry, but as the on duty Agent, I am more than capable of dealing with your clearance. Please remain calm while the beam scans your ship." With a few deft flicks of her fingers, the docking clamps latched in place and the power drains attached to the hull. The trader transport was not going anywhere.

What they couldn't know was that Agent Mornil had been detained by three strippers at the entertainment centre on the Drai orbital station. He would be coming late, if he could still come after they were done with him. The transport, Briax 2, signalled the end of her undercover operation, now she just needed to make the arrests.

Her hands skimmed over the toggles and switches as she said the two words guaranteed to send the transport captain into a frenzy. "Engaging scanner."

"Again, I protest! We wish to speak to Customs Agent Mornil." She hadn't known a male's voice could get that shrill, but he proved her wrong.

The scanner was giving her the feedback she was looking for. There were living beings on that ship that were stacked like cordwood in cold sleep. The transport was not graded for living transport and there was no stop on a colony world on their route. They were slavers.

"What is going on here?" A thunderous voice rang out behind her. It belonged to the diminutive Mornil.

"The Briax 2 is loaded with living cargo. They have no rating to transport living beings and no stops registered on colony worlds. They are slaving." She kept a close eye on him in the reflection of the vid screen. His face was running through a gamut of emotion. When it got to fury, she was ready. "It was bizarre, really. They kept asking for you for some reason. Don't worry, though, I had the station guards in place and ready to go. They are taking the crew into custody as we speak and rescuing the sleepers."

His first lunge at her took him past her and into the vid console. She had sidestepped him neatly. He took another run at her and she dodged him again. Finally coming to the conclusion that he could not grab her, he pulled his pistol.

It would have been intimidating if she wasn't ready for it. His thumb revved up the heat setting, he took aim and fired.

Finally. She had been waiting for this moment for weeks. A small flick of her mind and she bled the heat from the beam, turning it into the mere passing of air over her body. The air she gathered and shoved back into Mornil's chest. He was gasping for breath, so with a flick of her finger, she pulled the air out of his lungs and held it above his face. His eyes went wild and she could sense his question. She had heard it before. "I am an agent of the Drai, and a born elemental. You are under arrest." He had passed out before she had finished speaking and she absently forced the air back into his body.

Cuffing him securely, she watched the steady stream of cold sleep chambers moving out of the ship and onto the station. Those who had been enslaved would be freed, and those who wanted a cheap transport would be sent on to the next large port of call.

"Security, we have one additional participant for arrest. Please report to the customs office." With her assignment completed, she only had one more thing to do. "Transport Va'dil, please present for customs scan." There was no one to man her station and the goods and ships were still stopping in for refuelling and trade. Customs Agents waited for no one and they never traded shifts.

Mornil's shift passed with no other bits of excitement with one exception—a Draikyn arrived without notice and the officers fell over themselves to make him welcome. After the brisk scan and clearance of his shuttle, she only caught a glimpse of the black and silver of his form as he headed into the station. The tiny flicker of his shape was enough to chill her and heat her at the same time. He seemed horribly familiar.

"This is shuttle Morganti requesting clearance to the Drai station." The drone of the voice snapped her back to her duties. Daydreaming could wait—now was time for business.

"So, honey, how did it go?" Livin's mother was preparing dinner as she always did on the eighth day. Her Matya's pale skin gleamed in the bright light streaming through the window, showing proof of her diluted blood. It was the same light shade that Livin had, and it marked her as a mixed breed. Not exactly the most valued of the Draikyn. Her deep green hair accented her pale gold skin and was echoed in her offspring.

"Fine, Matya. About as well as could be expected. The rest of the shift was hard though—a personal craft was taking up one of the bays." She snuck her hand past the knife that was slicing cheese and snatched it back with her prize.

Her mother's sigh was almost deafening. It was a sigh of long suffering. "Honestly, Liv, couldn't you wait a moment?"

"Nope. I am hungry now. When is dinner?"

"Two hours from now, but wait, you had a call while you were out." Sivin turned her back to her offspring to protect the food and Livin tried to hide her smile.

"Was there a message?"

"Check your bed." Sivin threw a wink at her daughter and turned back to completing the elaborate Drai weekend meal.

Curious now, Livin ran up the stairs to check her room. She had heard from other species that it was uncommon for adult children to remain at home, but it seemed natural for the Draikyn to keep their families close. Parents who wanted privacy would arrange for a sitter and simply have their adult time away. The children would remain in the nest, no matter what the age, and sitters were mandatory. They were usually a mated couple who were friends of the family, and yet who had no children who were unmated. The rules and traditions of other races still confused her.

Reaching her door, she palmed the lock and winced as she saw the bed. It was an *Introduction* gown. Oh hells. She checked the invitation laid out on top of it and winced at the smell of ink. Whomever she was supposed to be introduced to, he had just arrived on Drai. At least she would have time for her mother's dinner. It was far more nutritious than anything that the Clan Leaders would have prepared. The *Introduction* was going to be set at the town hall. Livin could hardly wait.

Nothing like being rejected in front of a crowd. Just the thought almost put her off her feed. Almost. She threw her overnight bag onto the floor and fingered the elaborate embroidery that her mother had put into the gown. Sivin liked to tell her that the instant that she birthed a daughter, she had started on the gown. With the covering of needlework and gemstones, the gown almost stood on its own. It certainly showed the attention of a doting parent, but even her nest and upbringing had not brought her a mate.

She dreamed of seeing the male that haunted her nights speaking those fateful words, *"I dreamed of you."* If he reciprocated, then they were destined to be mates. If she could not find the courage to speak the words, she would remain alone. It wasn't a horrible thought. She could push for a seat on the council, or start matchmaking.

It was a family secret that her father had made the first move. Sivin had been too shy to approach him, so he had sought her out in a dark corner and whispered the words to her. She reciprocated and the rest was history. Sivin's lack of pedigree had never stopped Loson Hael. He loved her more with each passing day. It was gratifying to see her parents in love after three decades.

Perhaps it would have been easier if one of her ancestors hadn't mated with a genetically altered Terran. If she had been born a pure Draikyn, she might have had the dream that would lead her to her mate. As it was, her dreams were simply filled with wind and fire. Not too unusual for a woman who could call the elements to her. Now, if only she could call a man into her dreams, she would be set.

CHAPTER TWO

It had taken the better part of an hour to get her into the gown, but by the time she was in it, Livin was resigned to going to the Clan Hall. Her father handed her a bib before she sat down for dinner, and she was able to regale Loson and Sivin with the non-classified details of her assignment. "Why do they all try to use heat pistols?"

Her father barked a laugh. "Perhaps because no one knows that your talent exists, outside of the Clan Council." He rustled his wings in amusement and Livin remembered the envy she had felt as a child. She had wanted wings so badly, until Loson had sat her down to explain the facts of life to her. Boys had wings, girls didn't. When she asked why, she had been told that it was to keep the girls from getting away.

Sivin had hit him for that one, but as Livin grew, she realized the truth. It was indeed a mating response. Perhaps it was a throwback to the days when the Draikyn could shape shift into dragons. Nowadays, only the sleepers could do that—those rare Clan members who had flown to other planets thousands of years ago to sleep until they felt a call. Some said that they slept to wait for their mates, but some said that they would wake during a great cataclysm and come to repopulate Drai. That sounded a little too grim for Livin, who was helping herself to a third round of vegetables.

"So do you have a strategy for this evening, Liv?" Her father's fangs flashed with his grin.

"Yup, I am going in, saying hello, and getting out of there as soon as I can. I also am still technically on call, so while I am not hoping for a disaster, I would love a distraction."

Loson sighed heavily. "You are never going to catch a male with that attitude."

"I am not looking to catch one, I just want to meet a guy who doesn't ask me how far back the tainted blood goes. Sorry, Matya, Dakya, but it happens."

The first five times had come as a shock, but after that, the males had ended up trying to drink beverages that were either scalding or frozen solid, depending on her mood.

"I know, and I wish I could regret the blood in our veins, but I don't. Our strange talents have kept this planet free, even if only the Clan Council knows about it." Sivin smiled wistfully. Her own talent for telekinetic manipulation had saved thousands, and they would never know. She was simply a woman who was in the right place at the right time, carried on the wind by her mate.

"I do not regret for an instant choosing your mother, and we know that you are proud of her accomplishments." Loson reached out to take his mate's hand and they sat for a moment in familial silence. "Isn't it time for you to leave, Liv?"

"Wow, you are subtle. Goodnight, Matya." She leaned over to kiss her mother, "Goodnight, Dakya." She kissed her father. "I will return near midnight—please be finished whatever you are doing by then." She giggled as Loson swept Sivin into his arms and carried her into their private wing.

Livin was still smiling as she moved in her stiffly embroidered tunic and made her way into her personal flitter. The finely tuned hum of the engine made her warm inside. Her mother had done the maintenance while she was on Drai station. Her aging flitter now achieved altitude with no trouble and gained speed like a new machine. Sivin had done it again. No one had a touch like hers on mechanical objects.

Her smile lasted until she saw the Clan Hall looming in front of her. The occasional male looked into her flitter screen curiously, but flew off when they saw her face. She didn't look happy and she knew it.

Her gown rustled in anticipation as she locked up her flitter and looked up at the sky. Males of every description were taking to the sky in an effort to impress the females within. Many women dreamed of their mates in flight, so having them flying in the flesh made the matchmaking process easier.

Straightening her shoulders, Livin went to face her doom. She handed the invitation to the Council Guard at the door and was allowed entrance. The doors swung open and then closed behind her, effectively trapping the women in. Sighing and nodding pleasantly to the few acquaintances that she saw, she made a beeline for the punch bowl and settled in for the night.

Leaning against one wall, she kept a column of cold air around her to deter any of the males who came in through the upper windows. She was resigned to be a councilwoman or of perpetual use to the council. Her tainted line would die with her.

There was a cloud of women swirling around one of the males in the room. He must be the new one that she had been summoned for. There would have been no other reason for her to be sent an invitation as she had been written off as unmatched years before.

The ladies fawned all over him, each whispering in his ear that she had dreamed of him. Livin felt a pang near her heart as they touched his arms and leaned up to whisper in his slightly pointed ear.

"Livin! Psst." Horel jostled her elbow to get her attention. She and Horel had grown up near each other and occasionally played together at school. There had never been any animosity between them at these events as they were both seeking opposite qualities in their men. "Have you spoken to him?"

"No. Who is he?"

"One of the sleepers. Really, I am not kidding. My mother heard it from one of the Councilwomen. He had to pull some strings to issue the *Introduction* tonight, but they did it." They were standing with their heads together and didn't even notice when a dark figure blocked the light.

"Ladies, you are far too lovely to be standing here in the corner." He reached out to take Horel's hand and she flushed a becoming bronze. Her dark gold skin flushed in response as she returned his greeting.

As if it was unbidden, she spoke in a whisper, "I dreamed of you."

"I dreamed of you as well. My name is Jalok."

"Horel."

"May I escort you to the dance floor?" He tucked her arm in his and together they smoothly crossed the floor with a smattering of applause following them. Horel still looked stunned, but in a happy way.

A pang of sorrow hit Livin. It had been nice to think that she would not be alone as she aged, that there would be a friend nearby. She could see the match as the couple danced, it was obvious that they shared a soul.

She continued in her quiet corner and watched the women circling the newcomer. The sleeper. He was beginning to look frustrated by the attentions and his gaze was darting around until it alighted on her. A slow smile crossed his features and he moved out of the clutch of women to make his way to her.

Councilwoman Ratha intercepted him and he stopped for a moment to speak to her. He jerked his head toward her and when the Councilwoman turned to look, a blush flared over Livin's features. She was not used to being subjected to this kind of scrutiny. Ratha had the nerve to try and hold him back as he continued along his predetermined path. He shook her off and stopped immediately in front of Livin.

He extended his hand for a greeting and she looked at it for a long moment before she took it. "Livin Hael. I..." she was unable to continue as her emergency pager went off. With her right hand engaged, her left fished her pager out of her bodice. The message chilled her. "I am sorry, I have to leave." She tried to free her hand, but he was having none of it.

"You cannot leave—the doors are bolted until midnight. Where do you need to go? I will take you." He flexed his wings and scooped her into his arms without another word. She clutched his neck as he bent his knees and launched skyward from a standing position. Holy hells. She had heard of a standing launch, but most males couldn't manage it. It took tremendous strength.

"I need to get to Cleath forest. There is a wildfire that I need to attend to." She pressed her lips against his ear to speak and closed her eyes at the shudder that went through both of them at the contact.

"We will be there within the hour. Trust me?" His voice was in her ear and she shuddered at the heat that caressed her.

"I don't know you, but I trust you." They were the last words that she spoke in a normal tone as he hurled her upward and let her go.

She was falling, the ground was getting closer and closer and a scream was frozen in her chest. She summoned what air she could to slow her fall, but was terrified that it would not be enough.

I would never let you fall.

She could swear that she heard a voice, but when her body was caught in midair by a taloned fist, she shook with the ramifications. He really was a sleeper. He could shift.

A deep bronze head turned to fix her with one swirling gold eye. *I am and I can. I dreamed of you.*

She had dreamed of him, too, but thought that it had been residue of her history class. He carefully placed her on his neck and she clutched at him desperately, closing her eyes against the rising wind and hiding herself from the fear that his sentence had engendered in her.

So Councilwoman Ratha was telling me that you are an operative for the Drai government upon occasion. Would you be open to another job offer?

Do you have a nest? It was the most practical thing she could think of to ask. No male was supposed to be seeking a mate unless he had prepared a nest first.

Of a sort. I suppose that you would insist on a proper domicile. His thoughts were laced with masculine resignation.

Of course I would. I may not be a pure blood, but I have standards. If he thought that she was a quick tumble, he would be grievously mistaken. She would freeze his nuts off, no matter the form he wore.

Ouch. He wheeled into a higher position and she could see the faint glow in the distance of the fire.

"Set me down over there!" she yelled to be heard over the coursing air, not comfortable giving orders in her mind.

Why? You will be safer while riding me. He was right, but it was something she was unaccustomed to. *You will get used to it. I only just found you, I don't want anything to happen to you.*

I will be perfectly safe. Fire doesn't burn me. Water will not drown me. Air will not suffocate me and earth will not consume me.

But a Draikyn may eat you. There was a wicked connotation to his voice. It took her a moment and then she blushed to her roots. Fortunately, by that time they were hovering near the fire. He moved them slowly forward and she was able to draw the heat from the fire and have the earth turn to extinguish the embers. It was accomplished far more swiftly than if she had had to fly her flitter while trying to concentrate on taking the air from the blaze.

When he had made several passes, she took stock with her inner eye, looking for any hot spots. There were none. *We can go home now.*

Where is your home?

My parents' nest is on the Abercrombie pass.

Good location, did your father have to fight for it?

I believe so, but he doesn't mention it. He only mentions that the instant that he saw my mother, he fell in love. She dreamed of him and he of her. It was lovely to grow up knowing that they have such a strong bond.

It is that way between true mates, when the emotions generated on either side are undeniable.

Perhaps you should let me go to my flitter so that my parent's won't think anything is awry when I go home.

Oh, but I want to meet your parents.

Tough. They had a private night alone and are feeling mellow. I don't want to wreck that for them. To the flitter please.

Hers was the last flitter left in the lot and she slid down the neck of her ride for a better look at him. Livin whistled slowly as he preened for her attention. The fifty feet of dragon extended his neck and turned this way and that to show his entire morphed body for her. As she watched, he shrank to his bipedal form of seven feet of muscle and wing. He came to her and bowed low, "Our introduction was interrupted. I am Vasu and I dreamed of you."

"I am Livin and I dreamed of you, Vasu." She blinked up at him. "Now what? You are assigned off-world and I have an obligation to the Drai Council."

"I have a solution for that. There is a new branch of the Alliance called the Sector Guard. You have been chosen to become part of our elite team. The Drai have agreed to release you to join me."

Disappointment flooded through her. "Oh, so you only want me for my elemental talent. I guess I can think about it."

Vasu pulled her flush against his chest. She could feel his heartbeat pounding. "My mate was an elemental when I saw her. There was no other one for me. The fact that you are also Drai is almost too good to be true. If you accept the assignment and meet Hyder, you will know that he saw us together before he had even met me. If not for his guidance, I might not have returned to Drai to see if my match could possibly be here. You were." His head dipped down for a sweet kiss. In that kiss was protection, affection and a deep desire for more.

Shaking, she pulled away. "That was quite something."

"Indeed. Tomorrow I shall come to meet your family and explain the assignment to the Sector Guard."

"Fine. Goodnight, Vasu."

His hand caressed her cheek. "Goodnight, Livin. Dream of me." He chuckled as he took flight and she could see him in the rear view imager as she flew home. Her flitter kept steady and she felt strangely relaxed as she pulled into her landing zone. Seeing her safely home, he waved and flew off into the night, leaving her to deal with a riot of emotions and hormones that she'd thought were long dormant.

Bugger.

She dreamed.

CHAPTER THREE

"So how did last night go?" Sivin was wide awake and cheerful the next morning, making breakfast for her only offspring.

"Uh fine, is Dakya around?"

"He will be in, in a minute. Why?"

"I have something to tell you and I don't want to repeat it." She took her seat and started to butter her toast as her mother placed it in front of her.

Her father came up behind her and kissed the top of her head, as was his custom when she was home. "What is it, hatchling?"

"Matya, Dakya, sit down. This is kind of surprising." She waited until they were in a nice relaxed pose. "I met my mate last night."

Her mother squealed and her father simply looked at her in surprise. "Who is he?"

"He is a sleeper from off world. Vasu. I didn't get his last name."

"He may have left it when he left Drai. Are you sure he is a sleeper?"

"Very sure. He shifted." Liv met her father's gaze directly so that he would know she told the truth. "Dragons are larger than I had been led to believe."

Loson let out a long low whistle. "Really? Shifted? And you and he are a match?"

"Apparently. He certainly seems to think so." Livin shook her head. "That isn't really flattering, Dakya."

"I didn't mean it that way, I just meant that the sleepers were truly waiting for their mates and not the end of the Draikyn." Her father rushed to give her a quick hug to sooth the sting of his words.

She reached up to pat his clawed hand. "I know, Dakya. I was just teasing." He was so careful of the feelings of his women. It made Livin wistful to think it might be the last time that she felt cherished by a man in her life.

She had no idea what life Vasu would bring her, or how he would treat her. Livin wasn't even sure that he would come to meet her parents. Perhaps he had changed his mind.

Sivin had remained quiet this whole time and calmly served her mate and herself breakfast. When they were done, she nodded to her daughter and Livin took the dishes for washing. They washed, dried and put away all evidence of breakfast and were just preparing midmorning tea when there was a knock at the door.

Liv could feel the colour drain from her face as she heard Vasu's voice formally greeting her father. Her mother took her hand and she relaxed as calm washed through her. The tea prepared itself on the counter and she smiled at her mother. It was rare that she used her talent in the house. She said it was just as hard to do it by mind as physically, and if she used her hands, she could work off adrenaline when Loson had done something stupid.

They waited patiently for the men to finish their discussion, sipping tea in silence.

Finally, they appeared in the doorway, Vasu standing slightly in front of her father. She supposed it was his right as an elder, but it still bothered her. "Vasu, so nice to see you again."

"Did you think you would not?" He took one of the chairs designed for males and pulled it in next to her. "I told you I dreamed of you. I will not let you out of my sight that easily." He took her free hand in his own and rubbed his thumb along her palm. "Your father and I have discussed the offer of a position in the Sector Guard, but you need to agree and I get the feeling that your mother will have some concerns."

"You are damned right I have some concerns. Just what is the position in the Sector Guard that you are referring to? Will she be in danger? How far will you be taking her? Will you bring her back to visit? What of our grandchild, will you bring her to visit?"

He was a little taken aback by the direct tone Sivin took, but when he looked from mother to daughter, he saw the same questions in their eyes. "First off, she will first and foremost be my mate and under my protection. The Sector Guard is made up of mated pairs who are dispatched on assignment together. As the Guard assembles, we will reach a complement of one dozen agents who will be dispatched when the Alliance has need of us." He took the teacup that floated to him and sipped delicately at the contents. The grace and economy of his movements spoke of an earlier time and manners taught by a strict parent.

"As for the location, you can visit us on Morganti. That is where our Guard base is located. As for grandchildren, why do you assume there will be only one and that it will be a girl?"

Sivin smiled. "Our family has been a long line of females since the Terran, Cynthia Norman. When her blood mingled with her mate's, an unbroken line of females began. But only one per generation."

"I remember Cynthia. She was truly a courageous woman for one taken from her own time."

"What? You knew her?"

"She was the reason that I left to become a sleeper. I looked at her and knew that she was almost perfect for me, but she told me that it was her descendant who would be mine. She was a powerful seer who had an even stronger will. Garo was her mate and she pursued him with a vengeance. She obviously caught him or you wouldn't be here."

"How did she come here? I always thought that she was a captured human, a slave."

"No. She came through a rip in time, folded space and fell out of the sky into Garo's arms. She still had to go through *Introduction,* but Garo was her match. He had been dreaming of his pale princess since he was in council training. Even her diluted offspring could not deter him in the end and when they showed me their baby, Coral, for the first time, I knew that I had a long time to wait for you, Livin." His thumb stroked her palm again and she fought shivers. "So I went to Morganti and settled under a mountain. The avatar welcomed me and when the Sector Guard started amassing, he woke me and made me apply.

"The Guard is made of mated couples to ensure that the partners never need to go out alone. The fact that most of the couples will develop psychic links to reinforce their connection is a perk for the Guard." Vasu was smiling again.

"You didn't answer me about the grandchildren." Sivin was sitting with her arms crossed over her chest and not answering to Vasu's charm.

"Should any children be born, they will be raised at my nest on Morganti. You may visit as often as you wish. I will have a private shuttle delivered to you in a few months, I am assuming that you can fly?"

"I have only flown flitters and local shuttles. Nothing long range." Sivin was looking intrigued by the possibilities. "Loson doesn't fly. Well, not without wings. I suppose I could learn." She was showing signs that she had accepted her daughter's fated choice. Liv breathed a sigh of relief. So did Loson. It was obvious who controlled the family.

"You will allow her to leave your nest then?" Vasu's hand tightened on Liv's and she almost winced at the pressure.

"Provided that you have a formal ceremony when she gets to your nest, she can accompany you to Morganti, but no physical interaction before the ceremony."

Vasu's silvery eyes widened in his chiselled face. Liv fought the urge to stroke the thick black hair off his forehead. What followed was a frank negotiation of what was and was not allowed during the courtship. It was enough to send ripples of embarrassment through every pore on Livin's body.

She didn't know that her mother was up on all the slang for modern foreplay, but she certainly got an education that she had not been expecting. She and her father were both staring at the other two in amazement. Apparently, Loson was surprised by his mate's knowledge as well.

"If you two are finished with your graphic description of carnality, I would like to remind you that I am still on call with the Drai Council and I need to ratify that before anything else is said."

Sivin blinked. "Of course, Livvy. Councillor Ratha will be waiting for your call."

"I think this is news I want to make in person. Vasu, would you care to accompany me to the Council Hall?" Livin stood and looked down at her prospective mate with curiosity.

He blinked and stood rapidly. It was really quite endearing. "Please allow me to accompany you. I get the feeling the Councilwoman will not be an easy person to convince."

"I do not plan on giving her a choice," she whispered to Vasu as they left her home. She squeaked in surprise when he scooped her up. It was a common way to travel with one's mate, but it still felt a little odd. His legs bunched and he took flight an instant later. She closed her eyes and held her breath until he gained a steady altitude.

His eyes sparkled in amusement. "I am not planning on offering a choice either." Liv didn't know if he was speaking about the Councillor or her, but she was glad she had already decided to follow her dreams.

CHAPTER FOUR

"What do you mean, *you quit?* You can't quit. The women of your bloodline have served the Council of Drai for over a thousand years. You can't leave us." Ratha was taking it as well as could be expected. She was currently in complete denial. Her office was locked up tight, and aside from the occasional Draikyn flying past the window, they were alone.

"I beg to differ. If I have been called to Alliance service, it supersedes your claim to me. Aside from that, you have my mother on active duty still. Be satisfied with her telekinesis."

"*You* have not been called into service, Vasu has. You are not yet mated and therefore he has no right to insist on your presence." She almost crowed at that.

Vasu spoke now, "I dreamed of her a thousand years ago. Nothing and no one has the right to stop me from claiming her, or her from claiming me. It is written in the Draikyn mating codes. With our minimal birthrate, every match must be ratified if both parties agree to its validity. Or have the laws changed while I slept?"

Ratha's fingers formed claws and they scratched furrows in her desk. When she calmed enough to speak, it was through gritted teeth. "No. The laws have not changed, but with Livin's tainted blood, it may be possible that she may not be held to them."

Vasu snorted. "Despite what the archives would have you believe, many of us have blended DNA. Fifteen generations before my own, my grandfather fell in love with an Enjel woman. They loved, she died, but she birthed my next ancestor in the process. I can still shift, even with my *tainted blood,* but the modern Draikyn are far too insular to accept it." A harsh tone entered his voice, "And if you don't get your heads out of your asses, the Draikyn will die out as so many races have in the last thousand years. I have brought this concern to your Council heads and they are deliberating on the wisdom of melding genetics with some of the newer races. The Enjels and the Terrans have both been successful, but with the Terran penchant for psychic talents, I would put in a vote for preference on their front."

Liv looked over at Vasu in astonishment. If what he said was true, it would explain the difficulty in obtaining mates for many of the females of her generation, and the one previous. The majority of council positions were held by women, but if Vasu's DNA and hers could revitalize their breeding, it was worth a chance. If she could have more than one child, she would be the first woman in her family to do it in one thousand years.

Vasu took out a communicator and pointed it at the larger com unit on Ratha's desk. An Azon male immediately took up the display. "This is Hyder, acting head of the Sector Guard, Morganti base. Since Vasu has called, you are keeping him from claiming his match. We need her to fill our elemental post in the Sector Guard. The following attached communiqué is from Heror, Drai Representative."

A very angry Draikyn with smouldering eyes and midnight hair came on the screen. He looked a bit like Vasu, come to think of it—all muscles, harsh planes and angles. "Councilor Ratha, please be advised that in an attempt to spur on our flagging population numbers, Vasu Noln of Enjel descent has been granted complete permissions to seek out and mate with Livin Hael, of Terran descent. You will abide by this decision, Ratha, or feel the power of the Alliance Council." Leaving off her title had been a deliberate insult and Liv fought to keep her face still.

"I wish you well and hope you have a safe journey to your nest." The formal send off was bitten out, but as soon as she spoke it, they were free.

They held hands while leaving the Councillor's chamber and Liv's heart was so light that she almost skipped.

She was free of the Drai council and their demands for every little natural disaster. Other planets managed just fine without someone like her interfering in every little crop fluctuation. Besides, if they really needed her, they could call the Sector Guard.

"Matya, Dakya, I love you and I will call you as soon as I arrive on Morganti." She kissed her weeping parents and gave them each a hug. "I know that we thought this day would never come, but it is here today and we all need to embrace it."

"Livin, we hoped that this day would come, but feared it all the same." Loson's voice was sombre.

"We will be on our way for a visit as soon as the shuttle arrives." Sivin wiped away her tears and held her mate as he teared up himself for another round of sniffling.

"The shuttle will be sent out to you as soon as we return to base. Helen is the Pilot and she will give you instruction on how to manoeuvre it. We look forward to your visit, but now we must go." Vasu kept his arm firmly around her waist as he scooted her into the shuttle. With one final wave over her shoulder, she heard the door slide shut and her parents' nest was lost to her. Tears welled in her own eyes as she took the co-pilot's seat and strapped in for lift off.

"I would hold you, but we need to leave Drai. There is no telling when the Guard will be summoned and we need to get back to base as quickly as possible."

"I understand. It is just a final moment for me, picking you and a new life over the comfort of the old." She sniffled a bit and closed her eyes for the fight of the shuttle over gravity. The exit of the ship out of the atmosphere caused a sigh of relief. "That wasn't comfortable."

"You had best get used to it. Also, keep your eyes open while I direct the shuttle. You may have to do this one day."

Livin froze. "Where are you planning to be?"

"Perhaps I will just want a nap and you will be my obliging mate and let me have one." He sent her a twinkling grin, causing her answering smile. He really wasn't pretty. Vasu's features seemed honed by a hand used to granite, all angles and crags. Cheekbones were sharp, chin strong, and the brow line over his eyes threw them into constant shadow. His lips were the only sensual feature on him, that and the sleepy heated gaze that he controlled. One look and she wanted to be on Morganti, accepting his nest, even if it was only a lean-to on a rock wall.

"How long will it take us to get there?"

"Five days. Unless we hook up with an Alliance jump ship willing to take us." He smiled at her again. "The odds of that would be astronomical if I hadn't made a few calls." He smoothly piloted them behind the third moon and there was the enormous bulk of an Alliance warship with jump capacity.

"What an odd coincidence." Liv could hear the laughter in her own voice, but it was nice to know that Vasu was in just as much of a hurry as she was, only for different reasons.

He smiled into the mike as he spoke, "This is the Sector Guard shuttle, Dayi. Requesting clearance for Draikyns, Vasu and Livin."

A disembodied voice sounded in the shuttle speakers. "Welcome. Processing scans." The beams were invisible, but Liv could still feel the creeping of the energy across her skin. A different voice came to them. "Welcome, Draikyns, to the warship Conrandi. Please remain inside your shuttle while we head over to Morganti space. Keep your lunches inside your bodies at all times."

She knew what that voice was. "Thank you, pilot. Your attentions are quite flattering."

"I don't just run my beams over anyone." It was a masculine voice and was now dripping with amusement. Pilots were rarely identified physically, but this one had a familiarity in the feel of his voice, even though it emanated from a speaker.

"Pilot Sosan? Is that you?"

"Agent Hael! So nice to scan you again." Vasu was looking disconcerted by the conversation, but he kept quiet as he guided the ship to the open bay.

"Nice you hear your voice. You are obviously assigned to this ship, but what were you doing in that transport two months ago?" Her to-be-mate was looking embarrassed. He kept his gaze pinned to the view screens.

"Confirming your compatibility with Guard Vasu. Commander Hyder did not want to take any chances he would not find his match. I was the outrider."

"So you confirmed I wasn't hideous?" She crossed her arms and one foot began to tap lightly on the floor.

A warm masculine chuckle made it through the audio. "Something like that. I admired your undercover work as a Customs Agent. I have never had a customs search as thorough as the one you ordered."

"Oh dear, I hope the agents didn't put their fingers anywhere suspiciously irritating." Giggles were welling up, but the jump alarm going off held them back. "Warn me when we are going to jump."

"We are jumping." The pilot's voice reverberated through their hull and she squeaked as Vasu's hand gripped hers in support.

"Just breathe, Livin. It will be over in a moment." His voice came to her through her disorientation and then they were clear. "*S'hah*, I need my hand back to get us planet side."

She blinked and let his hand go, massaging her fingers. He had surprised her by using the archaic term for beloved. Vasu gripped the controls and requested drop clearance.

The pilot answered, "Clearance granted. Tell Helen that Sosan says hi. Nice talking to you, Livin."

"We will." Whatever else she would have said was cut off as Vasu shut off communications and dropped the shuttle out of the belly of the warship. Liv looked up to see the belly of the ship closing above them and the bulk changing direction. She only had less than a minute to look down to see her new home, all blue, green and purple, then they were in a controlled fall to the surface. "Is it a tech restricted world?" Some were and drop ships were the only methods of delivery for personnel or items.

"No. It is a sentient world and its avatar has allowed us to set our base here."

"I have never met an avatar. Is it male or female?"

"Male. His name is Kale and you will meet him after we mate."

"Uh, why not before?" She knew the answer, but wanted to hear it.

"Because you are mine and until we formalize our union, I am not letting you out of my sight." He glanced at her and she smiled brightly at him. It was going to be a fun trip.

CHAPTER FIVE

Waiting in a boardroom was never fun. Vasu and Liv had long expired the basic pleasantries and were now waiting for the head of the base to show his face.

His family was dead. He had one brother who had continued their bloodline, but he died in one of the planetary skirmishes, defending the Drai from encroachment almost one hundred years after Vasu had left to sleep on Morganti. The line had dwindled two generations later when a plague had taken many dream-mates. He was the last of the Noln, unless he had a child.

That was where she came in.

No one knew when the Draikyn had started to dream about their mates, but it had dramatically increased the birthrates and the era of divorce and separation became a faded memory. Mating with someone you had not seen in your dreams guaranteed an infertile match. It was why Liv had been hesitant upon meeting Vasu. Right up until he changed. She had dreamed of a bronze dragon all her life, and the instant he caught her body in his claws, he had taken her heart with it.

He already knew the basics of her family life and was impressed by her Terran lineage. Cynthia, the seer, was followed by Coral, the weather kinetic, who birthed Kayla, the convincer. Kayla was mother to Morwen of the power blast, who had Saliwen, the micro kinetic, spawning Haven, the pyro kinetic, who mothered Cailin, the water elemental. Cailin's daughter Oriwin was another seer, and the line culminated with Sivin who mothered Livin. Each woman in her line was full of power and none had more than one daughter, one long single line of undiluted power.

They had lapsed into silence for a few minutes when their new commander wandered into the meeting room. The Azon looked flustered. "Sorry to keep you waiting, Livin, Vasu. I am Hyder Mihal, Commander of the Sector Base Morganti."

They simply stared at him. "My mate is Pilot, also known as Helen. All members of the Guard are paired for stability." He looked at the door somewhat desperately. "She should be here soon. She was just out testing some repairs made by Fixer."

"Do all members of the Guard have multiple names?" Vasu looked over at Liv when she asked that question. He hadn't noticed, it seemed.

"You caught that, did you?" Hyder looked more comfortable. "Yes, it is more advantageous for some to have code names when they go on assignment. It keeps their friends and family from before the Guard safe and sound. You can also have a face mask on your uniform when you go out if you wish it." He slid her a data pad and nodded. "You can design the majority of your suits, but Fixer has been doing some wonderful things with the fabrics and reinforcement. The uniforms are sturdier than most armour plate in the Alliance, yet they breathe like gauze."

A woman burst into the room and ran up to Hyder, leaning down to give him brief kiss. She then turned to them and smiled. "I am Helen, or Pilot if you prefer." She extended her hand across the boardroom table and Liv took it, noting the Pilot jacks that dotted her arms and neck. "Has he introduced you to the others yet? Fixer and Shade, Thinker and Morph? No? Men." She blew her bangs up and flipped her hair back over her shoulder. "Wait, Morph and Thinker are off world. Dang it."

"That's alright. Dealing with too many new situations can blow my tiny little mind." Liv jerked her head at Vasu and Helen giggled.

"Well, Mala and Isabi are here and they are always up for dinner. Mala especially." The other couple laughed and shared a joke that the newcomers didn't understand. "Oops, sorry about that. Mala has a condition relating to her talent. The more she uses it, the hungrier she gets."

"Mala is Fixer then? That would make Isabi Shade?"

"Wow, Livin, you are quick. That is it exactly. Agreha is Morph and Haaro is Thinker. He is our telepath." Helen and Liv were dominating the conversation and the men were simply watching in amusement.

"I am kind of hungry. What time is it locally?" Liv's stomach lurched and snarled alarmingly.

"Three hours from sundown. We can either eat here in the facility or head into town. Your choice."

Liv looked to Vasu. "I have already seen both, would you like to see the town?"

"Yes, I would."

"Dinner in town it is then. I will summon Isabi and Mala." Helen tapped one of the connections on her neck and she was suddenly having a conversation with someone not in the room. It was short and to the point. It was also decided that they would be having dinner at Udi's.

"They will meet us on the way to the skimmer."

"Skimmer?"

"It is an open air standing flitter for short hops. Mala has worked hard on it and it now travels like a cloud." Pilot took the lead. Bemused, they trailed in her wake. As they reached the outer hanger doors, another couple greeted them and there was no problem telling them apart.

The unrelieved black of Isabi's flesh seemed to absorb light around it. Mala on the other hand was a bright rainbow of colour and movement. Her hair fell to her hips in a rippling multicoloured wave that had Livin hypnotized.

Introductions were made, then they piled into the skimmer. It had plenty of room and was off at Helen's touch. They floated on a cushion of air and it got them to the town in under five minutes. Helen had called Udi's during their approach and a table for six was on the way.

Everything in this new place had Livin swivelling her head. She wanted to see, to touch, to know everything that there was to know about it. It was only her second planet. Morganti was number two in her mental scrapbook.

Three moons were just becoming visible on the horizon and the sun was turning the sky a bright pink. It was a beautiful place to spend their off time, but there was a burning urge in Liv to see Vasu's nest. If he didn't show it to her soon, her head was going to blow off. A ticking time bomb in her heart had started the instant that they landed and was pulsing through her. If she didn't see his nest soon, she was going to have to leave.

Her mate-to-be shot her a look under his lashes—he had to know what was going through her head and body. It was standard Draikyn physiology. Join or part, you only had one chance at true love. Their chance was now on the clock.

"Welcome to Udi's. We have your table ready, Guardsmen." A creature that Liv had no name for bowed lower than she could manage if she was flat on the ground.

They were seated immediately and a light conversation ensued.

"So, Livin, have you given any thought to the name you are going to wear as a Guard? What are your talents exactly?" Mala was asking the questions, which made sense. Being mated to Hyder, Helen probably had the answers.

"I control some elements. Heat, cold, air and earth." She took a sip of the water that had been set in front of her. "I can't control water, though, and heat and cold are just opposite ends of the same molecular reaction."

"Wow. That is impressive. We have seen Vasu shift, of course. That is just as intriguing." Mala smiled brilliantly and her eyes sparkled in the subtle lighting of the restaurant.

"Thank you. Family heritage. All the women in my family have had some form of psychic talent. How about yours?" Turning the tables was fair play, and soon they were all sharing their personal experiences.

The meal was amazing, a variety of cultures represented that far exceeded the experience of Liv's palate. She watched to see what Vasu took and mimicked him in his selections. He had been off Drai for far longer than her less-than-a-day.

Watching Mala eat was a sport in itself. Isabi sighed and continued ordering as she consumed everything left on the table and then looked over at him expectantly. "Sorry to be such a ravenous beast, but I was working when Helen called and didn't have time to grab a snack."

Vasu was looking almost alarmed, "You eat like this regularly?"

Everyone at the table laughed.

"No, not regularly. Only when I have been working. Based on the specs that were sent to us by the Drai Representative, I knew what I had to design into your suit and into Livin's. So that was my project now that the scanners gave me your sizes." Mala popped another appetizer into her mouth and sighed heavily, pushing her plate away.

Her dragon was curious now, "Was it difficult to make fabric that shifted with me?"

"No. I had Agreha to practice on. Her body goes in so many different directions at once that it was a challenge to complete. She also needs it to go from air to water and to join together. That one was tough. The hardest part of Vasu's suit was the tail." The group chuckled again.

Hyder picked up the tab at Helen's urging. "Let the dragon get it, he has been sleeping on his money for years." He chuckled, which earned him a curious look from Liv. "Well, this has been a fantastic event, but I think we need to go our separate ways until the morning."

Outside the restaurant, night was in full bloom, the moons casting ivory wakes of light on the streets.

"Indeed. I don't want my lady to leave me because I haven't shown her my nest. So if you will excuse us?" Vasu held his hand out to her and she slipped her fingers into his warm, dry grip. "I have to earn my partner."

CHAPTER SIX

Outside Udi's, Vasu took flight with her in his arms. "I have been waiting for a thousand years to get you alone."

"Really? A whole thousand?"

"I first dreamed of you one thousand, one hundred and fifty six years ago. You were wearing fire with wind dancing around you. All that fury and no sound. It almost drove me mad not to hear your voice."

"Did my voice ever appear?"

"Three years ago, the day Kale woke me. As the ground pulled me from my rest, I heard you calling to me." He held her tightly to his chest and she relaxed, safe in his embrace. "You were freezing water then, pulling the fire from it and redirecting it. I could feel the power you were using and I wanted to help."

"I remember that. There was flooding on the northern shore. I froze it until the evacuations could be completed, but the heat had to go somewhere, so I pulled it in around me and wore it like a cloak. Funny, I had almost forgotten." She reached up to stroke the side of his jaw. He looked and when their gazes met, heat flared. "How far is your nest?"

"An hour with these wings, ten minutes with my larger ones. Are you in a hurry?"

"No, just enjoying being this close to you without breaking any of my mother's rules for contact." Liv giggled. "She would know, somehow she would know. Mothers always know."

"I am sure of that as well, or I would already have found some time to be alone with you."

"We are alone now, aren't we?"

"We certainly are. But I find that I am in a hurry." He flipped her into the air and this time, she was ready to be caught by the dragon on her way down. The ride was certainly faster, but he didn't speak to her the whole way. It was as if some strange urgency gripped him.

He circled for a landing near a ruin and that was when she saw it. His nest.

A crystal wall formed a palisade that kept out the wildlife. Within was a home made of the most glittering of quartzes. A large landing space in the courtyard lit from within at his approach and she looked over it all with a feeling of awe.

Large double doors swung open at their approach. *I enjoy the benefit of technology when it is available.*

"I can see that. Put me down, I want to look around." She didn't squirm, but her urgency was palpable.

He carefully landed on his hind legs, absorbing a great deal of the shock with his tail, and then lightly dropped to brace himself on his other foreleg. She smiled as he carefully set her down. She scampered out of his way and watched his transformation. He didn't shrink so much as blur until the aura he generated collapsed into his Draikyn form.

Once he was in his natural form and looking worried, she went exploring.

Room after room opened at her approach and she explored with the delight of a child. An impish idea flowed through her as she realized that there was no way she was going to reject this nest. In fact, she would be lucky if her mother didn't bump her off to get this home.

It took her the better part of an hour to sprint through the home, making a special note of the kitchen, the master bedroom, and the treasury. Finally, she had to face Vasu.

They faced off in the formal manner of the Draikyn. According to protocol, he was to speak first.

"Do you accept my nest and everything in it?"

"Are you within your nest?"

"I am."

"Then I accept your nest and everything in it, for I dreamed of you." She held her breath waiting for his next sentence. Their mating flight would commence immediately the following dawn.

"And I dreamed of you." Vasu took her in his arms and bent her back with the force of his kiss. She tasted blood, hers and his and her body surged to life in reaction. Their species did not drink blood as a rule, but a little mate munching was all in good fun. Now Liv knew what they had been referring to.

She wanted to run, to fight and to hold him to her forever. The fury of her lust swirled around them and sought the only outlet they could. The elements went wild.

The crystals of the palisade shivered and grew, the stones of the courtyard glowed with heat and a light snowfall commenced. The crack of one of the flagstones finally got Vasu's attention.

"I see that without the sound, the fury was free. I think that as a Guardsman, Fury should be your name."

"As you wish it, Beast." She chuckled at his look of shock.

"I have been a perfect gentleman!"

"And I wished you a beast, so Beast you will be." Laughing at his surprise, she stepped out of his embrace. "If you want to start the flight at dawn, we had best get to bed." It was also tradition for them to spend the night in the same bed without intimate contact, which was going to be a trial.

"I don't think I will be able to sleep."

"I will count the minutes until dawn myself. Tomorrow will come eventually." The jokes in her mind made her mouth twitch, but she kept them to herself. Vasu must have been harbouring the same thoughts because his own lips tweaked a little to one side.

They walked inside and Vasu pointed out his favourite amenities—the large bathtub that would fit his wings, and the larger bed. She skinned out of her clothing as quickly as possible, climbing into the enormous marble four poster bed with only a small outburst of gooseflesh.

Vasu turned his back while she stripped, more for his benefit than hers. He would only get more frustrated if he allowed himself to become more aroused than he already was. It was proof of his commitment to her happiness, and also his urge to make the flight long enough for a proper mating, that drove him now.

If they were on Drai, they would be coupling by now, but here on Morganti, a place where his basic instincts could run wild without difficulty, she had to play by his rules, even if it meant sleeping next to him when she wanted to be under him.

She sighed and snuggled into bed, torturing herself by watching him disrobe. He really had a marvellous ass. When he half-turned, she caught a glimpse of his erection and she groaned to herself. It comforted her slightly to know that mating would be the first thing that they did the next morning. Now if morning would only hurry up and arrive.

She was confident that she couldn't sleep, and that was the last thought she had until the morning.

The pale fingers of dawn were creeping through the window when some not-so-pale fingers grabbed her arms and dragged her out onto the balcony.

Face to face, belly-to-belly, they stood until the dawn bathed them completely in its light. She leaned up to Vasu and they shared a sweet kiss that spoke of years to come, centuries of life shared, starting at this moment. His erection between them seemed right, natural. She was almost humming with energy as the sun completed its morning emergence. His knees bent and then he cursed.

A blaring alarm was coming from inside their bedroom. A com unit was lit and the noise was coming from it. Words in ancient Draikyn spilled from Vasu as he stalked through the room with her in tow, one hand shackling her wrist.

"What the hell do you want, Commander?" The guttural snarl was not one that Liv had heard before. He was aroused, frustrated, and furious.

"We have an assignment for you two. I am sorry about the timing, but did she accept you?"

"She did. And my nest."

"So you are fixed for a few weeks then."

"Unfortunately, we are. But if you interrupt us again, I am shifting and then eating the base."

"When can you be here?"

"We need to dress. Perhaps ten minutes?"

"Great. I will have the briefing ready to go when you get here. Pilot will be accompanying you and Fixer has finished your suits. You are good to go." Hyder was trying to be cheerful, but Liv noticed that he studiously did not look over at her. Apparently a naked Vasu was taking up all of his attention.

"We have also selected our call signs. Livin will be Fury, and I will be Beast. And if you interrupt us before we mate again, you will see me live up to it."

"Understood. Looking forward to seeing you within the hour. Hyder out." The screen went blank and they sighed in consternation.

She grabbed her day suit from the night before and pulled it on, wincing at the residual stickiness that her body had caused during proximity to Vasu. Sigh.

He pulled on his pants and then jumped off the edge of the balcony, shifting on the way down. He literally pulled heat from the area around him to create the change and Liv just smiled and kept herself warm. He leaned up and presented his neck to her, then took off the instant that she was comfortable.

Her hair blew wildly around her face, tangling into a mass that was going to take an hour to undo. Perhaps there was someone with a comb at the base.

She would hate to go on assignment looking like a wild woman with gold skin and green hair.

There was a certain amount of propriety that she had been trained to uphold. Grooming was part of it. No one wanted to be rescued by a messy woman.

CHAPTER SEVEN

Hyder slipped them data pads and briefed them. "Xaheel 9 is heading for a disaster. Space-born particles were apparently eggs of some virulent form of locust. They are eating their way through the crops in their larval stage and will reach maturity in two days. You need to stop them."

Fixer looked over at their commander and asked what they were all thinking. Only Vasu and Livin had gotten the data pads. "So this is a solo mission for them?"

"You and Shade are better suited to repairs or espionage. For this we need Fury and the Beast. We need power." Hyder nodded to them and they nodded back. "Pilot will take you in the Class One and drop you on the surface. Beast, you can fly her to the infected area and help her to do a controlled burn. See you when you get back. That is all."

Liv took Vasu's hand as they headed to the shuttle bay. "I guess we will have to wait for our get together."

"It had better not take too long or Pilot is going to get an eyeful." He released her hand and curled his arm around her waist, pulling her against him.

Fixer beat them to the shuttle. "I adjusted the chair back so that Beast's wings will fit. We don't want him getting a cramp by holding them flat."

"Thanks, that was thoughtful." Liv gave her a bright smile and a pat on the arm, still admiring the rainbow shift of hair.

"Anything for the Guard. The Class One is a Reflex ship that works as a jump ship with Pilot at the helm. I am experimenting with a version that beings without the implants can use." She pouted and crossed her arms over her ample chest. "Isabi won't let me use it."

"Then he is smarter than he looks. Let's go Fury, the clock is ticking. Those bugs won't wait." Vasu reached out and pulled her into the ship. "See you when we get back, Fixer."

Fighting the urge to wave goodbye, Liv strapped into the shuttle. Pilot was already plugging in and Vasu was fitting himself into the modified seat. "This is really comfortable."

Pilot turned back and smiled. "Fixer does great work. She even retrofitted all of my plugs and now they are even comfortable. I don't need to contemplate having them pulled anymore." As soon as they were locked in, she began the pre-flight check. Toggles flicked without being touched and they lifted off in seconds.

"So, Vasu, does the feeling of lift off ever get less nauseating?"

"In time you learn to distract yourself while it happens." He held out his hand to her and she took it, clenching her fingers tightly over his as they gained altitude.

"How do I go about doing that?"

"Oh, imagine our first mid-flight mating and the logistics of me keeping both of us airborne." He chuckled at the shock that crossed her face. It was, however, a very effective distraction. She hardly noticed the exit of the atmosphere and didn't even flinch as Pilot pulled them into the jump. Liv was far too busy processing the image that was running through her mind.

Draikyn had stopped mid-air matings two hundred years before, when the population made privacy unlikely. The flitters were an issue as well. Watchers made the couplings dangerous since the male's wings lost control of altitude and attitude and the couple could drift miles from their original point. Since voyeuristic couples in flitters tended to lose perspective, mating fatalities had occurred and flights were abolished. Vasu wanted to continue his traditions and it was causing an answering pound in her pulse. She was getting nostalgic all over, and it felt wonderful.

They could have been in the jump for seconds or minutes, but eventually the bulk of Xaheel 9 loomed in front of them.

"Is that the cloud that passed over them?" With swift movements, Liv let Vasu's hand go, unbuckled her harness and took a position near the view screen. A misty haze flowed through the solar system. It looked as if it had drifted away in the last week from its embrace on the planet. Now it lazily made its way through space, depositing the locust eggs wherever it went. Fabulous.

"It is. There is a team member on the way to Morganti who can take care of this, hopefully before it causes the same kind of problem on another inhabited world." Pilot took them around the planet once and they watched the scans for the cluster of the larval locusts that they were looking for.

"There they are! Beast, head out and shift forms when we reach altitude, then come back for Fury. I will hover here until you pick her up, then signal me when you are done. I will be in a low orbit, standing by." Pilot was giving orders in a terse voice, but there was a reason for it. The wind and atmospheric gases were giving them a rough ride down. "Sit down, Fury, or I will drop you where you stand." Their ship gave a tremendous shiver and Pilot swore.

"Yes, Ma'am." Liv scuttled back to her chair and strapped back in, winking at Beast. He merely sighed and shook his head at her. She knew she was enjoying this far too much, but Xaheel 9 was going to be the third planet her feet had ever touched. She was excited.

"Alright you two, suit up. I promise I won't look. You are going to need atmospheric filters, Fury." A partition concealed the rear of the cabin from Pilot's seat at a touch so they went past it to where a drawer opened to display their battle gear.

Her suit was beautiful, a swirling collection of blues, reds, golds and grays. The headpiece was designed to contain her communicators and frame her face at the same time. Her green hair would flow freely down her back and yet the frame around her face would keep it out of her way. It was stunning and she could hardly wait to get into it, but there was the small matter of Vasu standing right behind her.

"I promise, I won't look either." Vasu's deep voice made her jump. "I would rather have you aware of what I am looking at while we are alone. Since we are not alone, anything more would be inappropriate." He had his back to her and was already sliding into his suit. She stood stupidly and watched him cover the deep rich brown of his hide with the metallic bronze of the jumpsuit. When he started to work it around his wings, she turned to yank on the beautiful piece of artwork that she was supposed to wear.

As quickly as she could, she stripped to the skin and stepped into the legs, working them upward with rotations of her thighs and hips that would have made her self-conscious if anyone had been watching. The suit was tight and she was happy she had skipped the underwear, or it would have stuck out like a sore thumb. Supportive ribs were installed along the bodice so when she sealed the closure her breasts were held firmly in place. There was not one jiggle that would escape that suit. She was tucked in tight as a drum, but she had full range of movement. She bent, flexed and went up on her toes before stepping into her boots. Everything on her person was secure.

A long low whistle emanated from behind her. "Very nice. Fixer outdid herself on this one." Liv whirled to see Vasu checking out the rear of her suit.

"The colors are flattering and your hair is most striking against the swirls."

"Thank you. Yours suits you as well. The bronze matches your skin and wings most faithfully. It looks hard. Can I touch it?" She didn't wait for him to agree, but put her hands on his chest and stroked the texture of his body under the fabric. He was almost warm enough to scald.

"Hands off him, Fury. It is time for Beast to live up to his name." Pilot's voice came through the partition without any trouble. Liv felt her eyes widen and her face heat in a blush, "No, I can't see you, but it was a good guess."

Vasu brought her in for a quick kiss and then lifted his head, "Beast, ready for deployment."

"Fury, come up here, Beast, to the hatch and give me a ten count." A hissing from the hatchway denoted the release of the doors as Liv headed back to Helen's side. They listened to his countdown and on ten there was a click as the door released him into the atmosphere of Xaheel 9.

"Do you think he will be okay? It isn't a pleasant atmosphere after all." She was tugging at her gloves and wishing she could chew her fingernails as they waited.

"He will be fine." A blip on the screen grew rapidly larger and approached the shuttle. The dark bronze of his hide flashed as he flew past the nose of the Class One. "What is he doing?"

Deep sweeps and turns of his wings flashed and flared in the weak sun of this alien world. He hovered in front of them, swept past them and looped around the ship, over and over. Liv realized what she was seeing and blushed again. "He's courting me."

"Oh, you haven't..."

"Nope. We got this call an hour too soon."

"Dang. Sorry about that. By the time Hyder and I finally got some time alone, I had forgotten why we were both naked." Pilot chuckled and gave her a small pat on her knee. "I will make sure you guys get a few days to yourself when we get back. We just have to wait for the others to arrive and we can be a full team with scheduled rotations."

A blue light began to flash on the screen. "Okay, he is ready for you to jump. Go get those locusts, Fury." The partition folded back into the walls and the path to the hatch was clear. Running so that she wouldn't change her mind, she crossed the length of the ship in under a minute and reached the hatch, jumping into the air of the strange new world and the arms of the dragon she dreamed of.

CHAPTER EIGHT

The air burned her lungs as she fell. Xaheel 9 was not a place she could ever set up a summer home. It was funny how these mundane thoughts flitted through her mind as she plummeted to her death. As suddenly as that thought came to mind, it was halted as a large body positioned itself beneath hers and slowed her descent before stopping her completely.

"Hey, Beast. You just had to let me fall for a few hundred meters, didn't you?" She patted the smooth heat of his neck as she settled into a straddling position on it.

I wanted to get your heart pounding a little, Fury.

"Then you should have remained in your human form and bent over in that tight outfit. Just the sight of your wings over your tight ass makes my heart pound." She chuckled at the shudder that went through the hide underneath her.

You could have told me that earlier. I would never have left the Class One.

He took a swirling turn and in the distance, she could see the cloud that was not endemic to Xaheel.

"And then we would not have been here in time to stop the locusts from spreading. If I don't miss my guess, they just finished their larval cycle and are now on the move."

It looks like you are correct, my dear. Plan of attack?

"Well, since they can survive in the cold of space, fire and water will have to do. Let's lay down covering fire and then loop back to survey the result."

Your fire or mine?

"Why not both?"

Excellent, Fury. On three then. One, two, THREE!

Hurling fire was not Liv's forte, but she needed to concentrate. The closer they got to the locusts, the more vile they became. The humming was deafening, even from the distance that Vasu maintained, but they rained fire. The beasts were affected by the fire, squealing and bucking as they burst into flames, but it was not enough.

It wasn't killing them fast enough. The drone diminished, but not even by half, and the locusts in question were well over four feet in length.

"Fire isn't working fast enough, we need more."

Ice? Can you throw it?

"No, but you have given me an idea, get me as low as you can as slow as you can." She really hoped this was going to work, because if it didn't, she was out of ideas. Instead of throwing heat, she pulled it out of each and every locust in the swarm. They were generating the heat with their munching, and pulling it from them turned them into brittle husks.

"Can you keep flying until we get them all, Beast?"

If you can keep it up, so can I.

"Then let's keep going until they are done, or we are." His great head nodded his assent and he continued to make slow passes across the plain of bugs and crops until there was no more residue visible. It took hours of gruelling effort, but she pulled all heat out of every one of the encroaching insects.

"One more pass to burn the carcasses. I don't want any eggs getting off this rock." She took the pent up heat and blasted the carapaces into oblivion. Fire shot from her hands, the gloves on her hands providing an insulating layer and the giving her suit support as she slumped in exhaustion. When a fine ash was all that was left of the swarm, she relaxed, "Take me home, big boy."

As my lady commands. He roared and gained altitude, heading for the clouds. He flicked her off his neck and she screamed weakly as her body flipped end over end.

In seconds, his body released the energy that it absorbed for transformation and she was in his arms again. She didn't even have the strength to punch him for his lack of warning. His heavy wing beats soothed her into sleep, and she woke for a second when their ship made the jump. "Did it work?"

"Yes, it worked, Fury. The Xaheel found two stragglers and destroyed them by freeze-drying and then incinerating the carcasses. Excellent work." It was Hyder's voice and she puzzled over that for a while.

"Why are you on the shuttle, Hyder?"

"I am not on the shuttle, you and Vasu are back on Morganti. He is in the bed next to you." The Azon looked over her vital signs and nodded briskly, "You were both exhausted and just needed some rest and fluids." He made his way out of the room as soon as he had finished his notes.

Livin sat and looked over at her soon-to-be-mate. He was pale, but seemed unharmed. He was also flat on his stomach. Carefully, she dangled her legs over the edge of the bed and got to her feet. She swayed a little, but made it to Vasu's bedside. "Hey, you. Time to wake up." She stroked the hard plane of his cheek and pondered how much her body hurt. She had never used her talent that long or that hard, and as for him, she had heard that breathing fire was stressful on the body and he had been doing it for hours.

He slept on and she moved her hand from his face to his shoulder then stroked the panels of his wings. He murmured gently and Liv continued, stroking his skin and rubbing the muscles between the wings. The motion was helping her relax as well, the heat of his skin running up her hands and loosening muscles. A massive shudder ran through him finally and he pushed into her touch and off the bed.

"You know, if I didn't feel like I was hardboiled and hit with a hammer, this would be the start of something interesting." He sat on the edge of the bed in the same manner she had, then leaned forward for a kiss.

The feel of his lips on hers shook her to her core. Low in her belly, a storm of heat began to swirl, but before she could lean into him to act on it, he pushed her away. "I am sorry, Liv. I am way to sore for any kind of fun, and I want our first joining to be memorable for something other than our requiring traction afterward." He rested his forehead on hers. "Give it a few days. We will have time."

Her breathing was shallow and she sighed heavily. "We will have time. Just remember, Vasu, I dreamed of you. I can wait."

He stood and hugged her tight against him, "And I dreamed of you, Liv, and kept that dream in my heart for a thousand years. I can wait until we have a week off."

"As can I, but if it takes longer than three months, I am gonna jump you in the shower, my Draikyn."

His chuckle warmed her. "I will make sure to have a firm grip on the soap."

SEERING ORDER

CHAPTER ONE

Sector Guard Base - Morganti

"Uh, it's wonderful to be back home." Aggie stretched and looked out the window, admiring the view of the Morganti base, then turned around and admired the view of her husband stripping off for sleep. Pretty. A flicker of light caught her eye and she turned back to the window. "What the hell is that?"

"If I don't miss my guess, it is Drai in a mid-air intimacy. I would avoid flying if you don't know where they are. That is a surprise you don't want." Haaro came up behind her and watched the pool of fire and wind in the sky settle to a glowing point that trailed to the dragon's home in the hills.

"Mid-air mating, huh? I wonder if we could try that one day." She turned in her mate's arms and ran her hands over his skin, relearning the planes and angles of his body. She never tired of him. It was a round of study that she would always embrace.

"We will have to make sure that they are off planet. Mid-air interaction is not for the faint of heart. It may take a bit of practice before we can get it just right." His hands pulled her hips against him. His eyes and horns gleamed in the dim light of the oncoming sunset.

"Well, my husband, let's get practicing." They laughed, together and then laughter stilled as they kissed and tangled together, practicing.

Planet Calor

Reva sighed and looked at her herd. She took a deep breath and gave them her *order, "Hands off, stand together and line up. Time to leave the market."* The fifty minor members of the Roci family lined up and prepared to return to their home.

It never failed to amaze Reva that her odd talent was best used as a nanny. Occasionally, the Matriarch would call for her service when she was laying a particularly difficult clutch, but other than that, she was left to the care and wrangling of the Matriarch's brood. Not a bad job for a slave from Geehoe Nine.

Reva had been born and raised as a slave. She had survived situations that should have driven her mad, and after years of assorted servitude, she had ended up on Calor, watching the young of a species that used to frighten her with its ferocity.

The first time one of her charges ate one of its siblings, she had cowered in fear of her owners destroying her for dereliction of duty. They had merely laughed and patted the aggressor on the back, saying that he was almost an adult now and would soon need to leave the nest. K'ket children had the snapping claws of their parents, but did not develop the venom until in their second year of adulthood. Their arching, stinging tail was their primary weapon in mating battles. It also served them well in trade. No one wanted to piss off something that could, and would, stab them through the heart with little or no warning.

Her herd of deadly children moved swiftly through the streets, pausing now and then to examine something that caught their eye, but a sharp admonition from her and they rapidly lost interest. It took less than an hour to march them home, and as soon as she counted them, shepherded them into their heat lamp appointed and hot rocked rooms, she rested in her private room until feeding time.

She was embroidering a tunic for herself, the delicate needlework keeping her hands busy while she tried to plan her future. There wasn't much to do on Cador. The Roci clan was nice enough, but it wasn't sufficient. Being born a slave had been a harsh sentence for her. Her life lay in the hands, or claws, of beings who could kill her in an instant, because she legally belonged to them. It wasn't enough to wait to die. She needed to get herself together and run.

The knock on her door was unexpected. "Nanny Reva, the Matriarch requests your presence."

"Just a moment." She set aside her embroidery and straightened her tunic. A small mirror had been placed in her room for just such occasions and she quickly ran a brush through her ivory hair. She could remember it being red when she arrived years earlier, but the acid agent in the water on Calor had bleached her hair and skin of its pigment. When her hair was neat and her tunic straight, she opened the door and let one of the Matriarch's oldest children escort her to the breeding queen. It was a career option for the K'ket. They simply had to agree to be sterilized by their parent and they would receive the safety of the nest. Reva steered clear of the six ground limbs as they walked together to the grand receiving hall of the Matriarch. Apparently, there was a visitor.

As the doors opened for them, she noted the humanoid standing to one side of the Matriarch's throne. Reva approached and bowed formally. "Matriarch, you sent for me?"

The visitor was an Enjel. His midnight wings flared out behind him, matching the silken hair flowing from his forehead. His eyes were the same bright onyx as the K'ket, but his skin matched hers in chalky appearance.

"Yes, Nanny Reva. This Enjel has come forward to purchase you."

"For what purpose, Matriarch?" The glare she gave the winged man should have given him the hint that she was not up for any fun and games.

"As a breeding partner. He says you have complimentary genetics with his kind and he has been seeking one such as you for some time." The enormous Matriarch clacked her front claws delicately. "I have agreed."

"Pardon, Matriarch?" She couldn't believe what she was hearing. "I thought I had served the Roci family well?"

"You have, Nanny, but it was a very large amount of money." The oversized insect cackled and her stinger came shooting forward to the spot where the Enjel had been standing.

He wasn't there any longer. He was behind Reva, winding his arms around her waist.

"You have received payment, Matriarch. Attempting to kill me was inhospitable."

"You are correct. I was just trying to see if I could keep both my Nanny and the money. She is quite talented, you know. I am sure you will be happy together." Retracting her tail from the floor, the Matriarch settled back on her hot rock. "Be gone, before I change my mind."

"Farewell, Matriarch. Lovely doing business with you." The Enjel bowed formally and bent his legs.

It took all of Reva's self-control not to scream as he launched them into the air and took them out the window. With her talent for giving orders that had to be followed by all within earshot, she carefully did not follow her instinct to yell *let me down*. With the height at which they were flying, it would have been fatal.

She kept quiet. The rush of air past her face felt surprisingly soft, and at this height, she could not taste the insects that populated this world. It was refreshing. His wings beat steadily, keeping them aloft and transporting them to the spaceport on the far side of the city. A trip that took hours on foot was accomplished in fifteen minutes.

When her new owner landed in the open-air spaceport, he placed her gently on her feet and took her hand in his own.

"Come with me, Reva. The faster we get off this planet, the safer you will be."

"What? What do you mean?" She didn't dig in her heels, but she wasn't following him with the enthusiasm he apparently wanted, so he swung her into his arms and carried her into the shuttle.

"Strap in and I will tell you. But I do warn you that your orders won't have quite the effect you anticipate, so I would avoid using them until we are off this world." He dropped her in the co-pilot's seat and took his own seat in the specially made chair. It accommodated his wings nicely, but offered back support.

He ran through pre-flight checks in seconds.

Reva could only sit, bemused. This was not what she had experienced the last three times she had been sold. Those eager hands had caused her no end of stress. Her talent had bloomed by then and had kept her from their advances, but they felt a certain amount of uneasiness around her that had sent her back to the block. "Where are we going?"

He finished the checks, got clearance and lifted off before he answered. "We have been summoned to Sadril. They are evacuating due to a problem with their sun, and as members of the Sector Guard, we are going in to help with the evacuation."

That shocked her. She was the slave of the guard? "Sector Guard? You are a Guard?"

"We both are. The minute you crossed that threshold, Reva the slave ceased to exist. You are now a full citizen of the Alliance with the rights and freedoms included. Of course, if you try out your position in the guard and find it not to your liking, you can find employment elsewhere. We are always looking for support staff on Morganti." Most of his speech was said through clenched teeth as he fought the helm for control.

"Would you like some help with that? I am fully checked out on this style of shuttle." The offer came from the part of her that feared he would shake the ship apart.

"If you can help with the attitude, I would be most grateful." His teeth were still tight. He flipped a toggle to activate the co-pilot's controls.

Reva leaned forward to grip the controls as he relaxed. She smoothed their ascent and gently guided them out of the atmosphere. She brought them up and headed them to the slingshot point off the nearest moon, then turned to look at him.

His black eyes sparkled in the starlight. "That was well done, but I knew it would be."

She snorted in disbelief. "How could you have known I could fly?"

"Well, you can tell I can fly just by looking at me." He smiled at her surprised laughter. "Let me set the coordinates for our mission and then we can have some lunch and discuss how we came to be in this shuttle together." He competently entered their destination and set the computer for maximum speed. "Okay. That's taken care of that. Let's have a little talk now."

CHAPTER TWO

"So, Reva, you have been on the Alliance radar for some time."

He led her back to the tiny common area and gestured for her to sit on one of the benches. The Enjel still hadn't told her his name, but he moved efficiently and soon she was sitting with a selection of small snacks designed for bi-pedal humanoids.

"Eat, they are safe enough for you."

"Thank you. What's your name?"

"Thalik. Norelios Thalik. You may call me Nor." He saluted her with a vegetable stick and smiled. "Enjel Seer of the Fornar colony."

"Seer?" She munched the vegetable and drank some of the tea he provided. It went down without any of the acidic burn she was used to. It had a rich and soothing taste that relaxed her with every sip.

"I have a certain amount of foresight when it comes to my own life. I have been seeing you as my partner in the Sector Guard for quite some time." He shrugged, the black feathers moving with the motion. "Finding you was the hard part."

She swallowed through a suddenly dry throat. "You have been trying to find me?"

"Yes. Our Commander is a pattern Seer. He can see the way people and events connect. You and I were meant to be partners, as are the other four paired teams. They all have complimentary balances that make them very effective Guards."

"And you want to *pair up* with me?" Her outrage made him laugh.

"Eventually, yes, but until you choose to start that portion of our relationship, no. There is no rush here." He shrugged again. "Unless you want to jump me now and get it over with?"

Her snort was answer enough.

"I just thought I would make the offer." He smiled. "I have tracked you from the farm where you were born through every sale, wiping out all trace of you as I went. No document or file exists with your name or bio profile on it."

She put her plate aside. "So when you said that I was free now, you weren't just trying to get me to go along quietly?"

"Nope. Your talent depends on your being able to make noise, so I want you to make as much noise as you can." He collected her plate and placed it in the cleaner. "So, is anything I have said remotely tempting?"

"The word freedom is still ricocheting around my mind." She smoothed her hands down her tunic. "What kind of a dress code is involved?"

"Ah. That is the fun thing." He flipped open one of the benches, revealing two folded suits. "This one is mine, and this one is yours. It will go nicely with your hair when the color comes back."

"You even know about that, huh?" Her hair was bleached to ivory when she was bought by the K'ket. Their acidic water had a bleaching effect on her hair and eyebrows. The suit he tossed her was a matching ivory with a stiff feel to the fabric. There were boots, but no undergarments.

"Yes. I was very thorough. The suit has insulating properties and has been treated to be a light armour. There is also a mask, if you wish it."

"What purpose does a mask serve?"

"To hide your identity from those we serve, so that they do not become attached, to give you some anonymity when you travel away from the Guard, and to keep any family members you have from becoming targets."

"The fellows of my birth file are not a concern. As far as I am aware, I am the only survivor of my breeding parent, as well as the only genetic combination between those two particular breeders." Reva looked around and after some investigation, found the small sanitary chamber. Getting the K'ket's servant tunic and leggings off was extremely satisfying.

Pulling the new suit on felt right. There was a frame that would surround her face, which held her hair back, but it felt a little cumbersome. Tugging on the boots in the small space was a feat, but she had moved more in smaller quarters. Taking a deep breath, she slid open the door of the sanitary chamber. "How does it look?"

He wasn't wearing his suit. Nor wasn't wearing anything.

Fortunately, she knew just what to do. Ignore it. Right down to the portion of his anatomy that was happy to see her. "Nor? How does this uniform look? There aren't any mirrors large enough for me to check it out."

"It looks lovely. Perfect, and the framing surround makes you look like an ancient goddess from a coin. It houses some speakers and microphones to enhance your talent. If you would like to practice on me, I am willing." He held his hands out from his sides and gave her an innocent grin.

"Put some clothing on." Her order was an instinct and when he moved to tug on the smoke grey suit, she breathed a little easier. *"Don't forget your boots."* Five years as a Nanny was a hard habit to break.

His costume wrapped him in smoky armour from top to toe. Only his wings were left free and unprotected. Even his hands were gloved. He was fully dressed and at attention with his wings half-furled. "Clothed enough?"

"Yes. Thank you. Time in slave pens does not endear one toward nudity."

He looked shocked, as if she had just crushed one of his favourite toys. "There goes my favourite pastime."

Reva sighed. "I know. I have run into Enjels before. It is probably why the Matriarch agreed to sell me to one of your kind. They are well known for their dabbling in slavery. It wasn't too much of a jump to think you meant what you said about a breeding partner."

"That was the idea. It was why I selected that particular tactic. She would never have surrendered you if it was to join the Sector Guard. K'ket are not known for their altruistic actions. It was far simpler to buy you."

She could see the logic. Dressed in this suit, she felt a certain stiffening of her spine, straightening of her shoulders, and a strange energy invading her. She wanted to help, and to run and jump as well as fight, except she didn't know how to fight. "Can I get fight training?"

"As soon as we get back to Morganti. It is a little impractical in a shuttle."

"Alright. How long will we be in this shuttle?" She was never good at staying in one place for long, not even in a shuttle, without something to do.

"Another three hours. We should be getting a pickup signal in a few minutes. A jump ship will pick us up and transport us to the solar system holding Sadril. We will be spending two days there for final evac and then return to home base on Morganti, where you will meet the rest of the team." He stretched and smoothed the fabric of his suit.

She bit her lip as she watched those strong hands move over his chest and hips. Oh. He was dangerous. Reva whirled and returned to the co-pilot's seat. "Alright. We are waiting for a signal. Let's go wait." She fidgeted her way through six minutes and then a signal began to flare through the com unit.

"This is the Alliance Warship Olical, please identify."

Nor took the com. "This is Shuttle Four of the Sector Guard, Seer and Order at the helm."

"Order? Don't I even get to pick?" Reva whispered with her hand on the mic.

Nor whispered back, "No. I have foreseen it and some things are not meant to change."

"You are cleared for bay nine. We jump in four minutes. Better hurry." The humour on the other end of the line was obvious and Nor immediately started to align with the ship. The bay doors opened and they slipped inside.

Clamps locked them into position. "Sector Guard Shuttle Four in place, ready for jump."

The voice laughed. "Confirmed. Hang on to your panties, Guards."

It was all the warning they got as space folded around them and they were in two places at the same time for an instant. The inside of the bay was the same as it had been before the jump.

The chipper tone of the voice through the com made Reva smile.

"Welcome to Sadril space. Enjoy your evacuation. We will be running evacuees to a variety of systems. So hail me if you need me."

Nor laughed and hit the magnetic releases. "Thank you, Pilot. But just for the record…" he shifted the controls and they fell out of the belly of the warship as smoothly as they had entered. "Guards don't wear panties on duty."

Sniggering lit the com as their ship turned and headed to the planet's surface under his control.

As the warship glided off to pick up the small ships waiting at the rendezvous point, Nor turned to Reva. "We will need to meet with the ruling body controlling the evacuation. Are you ready for that?"

"I am still not sure what is going on, but I will come with you. What the heck, I have the uniform." She nodded.

"Excellent. I thought you might say that." His grin was infectious.

She smiled back and before she knew it, she was adjusting their trajectory through the atmosphere so that they would land at the evacuee centre.

"Oh. We aren't going to land. Far too many people would rush our shuttle. Set the shuttle to hover around the fifty foot mark."

Surprised, she followed his directions and set their conveyance to hover. "What now?"

"Now? We go and meet the director." Nor set the doors to open and affixed a remote to one of his broad shoulders. "How do you prefer to be carried?"

"Um. What is easiest for you?" After all, he was the one with the wings—she was simply the passenger.

"This." He scooped her up so that she could drape one arm around his neck and hang on. One of his arms was under hers and around her ribs, the other was under her knees. "And off we go. Close your eyes if you need to."

Instead of closing her eyes, she widened them as he simply stepped out the door and then spread his wings as they cleared the shuttle. Heavy wing beats propelled them through the sky and with smooth grace, he brought them down inside a retaining fence outside a government building. Seer nodded to the stunned guardsmen and set her on the ground. She walked next to him, head held high as they entered the doors.

Reva followed his lead as he strode through the halls as if he owned them. Enjels were naturally arrogant and he epitomized the race. A government official came out to meet them before they reached the large doors they were aiming for.

"You must be the representatives from the Sector Guard." The unctuous official reached for Nor's hand and he ignored it.

"I am Seer, this is Order. We have been assigned to assist your evacuation. What can we do to help?"

"I am Mish, Mayor of Ir, the capitol city of Sadril. We require you to move some of our more resistant citizens out of the restricted areas and onto evacuation shuttles." The nervous man waved a data pad at them.

Nor took it when she didn't.

"I see no more than a half dozen of the hold outs. What is making them stay?"

"They are geologists that claim the planet will adapt to the heat and we will all be able to live underground." He shook his head at the foolishness. "If you can convince them to leave their labs, it will be much appreciated."

"They are all located around the capitol, in the hills nearby. This shouldn't take too long." Nor nodded briskly, looked over to Reva and jerked his head imperceptibly toward the door.

She took the hint and strode through the building and into the flaring daylight. Reva waited, and when Nor moved to scoop her up, she didn't fight him. She held onto the data pad as they ascended and kept her silence as the crowds screamed for help, with their panic turning them into a writhing mob. She had to stop it. *"Relax. Walk in an orderly manner, and help those who have fallen. You will all be evacuated. Don't worry."* She breathed in a deep sigh and looked up at her Enjel to see how he was doing so close to her talent. Nothing. In fact, he winked and flew into their opening shuttle hatch with silent accuracy.

When they were both back on their feet, he looked to her and showed her the headpiece on the side of his own uniform. It covered his ears. "I can hear you just fine if you speak in a normal tone, but as soon as you start using your talent, it shuts off my hearing until you stop speaking."

"That is very clever. How did you figure that out before you even met me?"

"I *saw* it. Years ago. For some reason, in my first imaginings, I could never hear you yell at me. It perplexed me, until I started to see you using your talent. Then it all made sense." He took the data pad and headed for the controls. "The first scientist that we need to retrieve is only ten minutes away. We will head there first."

She slid into the co-pilot's seat and watched Nor manipulate both the data and their trajectory. "What does the data pad say?"

"It gives the locations of those refusing to be evacuated. Can't you see it?"

"I can't read Alliance Common. It is not something taught to slaves." She tried not to feel defensive, she really did, but a tear came to her eyes at her failing.

"I am sorry. I didn't know. I saw you and myself looking over a series of data pads, but didn't know why. I will teach you the basics on our way back to Morganti. Don't fret. We will get you all sorted out and up to speed with your education." He took one hand off the steering bar and held her hand.

More tears filled her eyes. The last time someone had been nice to her, she had been in some unnamed slave pen the night before her sale and another female had given her a blanket to sleep under. That was the last kind moment she remembered.

Now she had one more for her collection.

CHAPTER THREE

"*Staying here will only ensure your death. Pack only your essentials, and please, make your way to the departure station to prepare to evacuate the planet.*" Reva took in a deep breath. The glazed eyes of the scientist had flared as he fought her control. She had won, but it was a close fight.

Seer had simply stood by and watched her work, an indulgent smile on his face. Just like he had for the first four scientists. Each of them had piled into private vehicles and headed for Ir after their *talk* with Order. They stayed on the property until he had loaded his essentials into his vehicle, then Seer carried her into the sky and back to the shuttle where they continued to monitor the progress of their projects.

Tucked back into the seats, Nor updated the data pad. "Excellent. Three have come in on their own and two were arrested. We need only get the last one and we can continue on to Morganti."

"That's great. I am exhausted. This takes a lot out of me. It's like part of me is holding them until the need for control has been exhausted."

"I am sure that Commander will want to study your talent in detail. He is also our Medical officer." Nor smiled. "Only one more and we can go home. But be careful. There is a reason that they did not send the army for this one. He's tricky." He used the shuttle to get them to their next evacuee and locked the controls for hover. Again.

Reva just wanted to sleep. She had never used her talent this continuously. It was exhausting, but she stood, went to the shuttle door and waited.

"Just one more, Order. Then we can go to the base and you can rest." He lifted her slowly. Even he was getting tired after all the ups and downs.

"Promises, promises. I still haven't decided whether to join the guard or not."

"Fair enough. Hang on." He jumped out the shuttle door and spread his wings. They glided down in a slow spiral that let her see all the surrounding trees. Takeoff would be difficult, but not impossible, when it was time to leave.

The house they landed in front of had an adjoining lab, and it was from that angle that shots rang out. Nor dropped to the ground the instant the firing started and covered her. They were not injured, but Order's pristine uniform picked up some stains.

"Cease firing!" She was angry and it had always given her energy in the past. With Nor on top of her, she could only squirm a bit to indicate she wanted to rise. His lower body against her buttocks signalled a different kind of rising. That hard ridge sent a bolt of panic through her. *"Get off me."* Reva scrambled to her feet when his weight lifted, and took a few steps away. "I think we should attend to the evacuee."

Seer was still on his knees, looking at her thoughtfully. "Indeed. Since you have kept him from killing us, you may as well take care of him. His name is Professor Nakalish."

She nodded and moved away in the uncomfortable silence that fell between them. The professor was standing in the doorway to the lab, his rifle still on his shoulder. Order took it from him gently and laid it out of his reach. "Professor Nakalish, we are here to make sure you evacuate. The planet's surface will be uninhabitable within months, and you need to leave, or you will die."

He blinked out of his trance. "They are exaggerating."

"They are not. I have seen the mutations of your sun for myself as we entered your system. The light is sickly and will not support life much longer. A few more months here will turn no tides in research and may cost you valuable time in setting up your lab on a new world." She used reason, hoping that he would listen.

"You don't understand. My life, my work has all been about understanding this world, its moods and the forces that shape it." Tears formed in his eyes. "I cannot leave it."

"Can you leave probes? Monitoring equipment? I am sure that a relay satellite can be arranged to send you a signal wherever you end up. You can still continue your research, but you can compare a dying world to a living one." She really hoped that he would agree to it, but she saw the hesitation in his face.

"I cannot plant the monitors on my own, and my assistant has already gone off-world."

"I believe that Seer can help you. But you must not use your weapon on us again. Do you swear to leave peaceably when the probes are set?"

"I do so swear. How did you get me to stop firing by the way? I felt held against my will." He was frowning.

"The Sector Guard are not chosen for their looks." She smiled and turned to call for Seer, but he was standing behind her. "Well, some of them may be." He was really far too pretty to her eyes, and to know that his body responded to her, well, *that* took her mind down other paths. "Seer, the professor—"

"Has agreed to leave provided that I assist him in planting his probes. It will be done." Seer nodded to her and then to the professor. "Show me what must be done."

It took hours, and, though exhausted, Order kept a steady stream of tea and snacks coming from the professor's stores. Food was essential to keeping a keen mind. The men discussed coordinates, trajectories, and a number of phrases that slipped her mind. It was times like this that her lack of education frustrated her.

She could operate a shuttle because she had been trained to by rote, but she didn't know why the ship responded, the mechanics of the situation and equipment. Her ignorance was an irritation, but with the help of the Guard, it just might be remedied. When a grimy but cheerful Seer looked over at her, she smiled back.

"We are almost ready, Order. Just have to set the last few to burrow at the appropriate intervals and we will be good to go."

It was Nor's face full of relief at the end of their assignment that she saw the instant before the professor fired the gun. Seer fell heavily to the ground and Reva was left facing the barrel. "You promised, Professor! You said you would leave if your probes were left behind. You didn't have to shoot Seer because of it." She edged toward the door, trying to see if Nor was all right.

The professor began to move toward her. "I lied. My work here is too important, and now, thanks to Seer, I will be able to complete my measurements as the planet surface changes. It was too bad that I had to shoot him, but he would not have let me stay here." The professor was advancing with the gun.

Reva was taking in a breath to run when the professor fell to the ground.

Seer was up and looking pissed at the bloody crease in his shoulder.

"Let me guess, you knew he would strike."

"Yes, I just didn't know when until I saw you standing there with the grass stains on your suit. It had to be then." Seer came forward and hugged her lightly. "Are you all right?"

"Fine. But I would step back if I were you." She smiled through tight lips. "I am fighting the excruciating urge to kick you in the balls."

He stepped back.

"So what do we do with the professor?"

"Oh, he is getting delivered and you and he are going to have quite the conversation on the way to Ir."

Her smile was still showing a lot of teeth. "Let's get him in there. Fly up and bring the shuttle down. I will wait with the treacherous one."

He looked a little hesitant, but left them to fly back to the shuttle. He would have to land it nearby as the woods were a little heavy.

The instant that Seer cleared the door, Order scuttled to the professor's side and started talking, *"You will never pick up a weapon in anger again. If defence is required, you may use it as a cudgel, but not a firearm. You will always give the Sector Guard the deference that they are due. When they are mentioned, you will sing their praises. After Seer returns, you will walk with us quickly and quietly to the shuttle and leave your home world for another, without complaint or argument. Upon reaching your new world, you will start over, with a love for the new planet you call home. You will find contentment, and never raise your hand in anger again."*

The professor struggled and rolled over, groaning and rubbing his head. "Where is Seer?"

Her head ached tremendously. "After you shot him? Getting the shuttle. You are coming with us."

"Yes, of course I am. I will just grab some data packs and we can be on our way." The professor was good to his word, this time. He piled a few data chips into a storage unit and turned to face her.

The thrum of the shuttle was close. Reva looked out the lab door and could just make it out through the trees. "Come along, Professor. Your ride is here."

It had been such a simple command, but he followed it as if lashed. They walked in silence toward the shuttle.

Seer met them halfway. He caught their mood and simply led them to the shuttle and helped the professor take a seat.

Silently, Order took the co-pilot's seat and lashed herself in.

He took off and in less than an hour, they were hovering over Ir. "I will take care of our passenger. See you in a minute."

He left her alone in the shuttle, and she smiled as she used the monitors to watch him spiral to the ground with his passenger. The professor neatly lined up with others to be shown to his assigned evacuation shuttle. He was terribly polite and very quiet.

When Seer came back to the shuttle, he flew past the front viewer so that she could get a good look at him.

His wings held a steady beat as he grinned at her. Each of the muscles of his broad torso was highlighted by the fit of his uniform. It was an excellent fit. He only showed off for a few minutes before returning to the inside of the shuttle. "The professor is all checked in and ready to leave with the others. We have completed our little trip. We can go home now."

"I don't have a home." Her voice was so soft she almost didn't hear her own words.

Nor looked over and took her hand in his. "You will. Just let it come."

"You have seen it?"

"That I have." He winked. "Now, since you are so adept at atmospheric flying, you may take us up to the outer jump station. We are hitching a ride."

CHAPTER FOUR

Reva was bemused. Another shuttle was waiting for them at the coordinates Nor had given her. It was slightly larger than the one they were in, but the same manufacturer.

"Pilot, is that you?"

"It certainly is. You won't believe what Fixer has come up with. Dock with me, then get in here for the jump." The female voice paused, "Sorry. Where are my manners? Hello, Order. I am Pilot, your chauffeur for today. Please come aboard the Class One."

Nor took the controls from her and worked to line them up with the larger shuttle. The light collision was barely noticeable. They were under the belly of the other shuttle. A few flicks of his fingers and a ladder descended from the roof of the shuttle. "Go on up. The lights are on for a solid seal."

"This is a little odd. I didn't even know there was an upper hatch here." Reva stood looking up for a moment, then started to climb.

"These shuttles have a number of exits. Being trapped in a sinking shuttle is one of my nightmares."

Nor's completely frank tone belied the heat in his eyes when she caught him staring at her buttocks in the tight white uniform. She simply sighed and kept climbing. A release handle was at the top of the ladder and, holding her breath, she pulled it. A feminine hand reached down and pulled her through the hatch.

The woman had similar features to her own, but small ports installed on her wrists, neck and temples. "Hello, Reva. Welcome to the Class One. I am Helen, the Pilot." Since their hands were still joined, she shook Reva's, smiling all the while.

"Reva, I guess I am Order. Thank you for your welcome." She brushed at the stains on her uniform, self-conscious at meeting another female while wearing dirty clothing. She stepped aside as Nor came through the hatch and sealed the hatch of their shuttle behind them.

He locked down the inner hatch of the Class One and smiled at the two ladies. "Shall we get going?"

Helen looked at his nicked arm and shook her head. "Okay, but you may want to strap in. Reva, you can be in the co-pilot's seat because, frankly, Norelios can't sit in it properly during jump."

Reva could see that his wings would be a little awkward in the standard seat. "Why did we have to come on board? Nor would have been much more comfortable in his shuttle."

Already hooking into her shuttle via a series of jacks, Helen looked back at her. "Oh. Well, Fixer has rigged up a piggy back mechanism, but we aren't sure if it will hold during a jump."

"So you might drop the other shuttle while folding space?"

"Yes. This one is safe, but I can't vouch for the other shuttle. This is kind of an experiment." Helen shrugged. "We have been having a lot of those lately. Fixer is one heck of an inventor. A little scary, but extremely creative. Each of us has a uniform that she has worked to our particular needs."

Reva tried to look encouraging, but brushed at more of her grass stains. "I just wish she had made it a little more stain resistant."

"Well, you are wearing a prototype. She'll make the adjustments you want in the next one." Helen smiled. "Norelios, are you ready to jump?"

Reva looked back at Nor. He was wrapping straps around his wrists as he stood between walls. "You can go through a jump like that?"

"It beats the alternative. Banging my wings isn't fun." He gave a few experimental tugs. "All set."

"Okay. First we deploy the membrane that will bind the two shuttles."

She closed her eyes and there was a mechanical hissing.

"Alrighty, brace for jump." Helen didn't even move. The ship simply moved from one point in space to another, within the span of less than a second.

As always, when they came out of jump, Reva's head swam a little. She glanced back to see that Nor was in rougher shape, his skin chalky and his head hanging down. She unbuckled her harness and went to see if he was conscious. "Nor? Are you all right?" Reva stroked the hair from his face and raised his jaw.

He looked at her blearily. "Yes. Rough jump, though." He shook his head and looked to his wrists. "Can you help me here?"

"Of course." She put her much smaller hands up against his rough ones and pried the ties from his grip, then engaged in unwrapping his wrists. She had to rise on tiptoes to untie him, and ended up leaning on him for support. As soon as his first arm was free, she went to work on the second. Their bodies touched from thigh to chest as she blushed and hurried to work the wrapping loose. "Just hold still. There. All free." Trembling with something that terrified her to her toes, she stepped back and away from him.

"Thank you. My hands were getting numb." He rubbed them together and smiled softly to her.

"Take your seat in the back, Norelios, or kneel, but we are heading into atmosphere and its going to get a little rough," Helen called.

Reva looked around wildly. "Landing? So soon? Are we at Morganti?" Her questions tumbled out one after the other. "How are you going to land with the shuttle under you?"

Helen's eyes went wide. "Oh, shit. I forgot about that." The com light lit up and Helen barked, "Fixer! How do I land with this thing on?"

They were entering the atmosphere and Reva was thrown against Nor.

"Best take your seat, Reva. Something tells me that we are going to have to ditch my shuttle to land."

His voice sounded in her ear and the warmth that had spilled through her when she untied him came roaring back. Muttering an apology, she pushed away from his chest and made her way to the co-pilot's seat.

An unfamiliar voice was answering Helen. "You were supposed to drop the membrane in orbit and get Nor back in control of the shuttle. As it is, you might need to come in for a hover and ditch shuttle four from low altitude."

Helen sighed. "That I can do, as long as the weight doesn't throw me off. Wish me luck and see you in ten, either to shake your hand or kick your ass."

A snigger came through the com before it cut off.

"That woman is quite the smartass." Helen laughed and brought the ship into the lower atmosphere.

"She's one of the Sector Guard?"

"Yes. Partnered with Shade. He's a Selna."

A large expanse of land sped by beneath them. Helen slowed the shuttle until it was moving at a much more reasonable pace. "That's the base. That blob over there on the left."

The ship slowly moved toward it and before Reva knew it, they were hovering over the shuttle bays near the base.

"Are we there yet, are we there yet, are we there yet?" came from the back of the shuttle.

Helen smiled. "Quiet, you, or I am turning this thing around and going back into jump." She lowered the shuttle a few feet and gently disengaged the membrane that held them to shuttle four. Seconds later, she landed the Class One.

Sighing with relief, Helen unplugged her body from the shuttle. "Okay. Everyone is alive and the ships aren't un-repairable. I call it a success." A giggle broke from her lips as she finished her declaration, ruining the effect. "I love coming home. It's like leaving in reverse. Reva, welcome to Morganti."

Holding to honesty, she took a deep breath, "Thank you, but I don't know if I want to stay."

Helen looked a little confused as she caught Nor's gaze.

He simply smiled and said, "I am working on it." He held out his hand.

Reva took it, letting him lead her into the air of a new world.

CHAPTER FIVE

They left Helen and Fixer arguing about the practical applications of the jump membrane. The ladies were still going strong with their *discussion.*

"This is new. They were just digging for the pool when I left. Enjels don't swim very well." Nor was almost scampering like a puppy, but Reva was exhausted.

The pool did look inviting, and perhaps after a nap she would take advantage of it. "I am sure that they don't. The wings would probably be a bit of detriment to your swimming ability."

"They don't like getting wet." He shook his head. "One of the down sides to feathers." He laughed at his own joke.

She smiled weakly. "Is there somewhere I can lie down and take a nap?" Her head was spinning.

"Our first stop is Medical. Helen's mate is our Commander and Medical officer, Hyder Mihal." He led her to the door that read MEDICAL and escorted her inside.

She had just lain back on the examining table when an Azon came through the door.

"Reva. So nice to meet you at long last. We have longed to have someone with your talents on board. Most of the talents we have are environmental and not confrontational."

She nodded at him drowsily. "Do you mind if I sleep through most of the exam?"

"No. That will be fine. I will wake you when I am done." He shared a look with Nor, but the smile he got in return was enough confirmation of her odd behaviour.

Reva was out like a light. Her light snores made him smile. "Not what you expected, is she?" Nor was relieved that he had gotten her back to Morganti. It had been a gray area in his mind for some time.

"No. I expected someone with more presence, and a louder voice." Hyder smiled as he put the scanners into action.

The equipment around the base was all getting remarkable upgrades, thanks to Fixer, but even Mala could not repair what was wrong with Reva. Nor despaired over her getting her self-esteem into working order because only when she was confident to come to him under her own power would they become partners in life, as well as in the Guard.

"Did you know about the scar tissue?" Hyder's voice was quiet and Reva's even breathing didn't change.

"I suspected. She was sold to a member of the Moreski royal family when she was a young woman. He only kept her for a few months, but he is the likely suspect for the damage. He was known for his...unusual tastes."

"It is extensive it goes from her shoulders almost to her knees." He shook his head in frustration. "I can reduce it, but not entirely. Some of the marks have gone to the bone."

Nor nodded grimly. If he hadn't already taken care of the Moreski in question, he would have been inconsolable. "When she is awake, I will ask her. What generates her talent?" Distracting Hyder wasn't easy, but talk of talents usually did it.

He checked his little handheld readout. "She appears to have multiple layers of vocal chords. In her case, literal chords. They must vibrate to reach the primal brain of whomever she is giving the Order."

"Interesting. She certainly does affect the primal brain. When she was giving the orders to the evacuees, they snapped into attention as if her words were oxygen." Nor moved closer to Reva and relaxed as he watched her deep breathing. With her past, the willingness to sleep in a public place showed tremendous trust, or it showed that she just didn't care anymore. He really hoped it was the former.

"Is she going to have a problem with Mala?"

Nor hesitated. "I have no idea." Mala was a Moreski royal bastard, but had the distinctive rainbow hair of her father's family.

"Well, we will deal with it if it becomes an issue." Hyder shrugged. "I would like you to wake her. She needs some inoculations and I don't want to give them to her while she is asleep. It isn't sportsmanlike."

As Hyder prepared the shot, Nor approached his sleeping companion. "Reva. Wake up." He was not expecting her to bolt upright and stand next to the exam table.

"Yes? What did you need?" She flipped her hair behind her back and looked at him expectantly.

"Oh. Nothing. Hyder is going to give you some inoculations. He didn't want to jab you while you slept."

Reva smiled at the surprised Azon, who had jumped back a foot when she launched off the table.

Nor watched carefully as Hyder recovered and stepped forward with the injector.

"Can you expose your shoulder? It will absorb into your system more easily with direct skin contact."

When she opened the front of her suit, Nor had to admit his attention was riveted. The smooth expanse of flesh made his mouth water, and when she peeled the ivory suit off her shoulder, his wings trembled in response.

Hyder was unmoved. He swiped a swab across her shoulder and pressed the injector.

"Ow."

"Sorry about that, but now you are cleared for the variety of species here on Morganti."

She shrugged back into her uniform and closed the tantalizing glimpse of skin. "Wonderful. You have no idea how happy that makes me." She yawned. "Now. Where can I really get some sleep?"

Nor moved to take her hand. "I will show you to our quarters." At her narrow eyed look, he quickly filled in. "The Guard's rooms are off a central hub."

"Then let's go before I pass out." She looked up at him and curled her fingers around his. "I need to get some rest before I can deal with any more of this." She raised her lavender gaze and smiled tiredly.

"Done and done. Hyder, any further tests can wait until tomorrow. See you then." Nor nodded briskly to his Commander and escorted his partner down the hall and to the Guards' private quarters.

Her rooms were next to his and that fact was burning in his mind as he watched her close the door between them. If she didn't come to him soon, his life was going to be hell.

The scream froze in her throat as Reva sat up in the unfamiliar bed. Her heart was pounding and her hands shook as she tried to throw off the remnant of the nightmare. The door that connected her to Norelios was firmly shut and she wanted it to stay that way. Maybe if she could work off the stress, she could rest. An image of the pool flickered through her thoughts, so she slithered back into her uniform and padded barefoot to the area that was in her memory.

The water surged invitingly as the light of the three moons danced across it. With no swimming apparel, she simply skinned out of her uniform and jumped into the water. At first the shock of the water locked her muscles, but soon she was tooling back and forth with an even stroke.

It was freeing to be able to swim as much as she wanted without worrying about being summoned for duty to the Matriarch. Her muscles had a pleasant numbness that she had missed and she was on her way out of the pool when she realized she was not alone.

Dawn was visible on the horizon and the two females were silhouetted in its light.

"Come on out, Reva. We have towels and clothes for you," Helen called.

The other woman was holding the promised towel and approached her slowly. "Hello, Reva. Good morning. I am Mala, but you may have heard of me as Fixer."

The woman's tone was low and friendly, so Reva allowed her to wrap her in the enormous sheet. Shivering now that she was out of the water, she tried to get a better look at Mala. The woman was still backlit by the light, but a chill went through her when she saw the rainbow hair. "Moreski?" The panic in her voice was unmistakable and her back tightened before she could calm herself.

"Only half, raised in exile because my father chose love over bloodlines. He died years ago." Mala seemed to be expecting the fear.

"You read my file."

"Yes. Commander thought I might need to know about it in case you had a permanent aversion to my father's race." She stepped back and let Reva take a long hard look at her.

Mala wasn't imposing, as the prince who tortured her had been, but she still bore the unmistakable genetic stamp of royal Moreski blood. Her eyes were kind, and her mouth had the look of someone who smiled often. A bright intelligence burned in her and it was obvious for anyone who wanted to look for it. There was also no pity or judgement in her gaze, no contempt for a slave, or derision for one beneath her. "I will withhold judgement until we have a discussion about my suit. Really, white?" She snorted and instantly the two women laughed cautiously.

"Well, I am here to make amends. I have some clothing for you to shop in, and we are heading into town as soon as you get something to eat."

Mala handed Reva the clothing, then turned her back to give her a semblance of privacy. Helen followed suit. Grimacing as she pulled the undergarments over damp skin, Reva dressed as quickly as she was able. "Ready, but I need shoes."

Helen answered her, "There are boots by the door."

A few quick stomps and she was ready for action. They walked beside her to the commissary and it puzzled Reva as to why the staff looked at Mala with trepidation. They had loaded their trays and were sitting down when she felt confident enough to ask the question, "Why are they looking at you like you are going to eat the whole selection?"

Helen laughed and dug into her fruit salad as Mala turned a delicate pink. "Because she has. The side effect of her talent for manufacture is that she has to replace the body mass she uses with food. She has forced the catering staff to put in more overtime than any selection of dignitaries combined."

Mala sighed. "It isn't as bad as that."

"Yes it is." Helen was still chortling.

Reva dug into her breakfast and tried to think of another way to phrase her question. Finally, she blurted out, "How am I supposed to get clothing? I have no money, no credits, no possessions even. All that I own is my skin, and in some areas, people would swear that Nor owns it."

Cursing lightly, Mala dug in her jumpsuit for a credit band. "Sorry. I meant to hand this over when we were shopping and I didn't think about you needing it before. It has your first annual salary on it, plus a signing bonus. Your retinal scan will work for identification."

Reva took the band and slipped it over her wrist. She now had her own money to do with as she pleased. "Can I get my hair done?"

Helen leaned forward eagerly. "Of course. What do you want, a cut, style?"

"First, I want my hair and eyebrow color back, then we can discuss what to do with the rest."

"Oh. I thought that was your color. What is it normally?"

"Before the K'ket acid showers, it was a nice blood red, I think. It was so long ago." Wistfully, she watched the staff go about their morning routine. More people were entering the commissary, including Nor and a male Selna. "A male Selna?"

"Yes, my partner and mate, Isabi." Mala waved the men over and Nor came forward with a relieved smile.

Isabi didn't walk so much as glide toward them, the unrelieved black of his velvet skin covered by what seemed to be a standard casual wear jumpsuit. "And you must be Reva, the newest recruit to our happy band." He bent low over her hand and pressed his smooth lips to her knuckle.

Nor looked less than pleased.

"I am pleased to meet you, Isabi." She simply didn't react to the touch. It wasn't at all the way she felt when Norelios touched her. No heat, just the warmth of a heartfelt greeting. The thundercloud of expression on Nor's face told her something she needed to know—he didn't like the Selna touching her, but he was not going to speak for her. It was nice. He trusted her to make her own decisions. "Your mate has been kind enough to offer to take me shopping with Helen. We will be leaving after we finish."

"Then Nor and myself had best get our food together so that we may enjoy your company for even a fleeting moment." Isabi was turning on the charm and his wife was looking at him as though amazed. As soon as the men left the table, the ladies started whispering.

"I think Isabi is trying to get Nor to court you. Do you think it is working?" Mala hissed to the other ladies.

"I have never seen him turn on the charm like that, Mala, you are a lucky girl." Helen smirked a little. "If Hyder had pulled something like that, I would have punched him. You also have a lot of self-control there, Fixer."

"It is more of a trust issue. I can't afford *not* to trust my partner, so I know that he is just trying to force Nor's hand. But you have to remember that the Enjel have a formal courtship process."

"Right. With the coloured gifts that he has to give. How weird is that?"

"What you two are saying isn't making any sense, shh. They are coming back."

As the men took their places, Isabi next to Mala and Nor next to Reva, she thought long and hard about what she had learned from those few sentences. Did she want to be courted? Where could she find the rules? Nor's thigh along hers was warm, almost hot, as he pressed himself against her. She was glad they had chosen the bench seating, as his wings would not have been comfortable in the chairs.

"Did you sleep well?"

His voice surprised her out of her thoughts of his wings. "I slept until I woke, as is my custom. I am used to getting by on limited sleep." She felt she had to add the last because he looked at her sharply.

"I thought I heard you cry out."

She blushed. "You may have. I stubbed my toe getting out of that bed."

He seemed satisfied with that, and not the least bit suspicious that Reva had screamed herself awake, as she had so often in the past. The K'ket did not mind once they moved her to a far wing of the nesting house, but her previous owner had been appalled by the damage done to both her body and her mind.

She sipped her tea and looked over to her soon-to-be companions. They were both finished eating, and the men had slipped into a discussion of formal practices for battle and religion. It was time to go.

"Shall we, ladies? I am excited. I have never shopped for myself before." She put an enthusiastic smile on her face and stood. Helen and Mala followed suit. "To the hairdresser!"

Giggling like schoolgirls, they nodded to their counterparts and left the base for the small town nearby. Reva was determined to have as much fun as she possibly could with these women.

It might be her first and last time shopping.

CHAPTER SIX

"That colour analysis was fun. I don't remember it being this dark though." Reva combed through her restored red locks with fascination. The stylist had repaired her hair as well as restored it. The deep blood red hair now matched her eyebrows and to the other Guards' amusement, her private areas.

"It looks lovely, and very striking against your eyes. I have never seen eyes that particular shade of purple before. What species are you?" Helen was idly curious as they headed to the next stop on their journey. Clothing and footwear.

"I have no idea. Hyder was running the analysis, so I am hoping he will be able to tell me." She shrugged and let herself be dragged into a shop that had both gowns and casual clothing.

"Welcome to Zalbeeliyah's, nice to see you again, ladies."

The proprietor was a l'nal and so Reva nodded cautiously. "Hello. I believe I need to be outfitted from the skin outward."

The upper four appendages rubbed together greedily. "With your coloring, my dear, I feel a challenge coming on."

"Zabby, go easy on her. She's just learning her fashion sense." Mala sat back on one of the stools designed for visitors and prepared to watch a show.

The spider scuttled toward her, then rose up on its hind legs. "Just hold still now while I scan your sizes in." A few swift motions and the creature went to the back room, only to return with a mind numbing collection of fabrics. "Well, now. Up you go, onto the fitting platform."

A little bemused, Reva allowed herself to be bullied into the centre of the showroom. "Nothing with an open back. I have some scar damage that may be a little offensive to some."

"Pity. You would look striking in something that revealed as much of that tasty skin as possible." Zabby clicked her mandibles in a laugh and the other ladies shared Reva's uncertain look.

"Is there something here that I can wear today? I really don't have any clothing with me." Reva kept her gaze forward as the seamstress held colours against her and created two piles—disgusting and acceptable.

"Mala, are you making notes? No sissy whites or ecru. I have to deal with people at close range in riot situations. Angry people throw things that stain." Reva was thinking of her next assignment without even realizing that she was accepting her role as one of the Guard.

Mala laughed and winked at Helen. "Noted. I was also going to improve the armour on your suit, since you will be arriving unarmed for the most part."

A deep silver tunic with leggings was produced, with a matching belt. It was gorgeous and would highlight every portion of her body while leaving her free to move. "I love it. Can I try it on?"

"Of course. The changing rooms are to your right. Come back out so I can make any adjustments that are needed."

Scuttling off with her arms full of fabric, she eagerly stripped off the borrowed jumpsuit. The tights fit like a dream, and the tunic was a little shapeless until she fit the finely wrought belt around it. The brighter silver shone against the darker, and when she flipped her hair out and looked at her reflection in the mirror, a little bit of pride filled her soul. She put the borrowed boots back on and strode out to face her judges.

The silence that greeted her made her heart sink, until the applause started. "Wow. Fantastic. You look great!"

Even the seamstress was struck by her appearance. "Perfect fit. As if it was made for you."

"Now, Zabby is going to get on the casual and formal wear, and you are going to get some shoes."

"Indeed. Did you wish to pay for all of your clothing now, or when it is picked up?"

"Now, please. And can it be delivered to the base? I don't know when my next assignment will be."

"Certainly." The spider rapidly ran up the tally.

With a shaking hand, Reva extended the credit band.

"Excellent. Lovely doing business with you. I will make your new wardrobe my first priority."

"Thank you." She wore her new clothing with pride. "Where to next, ladies?"

They spoke as one, "Tal's," then burst into giggles.

"Tal's it is. Lead the way."

In the shoe shop, she selected sandals, two pairs of boots, some slippers and had her measurements taken for some additional boots to match her uniform, when Mala got the new one done. Reva wore the sandals right away—they were strappy, black and suited her outfit.

She paid for her purchases and the ladies dragged her off to one more stop, the best local restaurant in town It was only when they sat and menus were placed before them, that Reva had to admit her failing. When her two companions asked her what she wanted to have, she looked at them and said honestly, "I can't read."

Helen whispered, "Seriously?"

"It isn't a joke."

Mala smoothed it over as the server came to take their order. "Kevak, and a pitcher of juice and sweet tea."

The server nodded and swept their menus away.

Reva leaned forward. "What did you just order?"

Mala smiled and took her hand lightly, a friendly squeeze before releasing it. "Oh. Kevak is a selection of small dishes on the menu. On Helen's world, it is called Tapas. The food is served in small servings, like a tasting menu, so you can pick out ones you like, and we will explain what they are and what they are called. New worlds mean new food. I used to live on a space station, so the variety available is twice as good here."

"Really, a station? Where?"

"It was Kaddaka station. I left working in the docks to join the Guard."

"Huh. I thought all of the Moreski were wealthy and spoiled."

"Oh. My father wouldn't stand for that. He worked and supported us, and when he died, I took over my mother's upkeep. She had never been alone, so it was hard on her when I left to find employment. Now she has her social circle to keep her occupied so that she doesn't need to break things as often."

Reva laughed in confusion. "What do you mean by that?"

Mala tugged her ear and leaned to the side as the pitchers of tea and juice were brought to them. "Oh. She used to think that I would only talk to her if she needed me to fix something. So she took to bashing her appliances and pulling wiring. Unfortunately for her, I knew that kitchen so well that I could repair any appliance no matter how far away I was. She had to settle for annual physical visits."

"So you see your parent?"

"As often as I can."

"And what of you, Helen? Do you see your parent?"

Helen's face clouded over. "No. When the Terran volunteers left Earth, we agreed never to return to our home world." She held up a hand to expose the jacks in her wrists. "I no longer meet my species specs. I couldn't go home even if I wanted to."

"That's harsh." Reva would have added more, but the food arrived and all the women fell silent as the server explained each dish and its ingredients. She started with the simple and easily identifiable, then went for the exotic. A few times, the ladies collided over the last of one of the tidbits, but it ended in laughter. Mala picked up the bill when Helen snarked about it, and Reva stayed out of what seemed to be a long-standing argument.

"Geez, woman, you are so cheap, it amazes me. All this money spent on nothing. You could have purchased a small retirement moon somewhere by now."

"I prefer to live a thrifty life. That way I won't go without." Helen had a prim look to her.

Reva just blinked. She added to the conversation. "I have not had money before, but it makes sense to spend wisely. Food with friends is a good investment, not only in the food, but in the goodwill it engenders."

"Excellently put. Now. We are going to take you back to the Guard base before Karaoke night starts up. Helen introduced it to Morganti and the locals just love it. My ears do not."

She agreed and soon the ladies and their shopping bags were on their way back to the base, "What is Karaoke?"

Helen looked astonished and then launched into a fevered explanation of her favourite pastime. She explained the music selection and the words scrolling on the screen.

"Oh. That may have to wait until I learn to read Common." Reva shrugged and smiled. She didn't want to leave the afternoon on a sour note.

Helen flushed in embarrassment. "Sorry. I forgot that—"

"I can't read, yet. No problem. I will." Reva smiled at the Pilot. "This Karaoke will give me incentive."

They talked about inconsequential things on the way back, including the Drai couple who made up yet another pair of Guards, as well as the Dhemon and his wife. The Drai had a home off the base and they spent all their time there when they weren't on assignment. Livin and Vasu were reportedly very nice.

When they were pulling into the parking area at the base, Reva had a chilling thought, *what if Nor doesn't like my new look?*

CHAPTER SEVEN

"So. What do you think?" Reva spun on her toes and twirled in front of Norelios. The surprise in his eyes was more frightening than gratifying. "You don't like it?"

As suddenly as the surprise had risen, a dark heat took its place. "I love it. On Jela, red hair is prized."

"Oh. Thank you." Her blush rose easily in her cheeks. He had been sitting and watching a vid in the common room when she burst in. "I won't disturb you anymore."

He reached out and caught her wrist. "You weren't disturbing me. I am glad you are pleased. Come and sit, I think you will find this vid fascinating." He pulled her into his lap and settled her against him.

The silk of her new tunic warmed quickly against him, and she took a deep breath, revelling in his scent. Cookies and spice, everything she had loved when she was working in a kitchen as a child. The video was about Enjel mating practices, and the formality of the system was ironic for a species that was renowned for its sex drive.

All unmarried women on Jela were assigned to live in an Aerie. The men sent them gifts and the colour of the wrapping determined the intent of the sender. The women chose from the gifts and their colourations for their companion for the evening, then they met them for the agreed upon event. White was a casual afternoon, green an apology, blue was a romantic evening at the Aerie with dinner and dancing, and red was an overnight stay at the male's home. Black was reserved for final commitment, the Leap of Faith, as it was called. The female, if she was Enjel, had her wings tied and dressed in a formal gown. At the appointed time, she leapt off the edge of a very high cliff. Her male's duty was to sweep in and catch her, thus binding them forever.

"That's lovely. What happens if he doesn't catch her?" She was cradled in his arms like a kitten, her legs folded along one of his thighs and her buttocks perched on the other.

"Then she dies and he is sent to the priesthood, never to be allowed near a female again." His voice was a soft rumble.

She rubbed her chin against his chest. Thoughts she shouldn't be entertaining came rushing to the fore. She sat up and looked him in the eye. *"Kiss me."*

Nor's eyes widened, but interest flared as he held the back of her neck with one hand and lifted her up to him with the other. The kiss started as a chaste brushing of lips, but when Reva sighed happily, he deepened it. She tasted him and her mind spun with lust. He tasted perfect. When he pulled back, she whimpered and clutched at his hands.

"You ordered me to kiss you, but I won't do anything else that you wish if you don't tell me to do it."

She blinked owlishly. "So if I want you to touch me, I have to order you to do it? Don't you want me?" Her voice was plaintive to her own ears.

He sighed, ruffling her scarlet hair. "No, not order, simply tell me. You have had enough options taken from you in your life. Taking a lover should be your choice."

Reva sat back on the edge of his lap and thought about it. She wanted him, his touch, his companionship, wanted to feel his skin under her palms and know she could stop him at any time. That kind of power was heady. She wanted it. "Norelios, make love to me."

"Your command is my wish." He held her firmly and rose to his feet. They left the common room and Nor's door opened at his approach. Inside the room, he quickly divested himself of his clothing. Naked in seconds, as only a man in heat could do, Nor let her look her fill, turning slowly and flaring his wings while flexing his buttocks.

"Very nice, but I seem overdressed."

He took her clothing off with much less speed, stroking the curves and textures of her skin with deliberate intent. She purposely didn't let him touch her back.

"Sweet, I know about the scars. They don't bother me, aside from the pain they caused you." His fingers massaged her shoulders then moved slowly toward her back.

She stiffened, but didn't stop him. She knew what he was feeling, the ridges and scars left by her sojourn with her Moreski master. They were stiff and made it hard to move in damp weather, but otherwise didn't bother her too much.

His face tightened, the already harsh planes focused on the information his hands were giving him.

Reva was afraid to look down for fear his desire for her had faded with the reality of her body's damage. His hands came to rest on her hips and pulled her firmly against him. No, his interest had not been damaged—in fact, it was quite heated.

"I want you, Reva, just the way you come. Scars, attitude and big mouth all in one." He chuckled against the top of her head. "I have a present for you before we go any further."

She looked at her own naked form and his, then blinked. "Are you sure that you want to stop for a gift giving right now? I was kind of in the mood for something else."

Nor laughed and reached into one of the drawers near his desk. A small bundle wrapped in red emerged. "I don't know if you were paying attention during the vid, but this is a request for a day in my home, with me."

Her hands trembled as she took the parcel. "What is in it?" She had never received a gift before.

"That is why you open it, to find out." He seemed eager to watch her.

She climbed up onto his bed and knelt with the parcel in front of her. She pulled the fabric away from the box and looked up to see him nodding at her. "Well, I have accepted the wrapping, so that is a yes." She carefully opened the box and found a set of bracelets inside. A deep silver with black accents, they fit her wrists perfectly. "Thank you. They are lovely. I accept them gratefully."

It was the last sentence she would utter for a while as he took over the invitation she had offered to him, and used it to make love to her for the first time.

No part of her escaped his touch, the graze of his fingertips and the stroke of his lips. Her body was humming with the need to be filled, and when he obliged, she hung on to him as if he was the last man in the universe. She bit her lip as her climax hit her, afraid that she would tell him to stop. Her body rocked against his, and when he shouted his triumph in his own release, she smiled tiredly.

This voluntary sex was fun. She was definitely going to try it more often.

She was on her back and Nor was on his belly, one wing covering her completely. She was toasty warm. Not a horrible way to spend her first open day as a free woman. She could see why the Enjel got their reputation as lovers. He had been most thorough, and each part of her body still tingled. "Nor? I appreciate this, more than you can know."

"Oh. I think I am the one who has to issue thanks. I have never before made love to the perfect woman." He lifted his head, then brought one of her hands to his lips. "It is an experience I wish to repeat. As often as possible." He waggled his brows.

She laughed.

He propped himself up on his elbows. "Would you care to go for a tour of the surrounding area? It looks lovely in the sunset."

"That sounds nice. But I have to get dressed, right?"

"It is preferable. There are several males on base that are not attached to anyone and I think the sight of you in the nude might irritate them."

"Irritate?" That was a new phrase. She had never been called irritating while naked before.

"That you are with me and not them. It is a source of pride that you came back to me after your day of discovery." He chuckled and stroked his hands down her arms. "As tempting as it is to keep you in bed with me, I think it you would better be served if we went out into Morganti."

Reva groaned as she pulled away from him. "Fine. But tonight you are mine." She located her clothing where he had flung it and was dressed in record time. "Let's go."

"Sorry. Images were in my mind after your last sentence." He blinked and stood, his body following where his mind had led.

She fought a giggle as he wrestled his erection into his pants.

Nor froze at the sound of her laughter. "I haven't heard you really laugh before. It's a wonderful sound."

She cocked her head and thought about it. When had she last felt the urge to laugh, the lightening of spirit and release of emotion that accompanied it? Years, maybe. The ladies had cracked her emotional barricade with their relentless good humour, and this time spent with Nor had melted the stone around her heart. She let her courting Enjel take her hand to lead her out into the sunset of Morganti. The sky was calling.

"No, no, no, no and no! My eyeballs will never be clean again." Reva turned on her companion as he howled with laughter. "Shut up, Nor! You are a freaking seer, didn't you *see* two fornicating Drai in the sky ahead of you?"

Nor wheezed out between chortles. "You certainly saw them. I am guessing you got a pretty thorough look."

They were running through the halls to the common room and Nor was having trouble keeping up.

"Time is fluid. I only see my own future. I was so fixated on you that I wasn't looking around. They weren't supposed to be back this soon." His breathing was still erratic. He was trying hard not to laugh. "Livin and Vasu retreated as soon as they realized they had an audience. We are having a meeting tomorrow morning. Do you think you will be able to look either of them in the eye?"

Reva continued to the common room and flung herself onto a sofa, glaring at him as soon as he came into view. Her reaction to the mating Drai was still rippling through her system, and she had never considered herself a voyeur before. She drummed her fingers against the arm of the sofa and scowled.

Nor came to her side and knelt. "I am sorry. I should have been paying closer attention, but I was so caught up in your enjoyment of the flight that I was distracted."

Mala and Isabi entered the room before she could tell him what to do with his *distraction*.

"Hey, Reva. I have something for you." Mala held a strange conglomeration of wires, headphones and a visor. "It's to help you with your learning issue."

Reva's eyes widened as she took the contraption, "It will help with the reading?"

"I have designed it to use light through your eyelids when you sleep, and an audio cue will read the word. It should work, but testing it on Isabi didn't tell me that much."

The graceful Selna smiled. "I am a poor test subject."

"So I put this on...when?"

"Now. It will start working as soon as you put it on, running through standard vocabulary and mathematics. We can get more advanced as you progress."

Mala helped her adjust it, and the fit became completely comfortable with only a few touches.

"Now, sit back and close your eyes. It will start right away."

Reva did as ordered. Words flowed onto her closed eyes and Isabi's calm voice said the word. "You used Isabi's voice."

"Him? You used his voice?" Nor wasn't impressed.

"You can give a sample for the next batch, Norelios. Isabi was handy and this was kind of an impulse thing." Mala's voice came through the drone of words. "Reva, your writing skills will have to come in the live world. Muscle memory is a harder thing to learn."

"Gotcha." She watched and listened to the Alliance Common alphabet. Keeping her eyes closed made it easier to concentrate, but she could still feel when Nor picked her up and draped her across him. She settled into a comfortable position and then focussed on her lesson.

It was a nice way to spend an evening, in the arms of a lover with friends around. It made a nice change from cowering, waiting for her master to decide that today was the day she would die. That had really sucked.

CHAPTER EIGHT

Her plans for the previous evening had taken a sharp turn with Fixer's learning machine, but both she and Nor had adapted to the change in the schedule. They would have other opportunities to wallow in each other, but one had better come soon or Reva was going to kidnap her Enjel. A warm hand caressed her shoulder.

"Time to wake up, Reva. We have a group meeting in an hour."

"Fine. What's the hurry?" She sat up and stretched. The sheet fell to her hips and she didn't bother to snatch it up. Nor tugged her out of bed and to her feet.

"Mala wants to set your new specs to the suit you had been discussing yesterday." He shoved her clothing at her and took a brush to her hair. "Let's get you moving so you will have time to snack before the meeting starts."

She gave a jaw-cracking yawn, pulling her leggings on while he fussed with her hair. "Were you a hairdresser in another life? Knock it off." She batted at him as she tried to pull her tunic on. "Let me pull this shirt on before you continue with the scalp torture, please."

"All right. But hurry." He watched impatiently.

She pulled the grey silk over her head and flipped her hair out. In less than two minutes, he made two small braids confining the hair on either side of her face and wrapped them around to knot in the back.

"There. That should keep it out of your face for the rest of the day."

"Thanks. Seer, Enjel, hairdresser, you can do it all."

"Wow. You woke up sarcastic today." He chuckled and hauled her down the hall to Mala's hanger.

"Shut up." Pouting did not seem the way to go, but she was out of witty comebacks. They had slept in the same bed and she hadn't even noticed it at the time. Her brain ached. Perhaps she had the learning machine on too long the night before. She rubbed at her forehead with her free hand as they passed MEDICAL. "Is Hyder up already? I was wondering about the results of my genetic scans."

Nor gave her an odd look and a quirky smile. "Hyder is up and preparing for the meeting. Here we are." He pulled her into a bay that announced itself as *Fixer's Lair.* "Here is your victim, Mala."

"Excellent. I was beginning to worry." Mala popped out of a nearby shuttle and scurried across the tarmac. "Reva, put this on and we can get to the customization."

A suit flew toward her and she flinched, but caught it. It was a beautiful charcoal grey with a rigid structure underlying the fabric. She looked to Mala, who gestured for her to use a changing screen at the back of the workshop.

The suit fit like a glove and it had a design of studs worked into it in separating bands. "It's great. What are the studs for?" Reva walked out of the changing area and into the gazes of one appreciative Enjel and a focused Moreski.

"Microphones and speakers." Mala only had eyes for the fit of the suit. "The suit will take an average projectile hit, and absorb a fairly powerful energy blast." Her hands ran over the suit, ensuring the fit. "The headset is over here. Smaller than the first one and much more powerful."

A tiara settled on her head with cheek pieces containing the microphone.

"I have something for you as well." Nor held out a package wrapped in scarlet.

Reva looked at it longingly. "If I accept, it may not be tonight that we spend alone."

"I can live with that, as long as you owe me one." He smiled.

She couldn't help it and giggled. "Fine. I accept. Now gimmee." She held out her hands and they shook as she opened the box. A beautiful set of boots greeted her. "Oh, Masuo. How lovely." She flipped off her sandals and tried them on. The living boots formed faithfully around her calves and took on the shade and pattern of her new uniform. The boots elevated her heels and she was soon in a comfortable, if occasionally precarious, position.

Mala gestured to the reflective surface on the outside of the privacy screen. "Take a look. Order, you look great."

Curious, she wandered over and struck a pose, hands on her hips. Her hair framed her body in a wild red wave, the two small braids holding the strands off her face. The grey fabric with silver studs was form-fitting and yet had a comfortable amount of flex to it. The boots were just beautiful. "This is wonderful. Thank you so much, Mala." She tried to check out her butt from the back, but the reflection wasn't cooperating.

"Your ass looks fine, Reva. Now, we have to get to the meeting, even Kale is coming." Mala chortled and shooed them out of her workspace. "The boardroom is in hall nineteen."

Together they walked through the halls and it was Reva who made the turn at the designated corridor. The boardroom was almost full. A Dhemon and a female that she hadn't met before were sitting at the table, looking exhausted. The offered her warm smiles, however, even though she was pretty sure that Enjels and Dhemons were enemies. The other couple she remembered with clarity. "Vasu, Livin. It is nice to see you…dressed."

Vasu barked with laughter.

Reva could feel Nor shuddering with the urge to laugh next to her. They took their seats and waited for Hyder while making introductions amongst themselves. Agreha and Haaro had just completed an assignment of a political nature and had just returned that morning. They wanted to sleep as soon as they were authorized to do so.

"Authorized to sleep? Are you serious?"

"Haaro is exaggerating. He drops off at the littlest bit of provocation. And he snores. Loudly." The group laughed at Agreha's comments and she was just taking a breath to pick on her mate again when Hyder and another male entered.

"Reva, I believe that you are the only one who hasn't met Kale."

The new male of unidentified species spoke. "Indeed. Reva, I am the Avatar of the planet we stand on. You are all gathered here today to help Morganti. There is a large comet heading toward our planet and I need to know what we can do to divert it." Kale reached out and triggered a display of an enormous ball of gasses and dirt with Morganti as the projected destination.

Everyone fell silent at the sign of natural destruction and looked at each other, then back to Kale and Hyder.

"I want all of you to think, in your travels, have you heard of anything that could possibly stop, or slow, this comet down?"

Mala cleared her throat. "I think I know what we need, but I don't know where to find it."

"What is it, Mala?" Isabi was a little surprised, but a coaxing note had entered his tone.

"A Star Breaker. I don't know what it is, but the W'Chan speak of it in hushed tones. They have used it on their mining colonies to break up asteroids."

"Where did you hear about it?"

"On Kaddaka. Drunk miners talk a lot. They were fuzzy on the details, but it is a good lead. In the meantime, I can work on some kind of a deflection array."

Hyder stepped forward. "No. We need to have an evacuation plan in place and that will include enough shuttle transport to get everyone off Morganti, if necessary."

"Alright, I will draw up plans."

Reva sat astonished as the Guard made plans for a future that might not come to pass. She looked to Nor and smiled. Whatever came of this event, she would have her Enjel and he would have her. She had already made her Leap of Faith.

STAR BREAKER

CHAPTER ONE

"So, to recap. We have an unstoppable asteroid heading for Morganti and no way to save the planet. We have five days to find a way to stop it, and only a rumour of something called a Star Breaker that we can't track down." Kale looked around at the members of the Guard who had stayed on to help with the evacuation. Their faces were solemn and serious.

As the living mind of Morganti, his very life was in danger, but Kale took the stand that the people of his world must come first. He could not evacuate regardless—he would die when the planet did.

"I think Mala has received more information on the Star Breaker. She was close to pinning down a location when last we communicated." Isabi spoke for his wife, Mala. Her work on the evacuation crafts had been tireless and the Guards just let her run with it. "She is going to try and make the meeting, but her schedule is a little hectic at this point."

"Noted. But any information she can gather on this mechanism will be useful." Gant pushed Kale back and spoke through their shared body, leaving his host to watch. "We need to engage in action as rapidly as we can. While I have enjoyed the last few months with you, I had wanted to look forward to centuries as host to the Sector Guard."

Isabi nodded in agreement. "We are pulling out all the stops, Gant. If anything can be done, it will be."

Mala darted in through the door, screaming, "I found it!"

Her husband was on his feet in an instant. "Are you sure?"

"Yes. Confirmed it with satellite scans in the area. We just have to hit the mines and negotiate with them."

"I will do it." All the faces turned toward Kale's body and inside it, he blinked in surprise. Gant never left the surface. He could, but he chose not to. This must indeed be very important to him.

Are you sure you wish to leave the surface? You have not done so in the whole time we have been linked. Kale wanted to make sure that Gant knew what he was getting into.

Yes, Kale. I want to, I need to do what I can to save this place and maintain the hope that the Guard is giving to the planets in the area. I know that you tune out the conversations I have with other worlds, but there is a feeling of hope now that has not been there before. I don't want my death to slow the spread of that hope. I don't want your death. We have been together for years and I have no urge to end my life at this point and time, in any manner.

Then let's get the shuttle warmed up and get to Mala's co-ordinates before you start to cry.

Shut up, Kale. The others were looking at him curiously. "I will need a shuttle. I believe my old conveyance is standing by."

"I have inserted a few upgrades to the navigation systems and have programmed in the co-ordinates that I was given."

Fixer was close and he could see the deep circles around her eyes. She was exhausting herself trying to save Morganti and the base. He could and would do the same. "Thank you, Fixer. Thank you all for your efforts on my behalf. I will endeavour to obtain the weapon with all speed so that we may put this matter behind us." Kale-Gant was sincere. Their attempts to help him were humbling. He would carry on with whatever information they could give him.

Flying in silence for two days had been enough time for Kale to start talking to Gant out loud. He didn't mind sharing his body with the soul of the planet, but it was easier to pretend that they were separate beings sometimes. With the life or death of their planet at stake, he feared it could be their last chance to act as individuals in the same body. If Morganti was destroyed, Kale would follow, Gant could survive, but he would have to wait until the surface was habitable again before he could take on another avatar.

Kale had already outlived his Berhar lifespan by over a hundred years. His agreement to become an avatar had come after he had been thawed out by the Alliance and offered this posting. The power of a planet would keep him alive and fend off the plague that was originally due to end his life in a matter of days.

Being the last of his species was quite the burden, but with the Berhar viral plague in his system, it would never be possible to have offspring that would be healthy. Gant's energy kept the virus at bay and contained, but if Kale died, the body would be immolated the instant the asteroid hit. The disease containment was part of the deal he had struck with the Alliance. No part of his body or the virus would be allowed to survive. Fortunately, it had been designed to destroy his kind and his kind alone.

Bio weaponry of that kind was now forbidden and punishable by planetary containment, but there was no way for Berhar to defend itself against the virus released by one of its own. As a scientist, he believed that the only way to save their society was to enact a survival of the fittest. The irony was the plague was one hundred percent fatal. Kale had been found dying by one of the Scorchers sent to the surface to burn off the infected dead. The woman had taken pity on him, a young man dying with his family, and arranged a cryogenic chamber for him. Telepathic communications had allowed him to stipulate the agreement between himself and the Alliance, including the conditions of his awakening. When all the conditions were met, they woke him up and he met Gant in a flurry of power and energy. He came to life that day and Gant kept him and everyone around them safe from the virus that surged through his blood.

While the Alliance administration was aware of his origins, none of the other Guards had come close enough to him to find out where he had come from. He just blended in with their conferences and kept to the administration of the planet.

Controlling supply shipments to the base, assuring an influx of new businesses to support the increasing staff and negotiating with the Citadel for a training base were all part and parcel of his duties as the avatar of Morganti.

It was boring work, tedious work, but it was steady and it was what kept the first complete Sector Guard base functioning. And it was his responsibility. It made him feel part of something for the first time since he learned that his planet and all others like him were dead. Kale had been the only survivor. Gant's loneliness had called to him and he had answered.

Now they were on a mission to insure that their collaboration did not cease. Kale had never felt less like the last one of his kind. The Sector Guard were his kind and they needed his help.

CHAPTER TWO

"This is it?" The scepticism in Kale-Gant's voice was palpable. His tour guide smiled at his surprise.

"This is the Star Breaker. In use for over four hundred years by my people, it has kept us safe from damage caused by encroaching particulates and other races who would care to take over our mining operations." Dramek's chest puffed with pride at his race's accomplishments.

The item that they were discussing was hanging motionless off the edge of one of the mining platforms. It was a sphere fourteen feet in diameter with one opening port on the side facing the blackness of space. The port was closed and the mineral that the sphere was made out of defied their scans. Whatever was inside was as much a mystery as how to operate it. "How does it work?"

"You merely aim the port at the object you want to destroy and the port will open."

"What about maintenance? It has to have some repair access."

"We have one citizen trained to work on the Star Breaker, as his father was, and his father before him. You get the idea. No one except his family has seen inside this weapon for more than two hundred years. They took it over exclusively at that time."

"So what are the terms of the W'Chan? What do you want from me or Morganti for use of the Star Breaker?" Kale-Gant crossed his arms and prepared to fight for the use of the one item that could help them save his world.

"Movik the Keeper will come with you and maintain the sphere. Aside from that, we are forbidden to charge for the use of the Star Breaker." He looked uncomfortable, twitching and scratching at his neck with one of the three arms the W'Chan sported. "We expect to get it back in operational condition."

"I can agree to not breaking the sphere myself, but cannot swear to regular wear and tear on the mechanism. If that occurs, I will not be held by the agreement." They extended their hand and one of the grubby appendages of Dramek closed the deal. A deep sigh of relief flowed through the Avatar. He had the weapon. Now he just needed to get home and use it.

"Done. Movik is on his way up. He wants to be done with this and back at home with the Star Breaker as quickly as he can. Don't worry about his manner, he is always a quiet one." With that warning, Dramek left the observation deck of the platform.

Kale-Gant was left alone.

Did you think that it was a little too easy? They didn't argue, fight or try to kill us. Kale was bewildered. He had been prepared to spend the stipend that the Alliance had given to Morganti for the first hundred year lease.

Well, they are not being honest about the Star Breaker. I can feel something inside that sphere. It's calling to me.

He couldn't feel it, not even through Gant's senses. *What kind of a call?*

It is a humming in my mind, a tickling tease at my nerve endings. The last time I felt this type of a touch was a few hundred years ago.

What was it?

The touch of a star. There was a sentient planet symposium five hundred years ago—two stars attended and this is the same type of flaring energy.

Curious. *Could a star fit inside that sphere?*

No. Not even a portion of one. That is what makes the energy signature so puzzling, and so teasingly familiar. It can't be, but it feels like it. Gant's frustration simmered below the surface and continued as the scowling W'Chan called Movik appeared and carried tanks of fluids onto their shuttle.

"I am Movik. Let's get this over with." He gestured for them to board their shuttle.

Kale-Gant was perplexed as the W'Chan took charge of their expedition. Bemused, they followed him into the shuttle and watched as he arranged the grapples to pick up the sphere and fasten it to the bottom of their shuttle.

Kale took up his position at the helm and programmed in the coordinates to the first jump. The ship was handling as if there was no large weight attached. In fact, it was manoeuvring as if it lighter than usual. It was impossible, of course, but a steady feeling.

Moving through the mining area was tricky, but with his ship handling so delicately, it was much easier than the journey in.

Ships pulled out of their path, silent fish in the reef of the ice and rocks of the W'Chan mines. Movik didn't say anything. He simply took over the only cabin and locked the door.

I guess he doesn't want to talk. Kale shook his head at the antisocial behaviour. He still had questions about the Star Breaker, but he now could not ask them until the W'Chan reappeared.

I suppose not. But the feeling that I mentioned earlier is getting stronger.
What kind of feeling?
Anticipation and amusement, mainly. Whatever is in that sphere has a sense of humour and is eager to try something new.
I wonder why I can't feel what you are sensing?
Perhaps it is because it is speaking to me on the same level as other planets do? You tend to tune those out.
Well, that is a deliberate evasion. This is odd. No matter how hard I try I can only hear static.
Stop trying so hard. Simply let it flow into your consciousness, just as you did with me. Perhaps that is the problem. Your mind is already full of mine.

As much as Kale didn't want to admit it, Gant was probably right. He didn't have much room in his mind for Gant, let alone another consciousness. He would have to deal with the buzzing in the back of his mind.

Movik remained in the cabin for two days. They were entering the final jump ship that the Alliance had arranged for them and making the leap into Morganti space when he emerged. "I need to run some diagnostics on the sphere. I need to get it into an orbital dock to check it."

Kale blinked. Those were the first words that the man had spoken. "There is no orbital dock near the planet, but we will arrange space on one of the evacuation vessels for you."

The W'Chan snorted and rubbed his hands together nervously. "I need complete privacy for the procedures. There is the matter of proprietary technology at stake."

"We understand, but Morganti does not have a station and you will have to make do." Kale-Gant was speaking and as such used *we* more frequently. "Your privacy will be assured."

He made the arrangements with one of the battle cruisers standing by to evacuate the inhabitants of the planet. They even agreed to cut off the recorders in the hold when Movik went out to manage the maintenance.

It was a bit anticlimactic. He put on an EVA suit, left the shuttle through the airlock and hauled along the fluids that he had brought with them from the mining station.

As Movik returned to the interior of the shuttle, Gant sent a broadcast of surprise to Kale. *She's awake.*

Kale was almost as surprised, *She?*

She was the avatar for a star. I don't know what happened, or why she is here, but that is what is inside that sphere.

How is she still alive?

A star's energy burns for millions of years. There is no reason that the avatar should burn out more swiftly."

Kale was shocked. To think that a living being was inside that hull of metal and unseen by living eyes was horrifying, but his agreement kept him from shattering the sphere as soon as he got it to the atmosphere of the planet. Frankly, he didn't even know what atmosphere she breathed.

Movik removed his helmet. "We need to head for the asteroid now. The Star Breaker is ready for action."

Back to the matter at hand. First they needed to destroy that asteroid, then he would work on freeing whatever was inside the Star Breaker.

CHAPTER THREE

She was moving. She could feel it, even without being able to see any of her surroundings. The stimulants that now coursed through her system woke her completely and rapidly to full alertness.

Her senses could not expand beyond the sphere that held her. She would have to wait until she was pointed at her target to find out what it was. There was also someone nearby—she could almost feel him as if he were in the sphere with her. A planet and his Avatar were near her. That was surprising. In all her centuries in this shell, they had never let another planet or star near her.

She would deal with that later. Now she could feel an approaching mass, faster and stronger than any of the passive meteors she had destroyed in the past. This would require a lot of skill to destroy. She was positively giddy at the prospect.

As they got closer, she began to project energy into the shell. It would hold it until she opened the port and directed it outward. Her mind assessed and sought the weak points in the rock, ice and gasses coming toward her. When the out-riding particles hit her sphere, it came as quite a shock. The pilot was risking his life to get her the perfect shot, not a courtesy that she was used to.

It was foolhardy. The shell she was in would survive a few hits by projectiles, the shuttle would not. If he was the Avatar that she was sensing, he had a planet to go home to. She would not let him waste his life in pursuit of the ideal attack point.

A surge of power released the magnetic clamps that held her conveyance and she used her power to shoot ahead of the shuttle. Flying blind was her favourite part of the job. Flying at all was a relief from the monumental tensions that pulled at her skin in an effort to split her apart. Working for the W'Chan miners had satisfied her urge to expel her power, but it lacked an emotional satisfaction that she craved.

Stepping between the shuttle and the asteroid satisfied that craving.

Opening the vent and seeing the asteroid she was about to destroy also held a certain attraction and the focus and direction of the energies of a star gave her a rush that had was unparalleled.

As her power flowed forth, she watched the disintegration of her sphere with some surprise. The remains of the asteroid flowed past her body in chunks and she felt what she had never thought to feel again. Home. The shattered rock had been her home.

"What was that? What happened? What did you do?" The normally taciturn Movik was frantic. When the sphere uncoupled itself, he had started to wring his hands and when it shattered into blazing particles that they could see from their vantage point above the breaking asteroid, he freaked.

"I did nothing. Whatever or whoever was inside that sphere is now out in the cold blackness of space."

"What do you mean *who*? What do you know?"

"The planet consciousness inside me felt the proximity of a star. That star is now humming happily as the creature from the sphere tears apart those rocks." It was hard to see, but here and there a form appeared, shattered a rock between its hands and then dodged away to strike another one. At the rate it was going, the great asteroid would be head-sized balls when it struck Morganti's atmosphere, easily destroyed by entry.

"An Avatar? Oh, nonononono." He was clutching at his head now, rocking back and forth, moaning as he watched the fragments of the sphere come apart wherever they touched the debris. "Where did the asteroid come from?"

Kale had to ask the base for that question. "This is Kale-Gant to Sector Guard Base Morganti."

Mala's tired tone came through the communications unit. "Go ahead, Avatar."

"Has an origin for the rock been determined?"

There was silence for a few moments while she brought up the information. "It has been travelling for just over four hundred years. Remnant of the Emhara system. Their white dwarf went black, the nearest planet to the star exploded, but everyone was evacuated. Is everything okay?"

"Yes. The bulk of the asteroid has been destroyed. Did you get the shield up and running?"

"Only just. When you get back, you are going to have to work on increasing food yields. I am afraid I had to replace quite a bit of energy and the commissary is pissed."

"Whatever you need, Fixer. Make me a list."

"Will do. See you when you get home. Sector Base Morganti, out."

Kale turned to Movik. "Whoever made the shell, made it from the same alloy that the occupant is so cheerfully tearing apart. The Emhara system ring a bell?"

If it was possible for Movik to turn any greener, he would have. As it was, he sat on the floor, rocking himself into a pattern saying, "Nonononononononono," as a constant chant.

With the momentum of the oncoming disaster modified by the lack of forward movement, Kale guided the shuttle closer. He wanted a closer look at the occupant. When she came out, he focussed the scans on her and took in the pale skin, midnight hair and humanoid body. It wasn't until she turned to wave at the camera that he saw the appalling truth.

She was a Terran.

With her job done, she propelled herself to the shuttle by unseen means. Being completely naked, she obviously did not have a rocket pack to assist, nor did she need to breathe.

A polite knock on the airlock had him granting access before he could think better of it. He opened the outer door and quickly had a full decontamination run done on her before he would open the inner door. She was fine. Completely clean and impervious to his scans.

When the inner door opened, she simply walked in as if she were a regular member of the crew. Movik was still rocking and moaning in the corner and she looked curiously at Kale-Gant before trying to speak.

She tried again, then paused and actually drew a breath. "I keep forgetting that you can't speak if you don't breathe. Hello. I am the Avatar to the dead star, Emhara."

"I am Kale, Avatar to Gant, sentient planet of Morganti. We are in your debt, Star Breaker." He executed a formal bow, not easy considering that his body was responding to her nudity in a most enthusiastic manner.

"It was nothing, but it does beg the question—how long was I in that sphere? I was set to remain for four hundred years or so. How long has it been?" She was asking Movik and he was squirming under her direct regard.

"It was four hundred and eighty two years, mistress."

"Did you plan to release me?"

"No, mistress. And there were many who made profit on your skills indirectly, mistress."

"Did you participate in these events?"

"No, mistress."

"Then you may live on. You did your duty and fed me as required. You are now released from your obligation and may seek employment elsewhere in the universe."

Movik grovelled in his gratitude. "Thank you, mistress. May I continue to serve you?"

"I cannot think of what capacity you may serve in. Perhaps these will have better employment for your skills." Her gesture took in Kale-Gant and it was a relief to know that she saw them both.

"Lady, as much as I am enjoying the view, I do have one question for you."

"Ask it." Her smile reached her eyes and the soft grey reached into Kale's soul to pull on his heart.

"How did you come to be in that sphere?"

"I think we need to sit and have a cup of tea. Hmm...I haven't had tea in hundreds of years. Make it a good one." She sat at the crew table in the common area, folded her hands elegantly on the table and smiled at the two men in the shuttle.

Kale went to one of the benches and out of the storage compartment and drew out a female uniform. "I would be much more at ease if you wore this, Star Breaker."

She started to step into the form-fitting leggings and pulled up the suit over all the portions of her anatomy that caused him distress. "Then I shall wear it. Now make that tea."

CHAPTER FOUR

"According to our documentation, Emhara was a white dwarf star that burned out over five hundred years ago." Behind Kale's eyes Gant was astounded. For an Avatar to survive without a host world or star for this long was almost unheard of.

"I suppose. I only know that I was Emhara and then everything went dark." She shrugged. "When I woke, the W'Chan were wiring me into that cage and started using me for their own defences. Or I think that is what happened. I am not one hundred percent sure."

Gant came forward. "Why were you away from your orbital station when she died?"

The woman cocked her head and concentrated, her silky black hair sliding across her shoulders and down over her breasts. "She sent me away. She gave me the power, took back her mind and sent me away." She sighed deeply. "I have missed her for a very long time."

He cocked his head. "That makes a certain amount of sense. Emhara is now a black dwarf star. No more life burns within her."

"That is sad. She was quite good to me, despite our rocky start." The woman smiled softly and they both basked in the gentle glow of her grief.

Gant nodded sharply and went back to the scanners to complete the work started in the cage. He ran the portable units over her, as close to the skin as he could manage without setting off one of those power sparks.

"What is that for?" She seemed only idly curious as Gant ran the scanner past her face.

"We are trying to confirm your original species and the changes made to you by Emhara."

"Oh." She blinked and then their Star Breaker was up and walking to the viewing window on the shuttle. "That knowledge was taken from me when Emhara died. My mind stopped and restarted at that moment. It took me years to figure out that the sphere was not my natural habitat."

Gant turned his back to her for a moment, letting Kale link the scanners to the communications unit. "Sector Guard base Morganti, this is the shuttle Netral. We have found the Star Breaker and need you to analyze the data that we are sending."

Hyder's voice came through loud and clear. "Data received and analysis underway. Is the Star Breaker everything you thought it would be?"

"The Star Breaker is beyond description. Contact me when the analysis is complete." He flipped the toggle for the communications terminal off.

"What do you think it will show?" She was next to him and he jumped at her voice.

Kale looked into those eyes whose grey lights were hypnotic and swirling with power. "I think it will show that you used to be a member of the Terran species of human. That you carry enough energy controlled inside you to burn a star brightly for eons."

"Terra? I remember something of Terra. I volunteered to come out into space. One of thousands." She sat in the co-pilot's seat and closed her eyes to pull the memories forward. "I was a courier when a wormhole pulled me to Emhara."

In the softest voice possible, he whispered, "What was your name?"

Her eyes snapped open. "It is gone. The star took my name." Sparks of power flowed into her gaze.

Gant was outraged. "That is impossible. I knew Emhara. She would never have done something so vile."

The Star Breaker scowled at him and a distinct heat began to build in the room. "It is true. I do not think I was a willing Avatar. Emhara used my body as her own. Until she finished with my body I was not allowed to surface."

Gant was reeling at the cruelty and breach of etiquette that had been perpetrated.

Kale spoke, "That is not how it is supposed to be between the Avatar and the host planet."

"I know, but I believe that Emhara was desperate. She needed to clear her system before she died. I just did not choose to join to her. Apparently, women who can link with stars are rare and a female was called for."

"Why a female?"

"Emhara had a strong feminine side that she wanted represented in her Avatar." The woman shrugged gracefully. "Apparently, I fit the bill."

"It is still appalling. Don't you think so, Movik?" The W'Chan jumped when he was directly addressed by the other male. He seemed to be watching the

Star Breaker's face with a sort of worshipful attention.

"Uh. Yes. Appalling. Mind you, there were some amazing histories written of Emhara, showing her care for the people in her system until the very end."

That got the woman's attention. "Really? Where can I get these histories? I don't remember much of my early days, or the later ones for that matter."

"You would have to apply to the Alliance archive. They were all sent away centuries ago. I only know about it because of my place as the keeper of the Star Breaker."

"Well, that job is over now." She looked over at him with a scowl.

Movik shrugged. "And that may cost me my life."

Silence fell and Kale served tea. It was very odd. For the star to have taken an unwilling Avatar was strange enough, but for her mind to have been wiped meant that something else had to be in play. He was going to make it his job to find out what. In less than a day, they would be on his turf and he was going to find a way to track down her planet and her people.

Hyder's voice came through the com a few hours later. "I think we have found her identity, but we are having trouble believing it."

"What? Is she Terran or not?" Kale couldn't help but feel a little impatient.

"She is. She was one of the Volunteers. Four years ago. Two years ago a Terran courier named Carella Masal disappeared on a run, ship and all. A spatial anomaly was tracked in the area of her disappearance."

Wormholes were not unheard of, but the likelihood of it taking her through space and time was... "How did she end up in the past?"

"No one knows. She was delivering a data pack for the Alliance that was considered too sensitive for a burst transfer. She disappeared after making her last check-in at Research Station Thirteen." Hyder paused. "There was no contact with her after that, and no trace of her shuttle at the next station. She was presumed dead."

"Do you have a physical profile or hologram?"

The Avatar was leaning on his chair, tears shining in her eyes as she listened to their calm discussion.

The Commander was silent for a few moments. "Sending. Does the picture look familiar?"

Hovering in the air between them was a hologram of the Star Breaker. Her statistics scrolled down in a readout below her phantom feet. The height, weight, hair and eye colour matched hers to the letter.

The woman's hand shook as she reached out to touch the name. "Carella

Masal. I am Carella Masal. But I still don't know *who* I am."

"One thing at a time. We have your name. Your life may come to you through that." Hyder's voice was kind. There was a reason that he had been chosen as the Commander of their odd grouping. He was the most level headed of the bunch, and he had the ability to see patterns in everything. Seer had his own foresight, but it revolved around his own life and the love lives of others. Not very useful in the long run.

Kale-Gant was happy that he had offered Morganti as the first Sector Guard base. These women and men had been selected for the honour of defending worlds and it was interesting to see them grow into their talents. He was at a loss of what to do for the Terran female crying softly next to him. "Thank you for the information, Hyder."

"There is one more thing, Kale. Another, larger, asteroid has been spotted on the edge of the system. This one is a planet killer. Is Carella up for another workout?"

"Do I have a few days?" Her voice was husky from weeping.

"Four or five."

She gathered herself and cleared her throat. "No problem. I will see you when we land and we will discuss its trajectory then, Carella out." She flipped the toggle to disengage the com and then looked at her hand. "How did I know how to do that?"

"If you were a Courier, then you would have spent your life inside a shuttle. After a while it would have been like breathing." He tried to stay calm, wanted nothing more than to take her in his arms, but the protection that Gant afforded him stopped him. He could not touch another living being skin to skin. The energy keeping the virus within him wrapped him and kept him safe from everyone else in the worlds. He couldn't even offer comfort. "We will arrive in less than two hours. That is Morganti over there." To distract her, he pointed out the view screen and she smiled slightly, then took in the approaching planet.

"It's beautiful."

"Thank you. I am very proud of it. I was thinking of restricting tech on the surface, but then realized that it would preclude having any fun visitors."

"Wise choice." She laughed, a light and relaxed sound. Not true joy, but it still warmed his hearts.

They passed the hours in casual conversation about his planet's surface and his enthusiasm for returning. They did not talk of Avatars and Kale-Gant was relieved. She had reason to hate the living worlds, and that she seemed disinclined to do so showed that once upon a time, she had been a fair and open minded woman.

He only hoped she would one day be that way again.

CHAPTER FIVE

Meeting the Sector Guard had been a quiet introduction. The second asteroid that her senses had vaguely picked up was on its way and it made its sister look like a pea next to a walnut. This one was a planet killer.

She had three days to get ready to face the second asteroid and in that time, she needed to find out who she was and how she had come to Emhara. Not knowing who she was bothered her more than she wanted to admit.

The Guards had been polite but wary when they were introduced and as soon as the Azon known as Hyder ran scanners over her, the intermingling was over. She was sent to a shuttle hangar with Mala, the Fixer. Apparently, her radiation emissions were a little intense for the average living being. Fixer had a plan and it amused Carella to give in to the smaller woman.

"So what position were you in, in the sphere?" Mala had her diagnostic equipment at the ready. The hangar was unusually empty. The radiation that was being put out was tolerable, but only if Carella stayed calm.

Carella took up a spread eagle position and explained. "My hands and feet were bound to links inside the sphere to keep me lined up with the port. I would build up a charge and then blast it out the hole. It was easy, really. I didn't have to think, just started to build a charge when the keeper started the fluid drips. As soon as they wore out, I would fall asleep again."

"Wow. That's horrible. And you passed centuries like that?" Mala was darting around her with the monitors and making frantic notes.

"Apparently. The memories are slow to come back, but Hyder assures me that they are still there. I just need to want them to return." It struck her that Mala was a little too free and easy with the radiation. "Are you impervious to the radiation, like Kale is?'

Mala just chuckled. "No. I am alright for the casual exposure. My cells heal the damage as soon as it occurs. I will be hungrier than hell after this, by the way, but relatively unharmed."

"That's a good thing, I suppose. What are all the measurements you are taking?" She kept her arms and legs splayed for the examination.

"I am creating a suit for you. You can resume a normal pose now. I just needed to see how much of a passive charge you put out." Mala nodded to her and shot her a happy smile. "I do more tailoring for this place than other work, but it does present some unique challenges."

Carella saw a mound of silvery fabric with some black starbursts on it. "Is that it over there?"

"It is. The studs are conduits for your power and the rest of the material is designed to retain your ambient radiation. Your face does not seem to emit as much power as other parts of you, just in case you were wondering."

"That's comforting, although I have always wanted to have laser eyes." She tried to make eye contact with the woman, but she was busy fiddling with the fabric. Chunks of sheet metal dissolved at Mala's touch and became part of the suit. It was fascinating to watch. Carella was a little surprised when Fixer turned and threw the suit at her.

"Try it on. I can make any adjustments to the fit and then we will work on the exposure and release problem."

Eager to put the suit on, Carella stripped and began tugging on the thick material. It was softer to the touch than she had expected and the star bursts of studs across the suit were beautiful and elegant. Silver and black pulsed on the suit as she settled it against her flesh with a final pass on the seal.

"How does it feel?" Mala was behind her in an instant, smoothing the fabric and tugging it into place. "It looks good, and your ambient radiation levels have dropped to a normal level."

"That's good. What do the studs do aside from look pretty?" It was impossible to keep from running her hands over the raised dots. They were fun, spiralling across her arms, gathering in a peak over the back of her hand and doing the same across her chest.

"They are vents for your power. If I guessed correctly, you will be able to point your arms and emit a beam of radiation through the vents."

"Really? That is so cool." It was tempting to let fly with a blast to test it, but with Mala so close, she didn't want to hurt the creator of the suit that gave her the possibility of control.

"Don't worry. Kale-Gant is working finding a place for you to try your talents out. You need some control practice and he needs to make sure that no living things are harmed while you get a handle on the funnel effect of the suit."

Finished with the alterations, Mala came around her and smiled brilliantly. "The basics have worked. You are emitting a regular level of radiation, no more than the average human."

"I had to be average to be accepted as a Terran Volunteer, but I don't think I have been human for a very long time."

"It will come back to you. We will make sure it does."

In a move that surprised them both, Mala rushed forward to give Carella a solid hug. Carella stood quietly before returning the embrace. This was the contact that she had needed from Kale and his personal shielding had kept her from it.

Wiping tears from her eyes, Mala leaned backward and smiled. "Do you like the colour? I can change it."

"It is lovely. But perhaps some red and blue for formal events? I don't want to scorch anyone by accident. Plus, every girl needs a change of clothes." The form fitting jumpsuit made her look like a superhero. Hell, it made her feel like a superhero, just the like the ones she read about in comic books growing up. It suddenly struck her. "I remembered comic books!" She laughed out loud and clapped her hands.

"I will imagine that that is a good thing."

"It is a part of my childhood. A snip of a memory that just came back." She hugged Mala again. "It means that my mind still has pieces of my past inside it. Emhara didn't wipe me clear." Impulsively, she swung the smaller Moreski in a circle while laughing and crying at the same time.

"Carella, I am happy for you, but put me down or I am going to puke." Mala stumbled back as she was suddenly released and laughed out loud. "You have no idea how excited we are to have you with us. Kale is very pleased that you agreed to come and make your home on Morganti."

"It seems like a lovely world. His offer of a home was very generous, as was Hyder's offer to let me join the Sector Guard." A thought occurred to her. "Does this suit work in space? Does it freeze? I need to work up a plan of attack for the big sister of that asteroid. It's still a few days or so away, but I can go naked if I have to."

Mala chuckled. "You don't have to. This suit will keep warm as you move. It will insulate your body and let you channel your power freely. Did you want to try it? We have set up targets."

"We?"

"Helen and I. She may not have told you, but she is from the same Volunteer section as you. A true Terran. Human, through and through."

"I am sure that she would have mentioned it if she thought it was important. Maybe she knows what comic books are?" It hurt that the woman who knew what she was and where she had come from was keeping it to herself. Pilot had been cold and polite when they met, earning several curious looks from the others. She had mumbled about getting the evacuees to stay put and had left the room.

"She probably does. I seem to recall her mentioning something along those lines when I created Morph's first uniform." Mala snickered. "That one was a lot worse than yours. She needs all kinds of flaps and closures that you could not even imagine."

"Very skilled detour of the conversation. Can I fly in this?"

She looked confused and stopped her fussing. "Like in a shuttle?"

"No. Atmospheric flight. I used to be able to."

"The suit shouldn't restrict you. Give it a whirl."

When Mala stepped back, Carella took a deep breath and concentrated. Power flowed through her arms, swirled in her abdomen and focussed out through her feet. Slowly and carefully, she released the power into a concentrated swirl of energy and air under her feet and around her body. Up she went. "Cool. This is great."

"Does Hyder know you can do that?"

"I don't have to breathe in space and am self-propelling, so I think it may be a little self-evident. If not, one of us can tell him later." She stretched and turned slowly about six feet up. "How does the suit look from that angle?"

"Great, and I am glad I didn't put you in a skirt. Go ahead and fly around for a bit—we are sharing a meal at six and if you are late, you will get to experience your suit's communication system." A flip of a switch and a skylight opened above them. "Off you go."

She squealed in delight and waved goodbye as she shot skyward. Time for some alone time.

CHAPTER SIX

Free. Flying through daylight, then night and then daylight again. Frightening flocks of birds, watching her image in the water of Morganti's oceans as she blazed past. Her mind spun with the feeling of joy that being able to fly was giving her.

All those years. Those centuries of being locked inside the sphere and she hadn't gone mad. With everything going on, she hadn't even wondered why she hadn't gone insane until this moment flying over a field full of flowers. Why hadn't she? Did Emhara leave enough of herself behind to keep the madness at bay?

Carella came in for a landing and just walked the surface for a while. The feel of the air in her lungs caused memories to flicker to the surface. Daisies, bluebells and the sweet smell of clover were the scents she was used to. The flowers of Morganti were close, but not what she had grown up with. Memories. She was having a memory of a meadow like this one where she grew up. Damn!

Taking care not to hurt the flowers or the meadow, Carella gently lifted off and flew to an area that she had passed earlier. Deserted and raw, this was a place where she could practice her art.

The first blast went wide, her right arm shaking with her frustration. The second and third blasts were better, closer to the charred and blackened tree. Finally, it exploded in a burst of charred wood and dust.

She was satisfied, but not happy. Why did that one memory come to her when the others were still hidden?

"Sector Base to Star Breaker." The voice was emanating from her own throat, using her body to produce the sound.

"Star Breaker, here."

"You are late for dinner. Please stop blowing up trees and make your way back to the base."

"Will do." She didn't even ask how they knew. Kale-Gant was the planet and Avatar and he would know when her power touched his surface or atmosphere.

Since they had rung the bell, it was only polite for her to show up.

Dinner was being held in the commissary. It was the only place large enough to comfortably accommodate the twelve of them and the table full of food that Fixer required. "You were not exaggerating. You do need a ton of food after that kind of exposure."

Mala nodded through a mouthful and waved at her to sit. The women and men preparing food were moving with military precision, prepping and presenting dishes as each person took their seats. Apologetically, Carella's server said, "We didn't know what you liked, so we gave you some Terran specialities."

The plate was filled with readily identifiable foods if you squinted a little and used your imagination. A hamburger was holding court, with some orange fries and a purple pickle. Taking a leap of faith, Carella bit in. It wasn't bad. It wasn't good, but it wasn't bad. She smiled and nodded at the servers who seemed relieved. She muscled through the meal while deliberately pushing the thoughts of the consequences of consumption out of her mind.

When she and the others had eaten their fill, Hyder stood up at one end of the long table. "I would like to take this moment to thank Star Breaker for agreeing to join our Guard. We have needed a space-capable talent and are delighted that you are with us.

"I would also like to thank you for the quick work you made of the asteroid. We are impressed with both your abilities and the talent that you have to wield them. Carella, I thank you from the people of Morganti." He raised his glass.

She sat bemused as the others followed.

Kale-Gant stood. "As the Avatar and living presence of Morganti, I would also like to thank you, Carella. Your efforts on our behalf, both past and future, will be remembered by this world."

"You are assuming that I can take out the next asteroid." She shrugged. "I will try, but it is in no way certain. You had best keep your people at a safe distance while I try it. Speaking of people, where is Movik?"

Haaro rubbed at the back of his neck, his wings fluttering. "He seemed fairly competent so we sent him to the orbital station to work on the shuttles."

"Good. That will keep him out of the way." At their startled looks, she expounded on her sentence. "He was my keeper. The keeper of the sphere. When the sphere disintegrated, he was out of a job and a danger to the W'Chan. He knows what the Star Breaker truly is now and having a Terran in confinement warrants a death sentence. He would know that and it would explain his pallor when he first saw my tattoos. So either our people will kill him, or his will. He doesn't have a lot to live for."

They looked surprised. Kale especially. "You have tattoos?"

She chuckled. "Obviously you were looking at my face when I came aboard. I had just gotten my standard Terran tattoos on my abdomen when I left on the mission that ended at Emhara." Carella blinked. "How did I know that?"

"Your memory is coming back. It may have something to do with being in your proper time or just the death of the star, but it does seem to be coming back." Hyder looked pleased and Helen had a hopeful expression on her face. That still bugged Carella, but she couldn't say why. She knew Helen from somewhere and just couldn't put her finger on it.

"Back to business. Why do you want me to wait until the asteroid is closer?"

"We didn't want to chance your first attack draining you."

"I feel fine, and with this lovely meal under my belt so to speak, I am ready for action. Just one thing for Mala, though." When the Moreski perked up and looked at her, she nodded to her wrists. "I need the ports on the hands moved more toward the index fingers. I don't point at objects with my middle finger, tempting as it is."

Chuckling, Mala got up and made the small alterations. It was amazing to be able to watch the material and metal flow at her touch, as if the particles had turned to water and then re-solidified. "Try some light."

Nodding, Carella held out her hand toward a dim corner of the commissary and projected a beam of light radiation. The particles clung and then dimmed in a moment. "Much better. Thank you."

Hyder sighed and came around the table. "You are not going to take off until we can get you a full physical workup. I want to know everything that Emhara did to you before we send you to blow up a small moon."

"Then let's get me up on the table. But no stirrups." Shaking her head at Helen's laugh, Carella couldn't help but wonder, what the heck were stirrups?

The physical consisted of clipping monitor leads to her collar and cuffs.

"With the radiation that your body puts out, this is the safest way to examine you. Out in space, we won't be able to communicate so I will be attaching monitor pods to you in an effort to find out how it is that you do what you do. Also, there are traces of alterations to your physiology and a power signature that isn't yours in your body. Residue of Emhara, perhaps? We will run all of the tests that we can and hopefully, when you get back, we will have some ideas about restricting your emissions without keeping your wrapped in a suit."

"The suit is very comfortable. I have asked Mala to create a few more in more festive colours." Another flickering memory came to her. "No one wants to blend in with rocks in the vastness of space."

The Azon pulled his feline features into a scary fanged laugh. "That is a valid point. Perhaps some flight lights or something on the focus nodes. Are you really planning on leaving immediately?"

"Of course. Well, as soon as I throw up the meal I just ate."

He was reaching for his scanners in an instant.

She swatted his hands away.

"Are you unwell?"

"No. I haven't eaten in over four centuries. I needed to start with some liquids, but I didn't want to offend anyone. So I will just hurl and fly. Hopefully in that order." Carella felt her stomach flip. "Right now in fact."

It only took a minute to expel the food that had taken the better part of two hours to eat, but she felt a little better for it. She rinsed her mouth with water and then walked out the nearest exit. She touched the com device that she had used before and spoke, "This is Star Breaker, on the way to meet the big one. Wish me luck."

Focussing her energy around her body in a shield, she rose from the ground and took off. She was half a mile up when she remembered, "Which way am I going?"

It was Kale who answered her. "Three degrees from the left side of the pink moon. Good luck, Star Breaker."

CHAPTER SEVEN

"She aimed her body carefully, propelling upward until she exited the atmosphere and when she achieved weightlessness, she aimed again and pulsed out her power.

While atmospheric flying was fun, open space was just amazing. Once she got up to speed, she could just cut the power and glide at the same rate until affected by a gravitational body. It was beautiful in its simplicity. Straight lines were key as well. Since she was a narrow body of propulsion, she either went in a straight line or splayed her legs to steer to one side or the other. She had done this before the sphere. These familiar actions had her sighting the asteroid. Her stern resolve moved her toward it at an ever increasing speed.

Her mind searched the rock, looking for patterns, cracks or anything that could prove to be a weak point. The mineral was the same as her sphere, the same as the first rock she had pulverized, only larger. Much larger.

Attacking from behind seemed like a viable option, so she swung around the mass and paced it, looking for that danged weakness. She didn't find it, but did figure out that if she struck it from behind, she would accelerate the debris into the planet.

Front-on assault it would have to be.

She propelled herself through cold nothing until she had enough space to turn around and become a living battering ram. Tensing her muscles, Star Breaker let it rip. Wrapping her body in as many layers of energy as she could, she ploughed into the centre of the asteroid. It was denser than she had imagined and she ran out of steam half a kilometre in.

Buried in rock she could not really move until she carved space out for her limbs. There was enough gravity for her to stand lightly inside the planet killer and she tried a new plan of attack.

If she couldn't break it apart with her energy, perhaps she could absorb whatever was propelling it. It was worth a shot. Standing in the centre of the asteroid, she concentrated on pulling energy *in*. Nothing happened at first. But she persevered. A rapid crumble started around her and spread outward. The rock turned to dust and in a few minutes, she was standing in a space larger than a garage, then a basketball court, then a football field and then space could be seen through the open gaps. She kept pulling inward, stockpiling the energy that she was not designed to hold.

Her limbs were shaking with the effort it took not to fly apart. The power wanted to break loose, but she needed to keep it in just a little longer. She was almost finished eating the molecular bonds that held the rocks in place. Stealing the energy from the rock would not have occurred to her until she had ended up inside the rock wondering what to do. As she dissolved the last of the rock into small shuttle-sized chunks, she could let go.

She stood on a last chunk of rock and spread her arms, releasing the pent up energy into the immediate vicinity. Debris popped and exploded all around her as she rode the last vestige of the asteroid through the vacuum of space.

It was wonderful, it was freeing, it was exhausting. She stopped the power flow and crouched on the tiny rock, trying to get her bearings. She was deeply exhausted, and disoriented. Despite her attempts to cling to the rock, she floated free.

The blackness of space blended with the blackness in her mind, so when she saw an EVA suit coming toward her, she tried to fight. Her rescuer was determined though and hauled her into arms that held her tight as the cable on the ship reeled them in.

The airlock cycled and Kale took off his helmet. "Gotcha."

She dropped her shielding enough to breath. "I am sorry you had to come for me."

"If Hyder hadn't been watching the readouts so carefully, we never would have made it in time."

"I thought you didn't like to leave the planet."

"I don't, but I was the only one who could track you. A planet can always find a star." He was crouching next to her and smiled gently. "You did it. You lived up to your name. The asteroid is no more than a few small rocks that will burn up on entry to the atmosphere."

"Fabulous. So why can't I stand up?"

"When you ejected the energy that you absorbed, you didn't stop there. You started on the personal reserves that keep you alive. Without Pilot doing an in-system jump, we never would have been here in time."

She raised her voice to be heard in the cockpit. "Thank you, Pilot."

"It's fine, Star Breaker. You did a good job. You didn't deserve to die, again."

That last word escaped Carella as she let her nice, safe body slip into a deep and regenerating sleep.

The glaring lights of the medical bay greeted Carella when she woke. Hyder was shuffling around with a number of monitors and watching readouts all over the room. As soon as she tried to sit up, alarms went off.

Hyder was immediately at her side, forcing a cup of water into her hands. "Drink it. We were both stupid. When you started eating, it started your metabolism. Your body ran out of biological energy, not radiation. So we need to get you eating regularly as soon as we can."

"Really? I passed out for need of a carrot stick? That's sad." She sipped at the water and felt the moisture re-hydrating her mouth. "What else is on the safe food list?"

"Soft foods, pastas, breads. And chew your food until it is almost eradicated. That will help you build up your stomach acids. I know it isn't appetizing, but the faster you can move to solids, the happier we will be."

"By we you mean you."

"Yes. I am trying to spend more time with Helen, but with all of the incoming Guards lately, it has been difficult. She has been going through quite a bit lately."

"Yeah, I can sympathize." She had a thought that might help her out. "Can you get me access to my Terran Volunteer records? It might help jog my memory."

"That sounds like a good start. Come with me."

He took her to the conference room and set her up with full access to the Alliance records involving Terran Volunteers. He was probably breaking about ninety protocols, but it didn't seem to concern him.

That they had declared her dead was the first thing that she saw. The rest was a rundown on her training, her short career and a footnote on her disappearance. It was less than informative.

She finished reading up on herself, her job and the Terran Volunteers in general then went to confront her demon.

CHAPTER EIGHT

"I went to your funeral." Helen was holding herself and rubbing her arms as if they had gone cold. "They told me that you were dead and I was at the memorial they had for you. You were yet another Terran to disappear in the line of duty and you were presumed dead."

"Oh, god, Helen. I didn't know."

"All of us within a week's travel came and put flowers on your memorial. It still gets regular visitors when Terrans pass by." Helen was looking out the window.

Carella didn't know what to say. "Really? Visitors?"

"People liked you, you know. You were an easy friend, always cheerful and ready for a laugh. We missed you when you were gone."

"I didn't know I was gone. I am fairly sure that Emhara was trying to put me back where she found me, but missed because of the W'Chan's greed. If things had gone according to plan, I would never have been missing, but I still wouldn't have had my memories. I would have been released and hopefully returned to the Alliance, but I don't know. I can't feel bad about something I didn't have control over and you are just going to have to give up your grudge, Bells." Another memory. Carella used to call Pilot Hels Bells, Bells for short. "I am back and I am not leaving."

"Oh lord, I don't want you to go! You were my best friend. We went through basic together and you took on Courier when I went to Pilot. Every chance you had, you hooked up with my ship and hitched a jump while we caught up on gossip. You painted happy faces on the outside of my monitor tank and kept me sane during the long cold first year in space." Helen turned back and tears were streaming down her face. "You aren't the *you* I remember. Star Breaker is a new woman in my friend's body."

"Helen. I get more of my memories back every day, but I need people around me to jog my mind. I want to remember being human. I want to remember Terra. Did I have a family? Why did I leave in the first place? I didn't have any particular skills that I recall. I could barely do the job of Courier without getting lost." That had been nagging at her since she started to come to herself. That one memory was missing, the audition that she had read all Terran Volunteers went through.

"I have no idea. You didn't really fit in, but you also didn't stand out. You were remarkably unremarkable. They had you marked for Courier from the moment that you left the planet. If I hadn't been in Pilot training, we never would have met." Helen finally seemed to relax. Her tears had eased.

Carella put a hand on her shoulder. "I think I know who to ask the next questions of. Just bear with me as I figure out who I was. We may both like who I am becoming." She smiled and then giggled. "But I am going to have to work on my wardrobe. This bodysuit thing is a little too form fitting for me. Get me some sweats and I will be yours to command."

Laughter lit Helen's face. "I know just the l'nal. Her designs could cover a jump engine on your back. Tomorrow at noon?"

"Done. Be there or I will hunt you down and take you flying without a ship." A quick hug was dicey, but when the other human's arms closed around her, Carella smiled through her tears. "Enough blubbering, I have a man to ask about a delivery."

With promises to meet tomorrow ringing in her head, Carella went to talk to the one man who had access to all the answers. It took a little bit of effort since he lived off the Guard Base.

Flying through the fragrant air of spring, she gave in to the urge to do a little bit of fancy manoeuvring. Loops and swirls in the atmosphere were lovely and she almost forgot her purpose when the sun began to set. "Damn."

Quickly, she stopped her silliness and flew straight to the neat house overlooking the cliffs. Landing at the edge of the walk, she made her way to the door and knocked in a polite manner. When he opened the door, she lost her urge to speak for a moment. The planes and angles of Kale's face and body had been chiselled by the gods. The Berhar were truly a lovely race. It was horrible that he was trapped behind Gant's field for the rest of his life, all due to a madman on his homeworld.

"Hello, Kale. I need to use you."

He quirked an eyebrow at her. "Do tell?"

Her blush heated her skin and the air around her. "Um, yes. That came out badly. I was wondering if you and Gant could use your connections to find out why I was chosen as a Terran Volunteer."

"Please. Come in." He waved for her to enter his home.

She walked forward curiously. The home was sparsely furnished, but it had a number of wall hangings and touches that spoke of his Berhar heritage. "Is that a Berhar wedding prayer rug?"

Kale looked more than surprised—he looked shocked. "Yes. How did you know?"

"In basic training we were told to research an extinct race and culture. I picked Berhar. You came from a fascinating race. Unlimited technology level. Evolved open religious tolerances and a wicked set of recipes. I made three for my final exam."

"You can cook Berhar food?" He sat heavily in the only chair in the room that was built for him. The rest were far too dainty.

"Well, I could. It must have been your face that brought back the memories. I don't know if I still have the recipes in my mind." His desperation for pieces of his home world was palpable. "I will try as soon as it comes back."

"Thank you. That would be wonderful."

She took a seat and squirmed a little as silence dropped in between them.

"Did you come here for anything in particular or were you just flying by?"

"I came to ask Gant for a favour."

He looked disappointed, but soon Gant was looking out at her through Kale's eyes. "Yes? What would you like?"

"I would like you to use your status as a sentient planet to search for *all* of my records. Someone sent me to that spot. Emhara didn't get possession of me by accident. I need to find out what happened to me." She took a deep breath. "Will you help me?"

"I have wondered if you would come to me for this and I am glad you did. Come with me." He rose from his comfortable chair and strode into an adjoining room.

Bemused, she followed. Inside was one of the most complex communications consoles she had ever seen. Gant was seated at it and triggering a connection.

"I am contacting the Alliance Archive. They should link up in a few minutes."

"Why is the shield in place around Kale all the time?"

"The virus that he was infected with is still active. I can't drop the shielding if there is another living being in contact range."

"Doesn't it get tiring?"

"With the stamina of a planet at my disposal, it is just another life form that I maintain. Do not mistake me, I enjoy Kale's company, but he is no burden to me."

"You can drop the barrier around me, you know. The radiation in my system is enough to kill any interlopers into my system."

"That will be his choice, not mine. Kale's arrangement with me is dependent upon my keeping him inside that barrier."

The console beeped and an image appeared. The Ontex was a little cranky, his silvery skin and large black eyes screwed into a scowl until he saw Kale on the screen. "Yes, Avatar. What may I do for you?"

"I wish for records on a Terran Volunteer. Designation Carella Masal, Courier. All records pertaining to her life, death and transfer."

"Just a moment."

His head bent and he did something on a data bank that Carella couldn't see.

"I am sorry, Avatar, those records are sealed."

"I am not Kale, I am Gant and I demand the information in those records immediately." He slapped his palm down on an identi-pad and whatever the Ontex saw was enough to have a message flashing *data received* in a few seconds. "Thank you. You have been most accommodating. Also, you need to switch Carella Masal's status to active. Have a nice day." Gant flicked off the connection and loaded the received information onto a data pad. Turning in his chair, he handed the pad to her. "Here you go."

"Thank you, Gant. It was nice of you to help me." She leaned down and kissed him on the cheek, despite the barrier. She was stunned that she made contact with warm flesh. She drew back in surprise. "I thought you would have the barrier up."

"Gant did. I dropped it. I have waited a very long time for someone to voluntarily touch me, knowing of my condition. Your radiation won't affect me and my virus won't affect you."

He stood and held her by her elbows. She could have gotten away simply by heating up, but she didn't choose that path. Instead, she waited for him. The kiss that he pressed to her cheek mimicked hers, his lips warm and pliable against her skin. Carella heard him inhale and then felt the pressure of his mouth on hers. The kiss was chaste and sweet, the kiss of someone who was learning as he went.

When he leaned back to see her reaction, she smiled shyly, but stopped him as he moved in again. "Kale, I really want to keep kissing you, but I need to read the information that Gant just got for me. I promise, as soon as I read it, we will have an old fashioned necking session."

"That sounds fascinating. What is it?"

"While I am reading, you can check the Terran linguist archive and figure it out." She felt like she was dismissing a teenager, but he was almost a foot taller and his muscular frame outweighed her human body by over sixty pounds. He was also over one hundred years old. She was not robbing the cradle, he just lacked physical experience. Carella shrugged. For all she knew, she lacked it, too.

Sighing heavily, she went into his sitting room and started to learn about her life.

Anger and betrayal ripped through her as the Alliance portion of the story came out. She had been deliberately selected for her position as Courier, and then Avatar. The Alliance had watched for someone with her genetic signature and when she appeared, they grabbed her. She had volunteered with thousands of other Terrans, but she had won because of her DNA. Once she was in the Alliance, they waited until the day that they had been informed was auspicious and sent her out to find the wormhole. The information she carried was not high priority, it was simply banking information for Emhara. What a star needed with a bank was beyond her imagining.

It didn't answer the problem of her lost memories, but it did give her raw information and interviews that she had given before she signed up. Carella watched the body language and listened to the voice. It looked like her, sounded like her, but also sounded like she was going to laugh at any moment. The attitude made her smile.

"Something funny?" Kale had taken up his seat in his comfy chair and was watching her intently.

"Yes. No. I was watching some of my original interviews and something in my voice made me smile. I was happy, I think." She shook her head and put the data pad aside. "Well, it was a conspiracy, but I still don't know why. It is frustrating."

"Speaking of frustrating, I looked up necking." He made as if to stand.

She waved him back and instead, climbed on top of him and sat in his lap. "Ah. What did you find out?"

"It is the practice of kissing for hours on end, with no other purpose."

"It can be fun, you know."

"I would have to see it to believe…"

She silenced him with a gentle but firm kiss. Her fingers threaded through his hair and his hands tentatively came to her waist. She continued until his hands flexed on her and then she lifted her head. "So should I stop?" Laughter bubbled up in her and this time he silenced her with a kiss.

He lifted her and sat her across his lap so that he could wrap one arm around her waist while pressing her butt against his burgeoning interest. He caught on quickly and soon they were hot and heavy in a full blown necking session.

The temperature in the room was rising and Carella thought absently that she might be warming the area with radiation, but if Kale didn't care, neither did she.

Honestly, she had wanted to be this close to him since she met him on the shuttle.

CHAPTER NINE

"Star Breaker, can you get back to Base please?"

Gasping, she separated her mouth from Kale's. "Why, Mala?"

"The W'Chan are claiming that you are their property. They are on their way to Morganti and I thought you would want to be here for that." The light tone belied the seriousness of the message.

Moving out of his embrace, she carefully stood on wobbly legs. "On my way." Regretfully, she gave Kale another sweet kiss and then turned to leave.

"Would you like to use my personal shuttle? It will be faster and make it far less likely for them to try and snatch you out of the air. I can accompany you." He held out his hand to her. His skin was still as flushed as hers no doubt was.

She smiled. "Sure. That would be very helpful." She placed her palm in his and followed his lead underground and onto a monorail. Seated next to her, he pushed the button that would send them subsurface at nearly the speed of sound. His hand was overcome by his shielding as they approached the surface. She missed the fleeting contact, but knew that it would wait until they were alone once again.

Berhar courtships were long and if he wanted to pursue her, she was going to need stamina—or, she could just do things the Terran way.

For the W'Chan males she would deal with, she needed patience. Patience and her ace in the hole.

The monorail was incredibly fast and in only minutes they were climbing out and walking up the stairs to Kale's quarters on base.

"You keep a room here?"

"Yes. It adjoins yours if that intrigues you at all."

"On several levels." Their earlier kissing and cuddling was still very much in her mind. She was going to talk to Hyder about an antivirus or a cure as soon as she could. Her radiation protected her, but Kale wasn't going to take any chances with other personnel on the base. She couldn't help but admire and resent his honour and duty.

"This way to the conference room." He extended his elbow.

She took it, her hand resting half a centimetre above his skin. She knew that he meant it as a show, but she had no objections. She was his for all intents and purposes. No other man had made her heart pound in her chest like this and no one could withstand her radiation. It made for a pretty small dating pool.

The Sector Guard were all assembled with the exception of Commander. Pilot filled in, "Commander is escorting our visitor to the conference room. Take your seats." There were two seats open aside from the head of the table where Commander usually sat. Kale seated her and then took his own spot across the table from her.

Fixer sat next to her with her husband, Shade across the table. Shade winked as her gaze skimmed off Kale and rested on him for a second. The amber-eyed Selna was an incorrigible flirt, but it did keep her from snarling when the W'Chan Ambassador entered the room.

The Guard stayed silent as Commander introduced them. "This is Ambassador Shassik, of the W'Chan Mining Consortium. He is here to reclaim the Star Breaker."

Carella smiled. "He is, is he?"

"Indeed I am, Miss. Simply hand it over and I will be on my way." His six arms denoted his rank among his people. The more limb sets one had, the higher up the caste system one was. He had the same iridescent green flesh as Movik, but poor Movik was only a worker with two limbs. He must have been delighted to be the Keeper. It would have given him added social status.

"That will not be possible." She stared directly into his yellow eyes.

He puffed up with indignation and looked to Commander for help. When none was forthcoming, he said, "And why would that be?"

"Because I am not going anywhere."

"You? You are the Star Breaker? But you were in the sphere! How did you get out? Where is Movik? I will ring his neck."

"Movik could not have prevented it. The mineral that made up the sphere was the same mineral that comprised the majority of the asteroid I was sent here to destroy." She leaned back and drummed her fingers on the table. "Once free, I was able to return to the Alliance and to find out who exactly I was before I became the Avatar to Emhara."

"That's not...you can't...you belong to us!" His spluttering would have been funny if the topic was not so offensive.

Carella flared slightly. There was no other word for it. She got herself under control when she saw Mala flinching. "I do not belong to you. It is illegal to own a Terran in the Alliance, and I have just obtained proof that I am most definitely a Terran."

His mouth hung open, exposing rotting teeth. "That's impossible. I demand to know what kind of proof you could have."

Commander stepped in. "There is an easy way to resolve this. Star Breaker, open your suit to the navel."

Pilot smirked and chuckled. She knew what was up.

Shrugging, Carella opened the closure to her lower abdomen and then looked over to Commander.

"Part the suit over your abdomen for a moment and then reseal it." He nodded in encouragement.

She did as he instructed, hearing the laughter start in everyone who saw her flat belly. Looking down, she noticed an elaborate tattoo. "What the heck is that?"

Pilot filled in. "It's a Terran tattoo. We were all given them after some races decided to make off with our species. I have one as well." She opened her own suit and parted it to display the same tattoo of a star with nine orbiting bodies. "The tattoos are keyed to our human genetics and contain mineral components that cannot be duplicated. Minerals from our planet."

"There has to be some mistake. She has been in the sphere for centuries. There is no way she could be one of yours."

"I went through a wormhole in time and space to reach Emhara. I was sent by the Alliance at her request, I was selected at her specification. Don't tell me that she didn't leave you anything to tell you where I came from?"

Shassik turned blue. He was blushing. "There is a data crystal, but no one can use it. It's on a genetic key."

"Do you have it with you?" She drummed her fingers on the table again. "Is it by any chance that light blinking in your left pocket?"

He paled under her scrutiny. "It isn't blinking."

"Sure it is. Mala, you can see it right?"

"No. But if you say you see it, I believe you."

Commander piped up. "Shassik. Empty your pocket. Now."

"But I am an Ambassador of the W'Chan Mining Consortium. I don't take orders from you." He was trying to be indignant, but was far too pale. "Ambassadors have carried this crystal for four hundred years. This isn't right."

"The crystal." Carella held her hand out and as soon as the crystal hit it, she sighed. A light burst of power and a figure bloomed from the gold facetted surface.

It was disconcerting to stare at her own face and have no recollection of the speech that she was making. The golden tint to her eyes was new and must be the soul of the star bleeding through.

"Hello, Carella. I am hoping that this finds you well and that you have arrived safely in your proper time. You may have wondered why me during all of this and I can only tell you that most people are not designed to be a star's Avatar. You were born for that task and no other, but I could not find you in my time.

"A message was sent to the Alliance. They ran it through the Seers at the Citadel and agreed to provide me with the body I needed to finish my last works. I have known that I was dying for some time, and the Alliance of Federated and Sentient Planets was attempting to help me by finding you. You see, I needed a body to contact the citizens of my star system, one planet at a time. They had to be told to evacuate and most had opted to restrict their technology and had no interplanetary communications. I needed you to do that.

"What I am here to tell you is why your memories are blocked. Despite my ordering you like a slice of pizza as you said to me once, I never intended to keep you in the past and have you die here. With the W'Chan scientists assisting me, I have come up with a sphere that should keep you preserved physically, and blanking your mind will keep you from going insane. Your mind will not remember anything, but your body will react to any threat. A power valve has been added for your defence and the W'Chan are honoured to host you. They will release you when you are back in your timeline and you can rejoin the Alliance as a Courier or whatever you choose. Your memory will come back to you naturally after you are freed from the sphere.

"I am a sentimental star." Emhara rubbed at her shoulder. *"I have marked you with my symbol and hope that you think of me fondly. Your presence saved many lives and gave me a companion in my final days. Know that you will always have the heart of Emhara within you.*

"If for some reason the W'Chan have failed me, feel free to take whatever revenge is appropriate. You served me well and you deserve your freedom and your people."

The image flickered out and then surged back to life. *"I have been reminded by you that you have an account with the Alliance and with the*

W'Chan accumulating for every year of your life in the shell. This should ease your transition back into a normal life. Again, thank you."

The image was gone and the jaw of the W'Chan Ambassador was slack.

"I am guessing, Shassik, that you were not expecting that message. So where are my accounts?" Getting over the shock of seeing herself speaking with an alien consciousness behind her eyes was easier if she went on the attack.

"Uh, I don't know."

"Lie."

His mouth flapped open and closed for several moments. "We can't give you that money. Our entire economy is based on that seed of hard currency."

"Then transfer it. You used me for centuries to defend your mining colonies."

He was startled, "No. Of course we didn't."

"I remember the screams of the pirates in my mind. The endless trips into battle as you used my defences as a weapon of aggression. I didn't remember my past, but I did remember everything that happened after the wipe and after Emhara left me. I simply had no emotional response to it then. I do now." She slammed her hand down on the table in front of him and melted the surface under her palm. "The accounts will be transferred to Morganti in an hour, or you don't get on board your shuttle with all your limbs attached, and then I will seek out every W'Chan outpost and sterilize the population, manually if I have to."

Isabi came up behind the shaken Ambassador and escorted him to the com room. "I haven't known her long, but I don't think she is kidding."

As they trailed away, she heard Shassik whining and crying. She fought a smile and looked back at the others. "I will have the table repaired. I promise."

Mala smiled and put her hand next to the hole. "One dinner after I have been working all day. You owe me." The hole sealed up in seconds and Mala took what looked to be a ration pack out of one pocket.

Shuddering at the amount of food that it would take to satisfy Fixer, Carella nodded. "Fine. And I owe you for the suits. That is some excellent workmanship."

"Considering that you are getting five hundred years of back pay from two societies, you can afford it. I think some of the shuttles need new panelling."

The evil laugh that emanated from the normally affable Mala was completely out of character, but very funny. Laughter spread throughout the

Guards in the room.

It was a few minutes before someone noticed the tears tracking down Carella's face.

"Oh, honey. Come here."

Helen's arms came around her in sympathy and she bawled into Pilot's shoulder. Racking sobs for a life not lived and a star that burned out centuries earlier spilled from her throat, and one by one, the Sector Guard held her as she cried. They all took a turn, even Kale's barrier crackled under her hands as she mourned her losses.

Dragging in a deep and controlling breath, she stood back from the arms that held her. "Thanks. I needed that. It's been a while since I could cry."

"You need to hydrate more." Hyder's no nonsense voice made her smile. "You are an unbecoming shade of pink right now."

Kale handed her a glass of water from the pitcher on the conference table. The cool water soothed the burn left by her emotional storm. Mala pressed a wet cloth into her hand and gestured for her to blot her face.

Carella took a minute to compose herself and rehydrate, and by the time she was reasonably composed, a defeated Shassik was slinking back to the conference room. "It is done. The W'Chan miners now hover on the brink of insolvency, but it is done."

"Get along the same way you did before I was trapped into a mineral bubble. The W'Chan were successful before I came along and they will be after I am gone. You just need to start taking your own defence into your own hands."

"Yes, Star Breaker. Thank you for allowing myself and my crew to return home unharmed." He bowed deeply to all of the Guards and started to take his leave.

"Wait!" It suddenly hit her that Movik might want to go home. "If Movik wishes to return to the mines, he is released from his vow of service. He is on the orbital station that has been set up for the evacuation. Please communicate with him and offer him a position among the W'Chan."

Shassik hesitated and then looked around at the solemn faces of the Sector Guard. "Of course. Whatever pleases you, Star Breaker. Who knows, the Guard may be needed in our area of space one day." His six hands rubbed together in uncertainty.

Commander confirmed the situation for him. "And we will come when we are called. No grudges held."

"Excellent. I will be going then. There are several financiers that are about to commit suicide and I want to be home to watch it on the monitors." The morbid comment stunned the Guards to silence and they let him go without further interference.

Watching the shuttle take off, Carella felt lighter. She picked up the recording crystal and held it to her heart. Breathing deep, she repeated to herself that she was back where she belonged.

Back in her own time.

She looked to Helen.

Back to her friends.

Kale stood silently waiting for her next comment.

Back to all kinds of possibilities.

"So, Bells. Since I have come into some money, do you want to go shopping?"

"We have to wait for the shopkeepers to come back from the orbital station. They were all evacuated while the asteroids were flying at us." Mala snickered and gnawed her way through another ration bar.

"You can't ignore her, Car. Mala is a champion shopper. Just ask Isabi. He has had to surrender most of his considerable closet space to her." Helen waved her hand at the Selna who tried to look sad and dejected.

He ruined the effect with his snicker. "There are compensations." He bent double as Mala punched him in the stomach and once again the room exploded in chortles.

Hyder ruined the fun by putting his foot down. "Morph, Thinker, get the evacuees back here. Pilot, fly the big shuttle. Seer, Order, I want you organizing people on the landing sites. Fury and Beast, I want you moving people on the ground, get them home again. Mala, repair the ships as they return and keep yourself fueled up. Shade, run the communications station. Kale, meet me in the medical bay. Star Breaker, if you wouldn't mind, see that the W'Chan get away without any trouble or picking up anything they didn't come with."

Blinking in surprise, they scattered to their appointed tasks.

CHAPTER TEN

"Why the sudden change of heart, Kale?" Hyder prepared the clean room and used the waldos to extract a blood sample. Kale held still as the needles and scrapers approached him.

"I am interested in courting Carella. I can't do that if we can't even hold hands." He sighed in pure frustration.

"What does Gant think of this?"

The idle chitchat was obviously designed to distract him from the scraping of his dermis. "He has lowered the barrier for you to take blood and tissue samples so he likes her just fine."

The blood sample was carefully stored in a containment field and the tissue sample followed closely. "I am going to try to isolate the virus, but I don't know how long it will take me to find a treatment."

"I have waited over a hundred years for a woman who wouldn't drop dead at my touch. I can wait a few more months or years, if necessary." He shook his head as Gant healed him and the barrier snapped back into place. Three rounds of decontamination and he was able to leave the sterile room.

"Well, you may want to keep in mind that she is highly radioactive and can probably never have children."

"Do you think that it matters to me? I am the last of my kind. No half bloods exist and one man cannot reproduce a species. I want the chance for happiness and companionship that everyone else seems to have. Just that chance. And I believe that Carella is willing to try as well." The time that they had spent cuddled together burned in his mind, but if he was going to do this, he would do it by the rules of his people. After letting Hyder clap him on the shoulder, he turned to the most important thing on his mind. The first thing he needed to do was to find the most beautiful flower he could. Then he needed to learn the flute.

Star Breaker had to keep from trying to laugh in the vacuum of space.

Movik had decided to keep his position as support personnel for the Sector Guard. Her first clue had been when Shassik's starship began to shudder and buck, the fuel cells obviously contaminated. She hauled them in to one of the Alliance jump ships standing by and flew back to the surface of Morganti.

She wanted a shower and she needed a nap.

A member of the security personnel escorted her to her suite, and it was with a great deal of relief that she stripped off her suit and stepped into the shower. When she left the shower, she was faced with a conundrum, how was she to not contaminate the area while taking her nap?

Mala had been ahead of her and in the wardrobe were her rainbow of jumpsuits. Grateful, she climbed into a blue one and then dropped into bed. They would call her if they needed her.

True restful sleep was hard to obtain, but when Carella woke, it was a heady smell that teased her into consciousness. She turned her head and noticed the flower on the pillow beside her head. It was lavender, pink, and a deep blushing red with a smell that reminded her of a summer meadow.

The dark, heady scent made her smile and she sat up, pushing the sheets aside.

A sound was teasing at her. As if wind was blowing through the reeds. She looked around for the source and followed the sound to the adjoining door.

Pressing her ear to the panel, she listened as the music got stronger and a tear formed in her eye as she realized what was going on. She was being courted by traditional Berhar method.

As his song wound to a close, she looked around and cursed to herself. She needed to give him a token, but she didn't own anything. As her hair swung forward, she had a eureka moment.

Quickly, she made a thin braid and then knotted it and broke the hair above the knot. As his song started up again, she opened the door and sat watching him play. This time, when the song ended, she extended the braid.

He bowed and took the braid, then frowned and said, "It's not enough."

Her heart sank. She didn't have anything else.

"A kiss will even things out." His eyes were sparkling with amusement.

Taking a deep breath and letting it out with relief, she walked to him and drew him down for her kiss. His arm wrapped around her and held her tightly against him while the other hand threaded through her hair to keep her against him. Wow. He learned fast.

When he let her go, she was blinking up at him stupidly. "Wow."

"Thank you. I have researched kissing in the Terran manner and I have to confess that there are quite a few things that I want to try. But not until we are in a shielded environment and after I have completed my courtship."

"Are you really going to go through with the whole thing? The singing, the weaving, the hunting? Not to mention the metal work and making my wedding gown."

"Every bit of it." He extended a data pad to her. "These are a sampling of Berhar recipes. You once told me you like to cook."

"I do. Thank you. At least this will give me something to offer you after your courting. I was a little at loose ends. I don't have anything." She grimaced.

"You are all that I want. So I will continue to court you and you will improvise. I wouldn't mind more kissing."

That last was said with such a hopeful tone that she laughed. "I like it, too, but I think parts of you would start turning blue if we keep it up to long."

That apparently confused him, but he brushed it aside. "As long as you are the one that I get at the end of the process, I will happily put up with anything."

She pulled him to her again. "That deserves a reward."

She wasn't going to rush into anything, but if she still felt this way about him when her memory came back, she would be a happy woman indeed. Now if Mala could find a way to make lingerie that had radioactive shielding on it...she would have to ask her later.

ABOUT THE AUTHOR

Viola Grace was born in Manitoba, Canada where she still resides today. She really likes it there.

She has no pets and can barely keep sea monkeys alive for a reasonable amount of time.

In keeping with busy hands are happy hands, her hobbies have included cross-stitch, needlepoint, quilting, costuming, cake decorating, baking, cooking, metal work, beading, sculpting, painting, doll making, henna tattoos, chain mail, and a few others that have been forgotten. It is quite often that these hobbies make their way into her tales.

Viola's fetishes include boots and corsetry, and her greatest weakness is her uncontrollable blush.

Her writing actively pursues the Happily Ever After that so rarely occurs in nature. It is an admirable thing and something that we should all strive for—to find one that we truly like, as well as love.

Viola can be reached at this email:
viola@violagrace.com
Viola's website is located at:
http://www.violagrace.com

CPSIA information can be obtained at www.ICGtesting.com
Printed in the USA
LVOW090130160512
281802LV00001B/24/P